dark future

KROKODIL TEARS

AMERICA, TOMORROW. A world laced with paranoia, dominated by the entertainment industry and ruled by the corporations. Welcome to the Dark Future.

Krokodil is an ex-juvenile delinquent turned cyborg killer, out for revenge on the sinister preacher man Elder Nguyen Seth for wiping out her bike gang. However, many people want her dead too, and there are three assassins on her trail: a Californian Operative, a psychopathic killer and a foul creature from the Outer Darkness. What's a gal to do?

More communiqués from the Dark Future

THE DEMON DOWNLOAD CYCLE

DEMON DOWNLOAD
ROUTE 666
Jack Yeovil

PLUS...

GOLGOTHA RUN
Dave Stone

AMERICAN MEAT
Stuart Moore

JADE DRAGON
James Swallow

dark future

KROKODIL TEARS

Jack Yeovil

For Janet, something more than a star.

A Black Flame Publication
www.blackflame.com

First published in Great Britain in 1993. Revised edition published in 2006 by BL Publishing, Games Workshop Ltd., Willow Road, Nottingham NG7 2WS, UK.

Distributed in the US by Simon & Schuster, 1230 Avenue of the Americas, New York, NY 10020, USA.

10 9 8 7 6 5 4 3 2 1

Cover illustration by Jaime Jones.

ISBN 13: 978 1 84416 379 3
ISBN 10: 1 84416 379 2

A CIP record for this book is available from the British Library.

Printed in the UK by Bookmarque, Surrey, UK.

Publisher's note: This is a work of fiction, detailing an alternative and decidedly imaginary future. All the characters, actions and events portrayed in this book are not real, and are not based on real events or actions.

When it was first published, *Krokodil Tears* was set slightly earlier than now. For this new edition, Black Flame has gently revised certain dates to bring this title into line with the other extraordinary tales from the Dark Future.

AMERICA, TOMORROW

My fellow Americans —

I am speaking to you today from the Oval Office, to bring you hope and cheer in these troubling times. The succession of catastrophes that have assailed our once-great nation continue to threaten us, but we are resolute.

The negative fertility zone that is the desolation of the mid-west divides east from west, but life is returning. The plucky pioneers of the new Church of Joseph are reclaiming Salt Lake City from the poisonous deserts just as their forefathers once did, and our prayers are with them. And New Orleans may be under eight feet of water, but they don't call it New Venice for nothing.

Here at the heart of government, we continue to work closely with the MegaCorps who made this country the economic miracle it is today, to bring prosperity and opportunity to all who will join us. All those unfortunate or unwilling citizens who exercise their democratic right to live how they will, no matter how far away from the comfort and security of the corporate cities, may once more rest easy in their shacks knowing that the new swathes of Sanctioned Operatives work tirelessly to protect them from the biker gangs and NoGo hoodlums.

The succession of apparently inexplicable or occult manifestations and events we have recently witnessed have unnerved many of us, it is true. Even our own Government scientists are unable to account for much of what is happening. Our church leaders tell us they have the unknown entities which have infested the datanets in the guise of viruses at bay.

A concerned citizen asked me the other day whether I thought we were entering the Last Times, when Our Lord God will return to us and visit His Rapture upon us, or whether we were just being tested as He once tested his own son. My friends, I cannot answer that. But I am resolute that with God's help, we shall work, as ever, to create a glorious future in this most beautiful land.

Thank you, and God Bless America.

President Estevez

Brought to you in conjunction with the GenTech Corporation.

Serving America right.

[Script for proposed Presidential address, July 3rd 2021. Never transmitted.]

Tick-tock, tick-tock, tick-tock, tick-tock.

– J. M. Barrie, *Peter Pan, or The Boy Who Wouldn't Grow Up*, 1904.

September 27th 2020

THE BRUYCE-HOARE AGENCY

"Protecting Colorado From Juvenile Crime since 2015"

SURNAME: Bonney
FORENAMES: Jessamyn Amanda

GENERAL INFORMATION

KNOWN ALIASES: Jazzbeaux, Red Jesse, Juicer, J'Am, Minnie Molotov, others
DATE OF BIRTH: November 15th, 2004
PLACE OF BIRTH: Denver NoGo, Colorado
SEX: Fem
RACE: Cauc.
STATUS: Single, juvie
HEIGHT: 5' 4"
EYES: Green
HAIR: Black
BIO-IMPLANTS: Four red metal stars inset in subject's knuckles.
DIST. MARKS: Teardrop mole under left eye. Faint but numerous scars across back. Subject denies she has been beaten, but her case worker (Ref: DOUANIER, LYNN Dept. of Child Welfare) reports that

subject's father (see: BONNEY, BRUNO) has been issued with three prior warnings, re: child abuse. My conclusion is that the father regularly chastised the subject with a rod or a cane.
OFFICER'S REMARKS: Majorette type, but dresses like Morticia Adams. Cleaned-up, could pass for Rosanna Arquette.

A.T.O.A. DETAILS
CLOTHING AT TIME OF ARREST: Black fishnet tights (ragged), black pseudoleather skirt, black pseudoleather waistcoat, black pseudoleather boots, one black suede glove (with talons), copper chain-link belt, bra and underpants, long scarf (weighted at one end, i.e.: cross-ref under WEAPONS).
PERSONAL POSSESSIONS AT TIME OF ARREST: Black pseudoleather handbag, $765.84 in bills and coins, sundry items of correspondence, vial of pills (as yet unidentified), powder compact, hyposqueeze and two cartridges of smack-synth, three lipsticks (black, blue, red), pocket calculator, issue of Moscow Beat magazine, badge of tri-D likeness of Petya Tcherkassoff, hammer-and-sickle earrings (cross-ref under WEAPONS?), credit cards (American Express, Disneycard, MasterGrab), five ampoules of morph-plus, MP7 glasses (with five Soviet-import musichips), N-R-Gee candy, diary (locked), dampraguettes, clippings from Guns and Killing magazine.
WEAPONS AT TIME OF ARREST: 27 loose rounds of .44 Scum Stopper ammunition (subject had no gun A.T.O.A), straight razor, stiletto in ankle-holster, Swiss Army nunchaka, filed-sharp fetish bracelets.
OFFICER'S REMARKS: subject's clothing and possessions turned over to the care of the matron, weapons given in to custody of the court.

HISTORY AND SOCIAL STANDING
ADDRESS: NFA
KNOWN RELATIVES: Bonney, Bruno (father), deceased. Bonney, Robyn is the name under "mother" on her birth certificate, but no such individual is traceable.

KNOWN CRIMINAL ASSOCIATES: Jean, Andrew (member of Psychopomps gangcult); Threadneedle, Simon (biosurgeon); Kristaldo, Gaspar (pimp, drug dealer, assassin-for-hire).
KNOWN CRIMINAL AFFILIATIONS: The Psychopomps, Denver Chapter. Subject holds rank of a Provisional War Chief in the Psychopomps' Junior League Cadre.
OCCUPATION: High school student. Subject's counsellor (Ref; WESLEY, SANDRA JEANE, Barry Goldwater High) cannot recall ever seeing her on the premises.
CREDIT RATING: Fair
PREVIOUS ARRESTS: Possession and sale of controlled substances, possession and use of a deadly weapon, assault with intent to commit serious injury, grand theft auto, being in charge of a vehicle while under the influence of a controlled substance, destruction of state property, contributing to the deliquency of a minor, driving without due c and a, conspiracy to solicit prostitution, taking part in an illegal sporting event.
PREVIOUS CONVICTIONS: Taking part in an illegal sporting event (she's a warehouse gladiatrix), destruction of state property.
OFFICER'S REMARKS: Cute kid!

CURRENT ARREST DETAILS
CHARGE: Homicide
SITE OF ARREST: The Baboushka Beat Nite Klub, Intersection Peebles Drive and 124th Street.
ARRESTING OFFICER: Patrolman L. J. Leonowens (Patrolwoman L. G. Tuttle, Civilian Auxiliary, P T Garratt, assisting).
COMPLAINANT: State, on behalf of the deceased (BONNEY, BRUNO).
OFFICER'S REMARKS: Subject will not serve time on this one. No one reading this report or attending subsequent trial will have any doubts as to the facts of the case, and it is my opinion that subject will, repeat, WILL re-offend. But Jessamyn Amanda Bonney is thirteen years old, and Bruno Bonney was slime wrapped up in a human skin. The judge will give her a medal and a lollipop, the Provisional

War Chief will become a ward of the State, and she will be back out on the streets. This situation will obtain until November 15th 2022, when subject will reach her majority and cease to be the concern of this agency, wherupon I recommend her file be turned over to all major law enforcement operations in the South-West.

Signed, sincerely yours,
Lucius J Leonowens.

Report filed with Bruyce-Hoare Central 27-9-2020. Fax print-out copies cc: DOUANIER, LYNN (Dept. Child Welfare), WESLEY, SANDRA JEANE (Barry Goldwater High), RODRIGUEZ, HOLM (Dept. Corrections), BERGER, HAMILTON (District Attorney's Office), CLUTE, JOHN QUINCY (Medical Examiner), PRINGLE, DAVID (United Press International).

part one
Jazzbeaux

I

Dying is easy, as her old man used to say, it's the coming back that's hard.

Inside her head, there was darkness. A red darkness. She was sinking slowly into it. Her optic implant was dangling useless on her cheek, her durium skull platelocks were bent uncomfortably inside her head. That wasn't supposed to happen. They were under guarantee. Doc Threadneedle had used only the best scav medtech from the Thalamus Corp.

There were dead people in the road with her. The Feelgood Saloon was burning, and there were overturned ve-hickles all around. The whole town was going up in flames.

All you need to be a freedom fighter, Petya Tcherkassoff sang on his "The World We Have Lost," *is a fiddle and a bow and a cigarette lighter.*

Somewhere in the darkness outside her head, something – an animal or a person – was howling in pain.

There was a dull *whumpf!* as a gas tank exploded. Jazzbeaux felt specks of heat on her face. The hardtop shuddered with the impact of flying debris. She knew she was lucky not to have been cut in half by a razor-edged car door playing frisbee.

Her father, of course, was dead. He had never come back.

The longer she lay here, the shorter the odds became…

SHE TRIED TO open her eye – the right one, the one that was still there – and found it glued shut. She had blood on her face, dried-up and mixed with grit from the road.

The preacherman had hauled her out of the Feelgood and battered her face against the road. That was how she lost her optic implant, how her platelocks got knocked out of shape.

The road. All her pain came from the road.

Get your kicksssssssssssssssss, the preacher had hissed, on Route SixSixSixxxxxxxxxxxxxxxxxxxxxxxxx!

SHE HAD A skullcracker of a headache, and guessed she'd been opened in several places by knifecuts, branded in others by dollops of fire.

Sicksicksick, sicksicksick, sicksicksick, sicksicksick…

SHE KEPT LOSING herself, losing her train of thought. She wished she had listened when Doc Threadneedle tried to tell her about her brain. It's where you live, the Doc had said, you should take care of it. Well, she had tried. A durium skullsheath doesn't come cheap. A year's worth of fenced scav had brought her the treatment. It was supposed to be like armour inside your head. Guaranteed sound against anything up to a direct hit in the eyeball with a ScumStopper bullet.

But the preacherman had opened up a crack, and got into her greymass. Somehow, he had wormed his way into her private self, the place where she lived. And he had done a lot of mischief in there. She knew her body could be fixed, but she wasn't sure about the important stuff. Doc Threadneedle couldn't replace neurons and synapses. Even the GenTech wizards, Dr Zarathustra and WD Donovan, could only reconstruct a ruined face; they couldn't do anything about a shredded psyche, a ruptured personality, a raped memory…

SOMEWHERE IN THE distance, there was gunfire. Shots were exchanged. Then, nothing. She could hear fires crackling. The thing in pain was out of it now. Spanish Fork, Utah, was another ghost town. She was probably the only thing alive in it. Soon, the predators would lope out of the desert for her. On the road with the Psychopomps, she had seen some pretty weird critters, wolfrat coyotes, subhume vermin, sharkmouth rabbits. They had to eat red meat one day out of seven.

Jessamyn.

Amanda.

Bonney.

She held onto herself, trying to come to the surface of her cranial quicksand.

Jessamyn Amanda Bonney.

Nobody called her that any more. Nobody but cops and ops and soce workers. Not since her old man.

Jessa-MYN, her Dead Daddy whispered in her inner ear, *cain't you be more sociable?*

No, not Jessamyn. She didn't live here any more. Jazzbeaux. She was Jazzbeaux. That was her name in the Psychopomps, that was who she was. Jazz-beaux!

She brought her right hand up to her face. A numbed pain told her two of the fingers were broken. She rubbed her eye, and tried to open it again. The blood crust cracked, and she saw the night sky.

Star light, star bright, first star I see tonight…

★ ★ ★

PUSHING HARD WITH her elbows, she half-sat in the road. Her back ached, but her spine was undamaged. That was something. The Feelgood was a stone shell full of glowing ashes. A half-burned corpse sprawled on the steps, the top of its head gone. That had been the town's boss-man, Judge Colpeper. A wind had come through with the Josephites, and blown away the man's whole world.

...I wish I may, I wish I might...

THE STARLIGHT AND the firelight went to her head like a blow, and she blinked uncontrollably. Her damaged implant was leaking biofluid. Delicately, with an unbroken thumb and ringfinger, she eased the ball-shaped doodad back into its socket. The connections were loose, and the optic burner didn't respond to her impulse command. No prob. Doc Threadneedle could fix that. At least, he could if the fault was in the machine rather than in the meat.

She found her eyepatch on the ground, and slipped it on over her optic. She pulled her hair out from over the patchcord, and passed her fingers through it. Blood, dirt and filth came loose. Her broken fingerbones ground painfully.

...have the wish I wish tonight.

SHE WAS MORE in control now. Soon, she would be able to stand up, able to walk out of here on her own two legs.

The chapter was finished, she guessed. Andrew Jean, her lieutenant for the past two years, was a few yards away, skin in shreds, orange beehive hairdo picked to pieces. The corpse looked as if it had been attacked by dagger-billed birds. The 'Pomps who weren't dead had gone off with the preacherman.

The preacher. He was the start of it. Seth was his name. Elder Seth. The Josephite.

He had seemed to be such a nothing, meek and mild in his black suit and wide-brimmed hat, calm behind his mirrorshades, surrounded by his quivering flock.

Such a nothing.

THE MOTORWAGONS WERE *pulled over to the side of the interstate when the Psychopomps' advance scouts first sighted them. Jazzbeaux was on her way to a pre-arranged duel of honour with the Daughters of the American Revolution. There was a territorial matter to be settled. It was an important fight, and she shouldn't have been concerned with petty pickings like the hymn-singers. She could have passed by without rumbling the Josephites, or just given them a light pasting and taken their food and fuel. She had other business to cover, major league business. There was no need to take the time to beat up on the new pioneers.*

But there was Elder Seth, standing tall, and smiling just like her old man. On sight, she knew she would have to take him down.

The scav was pathetic. She took Seth's mirrorshades. At first, she just wanted to look into his eyes, to taste his fear. But there was no fear. She hadn't been able to read anything from the ice-chips that stared back at her. Not even when she had Andrew Jean and the others cut out a couple of the pioneers and pizza them across the two-lane blacktop. She remembered the names of the dead. Brother Akins, Brother Finnegan, Brother Dzundza. She never forgot the names of her dead.

She could have killed him then. Done it easy, shoved a gun into his mouth and squeezed off a ScumStopper through the roof of his mouth, exploded his brain.

But she let him live. She took his dark glasses, and let him live. Two mistakes. Bad ones.

CITIZENS, PSYCHOPOMPS, CAV. There were lots of casualties. Jazzbeaux had been out of it for most of the fighting, but she could tell from the leavings that things had got serious. Some of the people looked as if they had been torn apart by animals with more in the way of teeth and claws than the Good Lord intended for them to have. Cheeks, a gaudy girl who had been riding with the 'Pomps for the last few months, was literally crushed flat into the road, dead eyes staring from a foot-wide face. A farmer was burned to the bone inside his unmarked Oshkosh B'Gosh bib-alls. A black US Cavalryman was slumped against the front window of the drug store, dead without a mark on him. She unbuttoned his holster, and took out his sidearm. She had lost her own gun back in the Feelgood.

The official killing iron was heavier than she was used to, but it would do the job. She unbuckled the yellowlegs' gunbelt, and cinched it around her hips.

Then, she picked up a half-brick and threw it through the drugstore window. Picking the glass away from the display, she reached for a squirter of morph-plus. She exposed her wrist, and jabbed the painkiller into her bloodstream.

Her head clearing slightly, she filled her jacket pockets with pills and ju-jujubes. She popped a glojo capsule into her mouth, and rolled it around on her tongue, not biting into it. The buzz seeped through her body. Some of the pain went away. Some.

THERE WAS SOMETHING *strange about the preacher's shades. Jazzbeaux had been wearing them on and off for two days. They were clearer than regular dark glasses, and did funny things to her. Once or twice, she thought she saw things in the periphery of her vision that couldn't be there. Indistinct things, but somehow unsettling. "Whassamatter, Jazzbie," Andrew Jean had asked, "you a loca ladybug? You're spookola in spades this ayem..."*

After a while, she began to get migraines. She took the glasses off, and thought about throwing them away, driving her cyke over them. But she just slung them around her neck.

The world looked real again, but she found herself wanting to put the glasses on again. It was like when she was eight, and Dead Daddy put her on Hero-9 to keep her under control. She had had to wean herself off the dope over a period of years, and still felt the occasional urge for a H-9 hit. This was an irrational longing too, but after a while it became irresistible. She fought it for as long as she could, but it was such a silly thing. She was a War Chief. She wasn't afraid to wear a pair of glasses.

This time, the effect was different. Colours were brighter, but less sharp. There were shadows where there shouldn't be. It was a little like a Hero-9 or Method-1 buzz, but without any of the elation. Somehow, with the glasses on, she felt compelled to look back over her shoulder all the time.

Like one that on a lonesome road doth walk in fear and dread, Tasha sang on her Ancient Mariner Mambo album, and having once turned round walks on, and turns no more his head; because he knows a frightful fiend doth close behind him tread.

It was like that. You didn't see the frightful fiend, but that didn't mean it wasn't there.

The preacher was coming after her, coming for his property. That shouldn't have scared her.

But it did.

THERE WAS A well nearby. Her waterdetector – now lost – had twanged when they crossed the Spanish Fork city limits. She would need a drink soon, and food.

She couldn't find a ve-hickle that worked. She supposed Elder Seth must have taken them all with him when he left in his motorwagon train. He would be half-way to Salt Lake City by now.

Now, she was coming for him. He had done his best to destroy her, and she was still here. She was still Jazzbeaux.

She squatted by the mess that had been Andrew Jean, and said her goodbyes. Andrew Jean had been a good 'pomp, a good gangbuddy. Nobody deserved to die like that.

Except the preacherman. Elder Seth needed to die slowly. He had been invincible earlier, when he had changed – the real self pushing out from behind his human mask – but now he was her meat.

The preacher had taken a girl out to kill her, but had made of her a weapon which could be used against him.

Jazzbeaux walked away from Andrew Jean. Just off the main street, she found the first of the carrion creatures. It was a bad one, a mew-tater. There was some kind of housecat in there, but it was the size of a moose, had white skunkmarks down its back, and the buds of vestigial extra heads hanging in its neckfur. It had gathered three or four corpses, and was playing with them, slicing them out of their clothes. Its saliva was corrosive, and etched patterns in the pale, dead skin of its supper.

Jazzbeaux stretched her fingers and lightly rested them on the butt of her scavved gun. The creature turned its head to look at her with slit-pupilled eyes the size of saucers. It showed its needle-sharp teeth, and flared a furry ruff. It could have leaped. With her broken fingers, she probably couldn't have outdrawn the thing.

But she met its eyes. It recognized a fellow predator, and backed down, returning its attention to its food. She walked away.

For the first time since she iced her Dad, Jazzbeaux felt she really had a purpose on this dull earth.

She hoped the old man would be proud of her.

II

THIS IS ZEEBEECEE, *The Station That's Got It All, bringing you What You Want twenty-four hours a day, sponsored by GenTech, the bioproducts division that really cares…*

In just five minutes, it will be time for Keep Fighting Fit With Governor Arnie, and some helpful advice on the maintenance of muscle implants in the elderly. Then we'll be bringing you Johnny Knoxville's Wide World of Executions, with some remarkable footage of garotting in Morocco, burning-at-the-stake in Thailand and, for the traditionalists among you, an Olde Englishe Publicke Hangingge from Tyburn Tree in London, England. But, first, tune into reality with Lola Stechkin, bringing you the Pre-Breakfast Bulletin from the comfort of her dancercise studio...

"Hi, Early Birds of America! It's August the 27th, 2021, and this is Lola, inviting you to stretch and strain and lose that pain. Here it is, folks, all the news you can handle...

"Washington, DC. Last night, President Estevez fielded tough questions concerning the controversial economic policies of his administration. Accused by some factions of bringing the nation close to bankruptcy with the Big Bonus, his personalized combination of high spending, high unemployment and decreased taxation, the President claimed, 'We'll just all have to wait and see how it pans out, won't we?' Dr Ottokar Proctor, head of the presidential think-tank, and widely believed to be the architect of the Big Bonus, was unavailable for comment, although he is scheduled to make an appearance at a film festival in Tampa, Florida, where he will give a lecture on the Sisyphean influence of Wile E Coyote and the Road Runner on contemporary American culture.

"Salt Lake City, Deseret. The first wagontrain of Josephite resettlers, under the leadership of Elder Nguyen Seth, is due to arrive in the deserted conurbation sometime before noontime today. Elder Seth has vowed to reclaim the wilderness from the elements as the Mormons did before him. A bill providing, among other things, for the renaming of the State of Utah, has been passed unopposed through Congress. The recent demise of Representative Osmond of Utah, who had planned to speak against the bill, is still unexplained.

"The horror murders of the inhabitants of a quiet suburban estate within the Savannah PZ have been attributed by Ms Redd Harvest of the Turner-Harvest-Ramirez Agency to the serial murderer who signs himself 'The Tasmanian Devil'. T-H-R claim to be following several leads, and hope to make an arrest soon. 'The Tasmanian Devil' has claimed over 350 victims in all quarters of the United States in the last year, and is noted for the savage ingenuity of his frenzied attacks. Surviving eyewitnesses are few in number, and give contradictory descriptions of the killer, but all agree on his unnatural strength and viciousness. 'We'll get him,' Ms Harvest has sworn. More on this as it breaks.

"Moscow. Talks broke down today between the Soviet and Japanese delegations who have been negotiating over recent territorial clashes over culture-krill-harvesting operations off the island of Sakhalin. Premier Abramovich has announced that he still hopes to come to an amicable agreement with the Imperial representative and the board of GenTech. In an editorial statement later this morning, Akira Kobayashi, the Chief Executive Officer of GenTech East, will explain how unreasonable and inefficient the Soviets are proving on this issue.

"Don't you think it's unfair of nature to insist that humanity only have two dentitions? The set-up was fine when life expectancy was barely thirty years, but with modern advances in medtech ensuring that all solvent citizens can enjoy a full and active life well into their one-hundreds, one set of milk teeth and one set of adult teeth just isn't enough. Well, thanks to GenTech, you can now have sown the buds of a third, fourth, fifth and even sixth set of genuine enamel-coated teeth. For as little as $500 a tooth, we can get you great-grandpas back on the taffy and rare steaks. GenTech, the biodivision that cares...

"Glastonbury, England. Prime Minister Mandelson today opens the state-sponsored popular music festival, showcasing the best of British culture. He has announced that he will join patriotic singer Johnny Lydon, host of the popular British variety program *The Johnny Lydon Band Show*, in a rendition of the star's biggest hit, 'God Save the Queen.' Other British showbiz greats scheduled to appear include Gary Barlow, Shane Ritchie, Joe Pasquale, Bradley Walsh, Cat Deeley and the comic duo of Benny Elton and Ricky Mayall, with American guest stars Marilyn Manson and Justin Timberlake reaffirming the Special Relationship. Rumours that Hanson plan to come out of retirement for this one last concert have been denied by the reclusive multi-billionaire band's manager, Peter Hall. John Lennon, the leader of Her Majesty's Loyal Opposition, who was briefly a member of an unsuccessful group called The Quarrymen back in the 1960s, was apparently asked if he wanted to reform to appear on the bill. 'Nobody was interested back then,' he told our reporter, 'I don't see why they should be now, like.'

"Manila, the Philippines. President-for-life Imelda Marcos yesterday dedicated a new statue of her late husband, the former president-for-life, and announced, after singing twenty-eight patriotic songs to the assembled multitudes, that she would set in motion a new scheme to clear up the streets of the city by personally firing the first bullet. Rebel forces remain encamped in the North of the islands, apparently supported by a Chinese Guomintang warlord and a Swiss-based multinat. Imelda will be guest-hosting the popular ZeeBeeCee show, You and Your Shoes, for the next three weeks.

"Puerto Belgrano, Antarctica. Following President Maradona's 75% increase of the levy on non-Argentine mining interests around the South Pole, violence flared up again as British wildcat oilmen tried to even the score after their resounding defeat in the Malvinas War of 2011. 'Wild' Charlie Mander, the British consul, and Sheriff Felipe Almodovar, the self-styled 'Law South of Tierra del Fuego', met for talks in an attempt to reach a settlement, but tempers rose and shots were exchanged. Ice Kold Katie, the Scottish esperado who has robbed several Argentine-owned banks and trading stores on the continent, celebrated the increase by ambushing and killing a troop of Argentine snowcat cavalrymen on their way to Esperanza.

"Ladies, don't you wish you had breasts as nice as mine? Well, thanks to GenTech biodiv, your wish can be granted. Personally developed by Dr Zarathustra, winner of the Nobel Prize for Genetic Surgery, our pectoral pump treatments can yield astonishing results. Even Warren Beatty won't be able to tell the difference. This is Shiralee St Croix of Saginaw, Michigan. We treated one of her breasts with the GenTech pectoral pump, and the other with a product manufactured by one of our competitors. I think you can see the difference for yourself. GenTech, the biodivision that cares...

"Teheran, the Pan-Islamic Congress. Today, the Ayatollah Bakhtiar, chairperson of the Sword of Allah Jihad Committee, sentenced to death in absentia graphic novelist Neil Gaiman author of the award-winning *Tintin in the Land of the Ragheads*, which has been widely interpreted as a personal attack on the Moslem faith and the continuing Islamic occupation of Greece, Albania, Macedonia, Kosovo and Montenegro. Gaiman has gone into hiding, but claims to be still working on his next work, a reconstruction of the myth of Desperate Dan, portraying the comic cowboy as an Indian-hating mass murderer. Viewers are invited to fax in with their guesses about where Gaiman is holed up. The closest to the truth will win a thousand dollars credit at their local Titancorp comics store, a Captain Haddock T-shirt and an all-expenses-paid holiday for two in balmy Beirut.

"Vatican City. Petya Tcherkassoff, the Russian singing idol, today had a personal audience with Pope Georgi. Tens of thousands of fans thronged St Peter's Square to glimpse the pair. What was discussed between the two has not been revealed, although Tcherkassoff did modestly state to the press that 'the cheloviek in the white hat has a bigger following than I do.' Tcherkassoff's current album release, "Songs for Suicidal Lovers", has been at the top of the musichip charts for six straight months.

"The Isle of Skye, Scotland. Sad news for children everywhere. Despite the donation of more than thirty million European Currency Units raised by GenTech-sponsored concerts in America and the Soviet Union, Wally the Whale – believed to be the last cetacean in the Atlantic Ocean – died today of natural causes totally unconnected with the acceptable levels of pollution in the area. Iain Menzies Banks, mayor of the island, has mooted a plan for the preservation of the whale as the centrepiece of Wallyworld, a luxury tourist preserve and family theme park. The whale will be coated inside and out with acrylics, and Banks intends to open a restaurant called The Jonah Snackbar in its stomach. Wally will, of course, live on in our hearts and minds, thanks to his continuing adventures on our Saturday Morning cartoon show Wally and His Whalesome Pals, and his smiling face will still appear on the packets of Wally's Whalefood, the popular krill-based breakfast cereal.

"This has been Lola Stechkin at ZeeBeeCee, signing off. If it's all right with you, it's all right with us..."

Stay tuned to ZeeBeeCee, The Station That's Got It all, if you want to enter the competition of the day. You could be the lucky winner of a free course of pectoral pump treatments, or a brand new Cadillac convertible. All you have to do is answer three simple questions, complete the following sentence, "If I had bigger breasts, the first thing I'd do would be..." and send your answers in on a fax with coupons from any three GenTech products. The questions are: a) Which former Vice-President of These United States had a sex change operation under the aegis of GenTech's own Dr Zarathustra? b)Who wrote the words to the 'GenTech Merry Marching Song'? Remember, it's the lyrics we're interested in, we know Andrew Lloyd Webber wrote the music. And c)what is transhumance?

As you heard on the news, we at ZeeBeeCee have been saddened by the tragic passing of Wally the Whale. As a result, a three-hour tribute to the brave aqua-mammal will pre-empt tonight's scheduled address to the nation by President Estevez, which will now take place after the eleven o'clock nightcap news. A whole host of stars, including Drew Barrymore, the Mothers of Violence and Hayley Duff, will be coming into the studio to share their memories of Wally with English folk singer Gordon Sumner, who has composed a special 'Goodbye Wonderful Wally' song to mark the whale's death. But now, on a lighter note, heeeeere's Governor Arnie...

III

THE KATZ MOTEL was a klick out of town, and hadn't been touched by the firefight. There was an old wooden house perched on top of a small hill, and the featureless cabins were spread out across the property below. The Psychopomps had checked in and done some minimal damage two nights back. Jazzbeaux had left some of her stuff in the cabin, confident that the twittering, birdlike manager would be too afraid of the 'Pomps to bother lifting anything from the gangcult.

On the road out of Spanish Fork, she had become aware of a wound just above her knee. It was a deep cut, and made walking painful. She bit down on the glojo capsule, and the pain went away.

She got stronger as she walked towards the motel. Perhaps she should sleep a while, and recover some more. *Little girlie-girl, you've had a busy-busy dayyy*, sang Petya Tcherkassoff in her head.

It was nearly dawn. There was some light in the sky. Nothing had come out of the dark to bug her.

Her knee felt like a wet sponge. She was limping. The glojo buzz faded away, and the pain trickled back.

She hadn't hurt this much since Daddy Deadest was around, playing his games with his willow switches and aluminium rods.

By the time she got to the motel, it was daylight. The manager was waiting for her at the desk, deftly fidgeting with a half-stuffed peregrine falcon. Herman Katz was a thin, youngish man with nervous eyes and a slight stutter. He was wearing an apron which made him look like a housewife, and tinkering with glass eyes, taking them out of a box and holding them up to the empty sockets of the dead bird, trying to find a matching pair that fitted. It wasn't Jazzbeaux's idea of a hobby, but there were more dangerous people in the world.

"Morning," he said. "Quite a bit of noise, last night. Nobody else has come back from town."

She didn't feel like giving him the news. He would find out sooner or later that there wasn't any Spanish Fork any more. She wondered if he'd stay on in the motel business, or move out. Not her prob.

"Mother was upset. She couldn't get to sleep, what with all the shooting and shouting and I-don't-know-what-all else."

Herman kept talking about his mother. She was an invalid, stuck in a rocking chair up in her room in the house. Jazzbeaux hadn't met her, but she could imagine the type. A bitter old biddy, eating herself alive with bile, pretending to be crippled to tie her son to the old place, sucking all the life out of him. She knew all about demanding parents.

She'd learned about that back when she was Jessamyn Amanda and nine-year-olds had been worth a gallon of potable water on the streets of the NoGo. Ma Katz could hardly be more of a monster than Daddy Dear, Bruno

Bonney. He had told her she would have to be an outlaw because of her heritage. The old man had claimed kinship with Anne Bonney, the pirate queen of the Spanish Main, and William Bonney, Billy the Kid. One thing she had to say about Dad, at least he had prepped her for the world she was going to have to live in.

Other girls graduated from the PZ high schools and got Senior Proms, but she had known she was a grown-up woman the day she ripped Bruno's rotten throat out for him. She'd breezed through the courts, faking numbskull stupidity, and come out clean. Everyone knew what she had done, but no one was really that conce with it. A few looies spread around the Juvie Op Agency, and she walked free. She had been with the 'Pomps since then.

Yesterday, she had thought she might have a healthy career in front of her. She didn't believe she'd marry Petya Tcherkassoff and move to a dacha on the steppes any more, but she thought she might see twenty-five. Now, things were different. She would live as long as she had to to see Elder Seth dead, and then she would think again...

"It was a rough night. Don't worry about it."

"You want your room key?"

"Chalet Number One."

Herman fussed with his bird, needlessly wiping his palms on his apron, and took the key down.

Jazzbeaux took the key. "Is the shower working?"

"Sh-sh-shower?" Herman was spooked. That put her on her guard.

"Yeah. I'm a mess. I want to clean up."

"Sh-sh-sure, the shower's fine. I checked the systems myself only a week back."

"Terrif."

"It's a special service. Costs extra. Water's expensive. We have to get it piped in from town special. We have to pay one-third of our turnover to Judge Colpeper for the privilege, so you'll have to dig deep into your purse."

She pulled her jacket off her shoulders. Some skin came away with it, and her back stung. Her cutaway T-shirt was even more cutaway than it had been when she bought it. Herman's eyes popped. She couldn't work out whether he was ogling her breasts or appalled by the extent of her injuries. He tried to say something, but she walked away, towards Chalet Number One.

"I put in cuh-cuh-clean towels, mizz," Herman whined.

She ignored him, and unlocked her door. Inside, the room was a mess. She had partied with Andrew Jean, Cheeks and So Long Suin the night before last, and Herman hadn't even tried to clear up. One of Andrew Jean's beehive combs lay on the dressing table in a spread of pills and lipsticks. The pornovideo set was smashed, a high-heeled ruby shoe lodged in the cracked screen. Cheeks hated Billy Priapus flicks. The ice sculpture had melted, leaving a tray of warm water on the floor. That brought back interesting, if cool, memories. There were bulletholes in the ceiling – which might have been there before the 'Pomps checked inand the queensize bed was a tangle of ugly tie-died sheets and surplus clothing.

She remembered the night, the nights. Andrew Jean on top, Cheeks squealing, So Long rocking her to orgasm. She would miss her gangbuddies. The days of fun and frolic were gone for good. Shit, she was nearly seventeen. She should be all grown up. She'd never sign up for marriage and mortgage, that was for sure. But there was an adult place marked out for her.

The bathroom was better. Jazzbeaux took the rubber ducks and Wally Whales out of the tub and threw them away, then turned on the shower, letting the water run. Getting naked was a long and painful process, and involved finding out just how much punishment her body had taken. She had to cut her stockings off with nail scissors, and the fishnet pattern was stamped in red on her swollen knee. She wasn't bleeding any more, but there were huge scabs on her face, chest and back. She stretched, and little stabs of pain shot through her.

Jazzbeaux stepped under the shower, and sponged her wounds. The warm water washed over her face and body. She shook her hair, scraping the slime out of it. The remains of her whiteface make-up came off with the clotted badges of blood. The warmth made her sleepy, and she slipped down in the bathtub, lying under the shower jet, taking the water full in the face. Between her feet, water swirled down the plug-hole, taking red and black threads of blood and dirt with it.

She thought of sleep, but was too tired to make a move for the bed. Wearily, she sponged her torso and stomach, cleaning her wounds. They stung, but it was a healthy, healing pain. Doc Threadneedle had fixed her body up so she healed quick, and the stinging meant that the micro-organisms he had fed into her flesh were doing their good work. What you want is a parasite that works for you, not on you, he had said.

Her head lolled to one side, and her eye fluttered shut. Something moved, and she looked again. There was a shadow on the shower curtain, a human-shape holding something in an upraised arm.

The plastic dimpled, and a silvery point poked through. It was a long knife. The curtain tore, and the figure stabbed...

IV

HAWK-THAT-SETTLES, son of Two-Dogs-Fucking, was waiting. But he knew his wait was nearly over.

His people, the Navaho, had been waiting for nearly a hundred and fifty years. Brutally suppressed by bluecoats led by Rope Thrower, known to whites as Kit Carson, in 1863, they had been out of the major Indian Wars because the Reservation lands given to them were so arid and dreary that even the white man didn't want to kick them off to somewhere else. No gold, no oil, no food, no water: just Navaho, persisting as they always had done, getting drunk and stubbornly refusing to die out. Now, the whole of the West and the Mid-West was like the Navaho Reservation. Before Rope Thrower subdued the Great Chief Manuelito – among whose lieutenants was Hawk's many-times-great grandfather Armijo – the Navaho had been herders of horses and cattle, cultivators of corn, pumpkins, wheat and melons and famous for their groves of peach trees. The Navaho had respected Rope Thrower as a warrior, but could never forgive the destruction of their prized orchards. Removed from their fertile lands in what became New Mexico, the Navaho were transported to the Bosque Redondo and into the mountains.

Now, in Monument Valley, on the border between Arizona and Utah, Hawk pulled his stetson lower, to keep the glare of the sun from his face, and strode out of the drugstore to join the depressed knot of Indians at the roadside. The motorwagons were passing them by, a battered parade. Two-Dogs was slumped in his usual chair, with four legs of unequal length, sucking like a baby on the brown-paper-wrapped bottle he always carried. Hawk nodded to his father, the man who had tutored him as a Dreamwalker, and was not acknowledged. He knew all the others by name, by the names of their families for generations past. It was his place to remember the ancestors. He was the medicine man, now that Two-Dogs was the whisky Navaho.

Bowed, weary, and with deeply-lined faces, the Indians all looked ancient, even the children. If possible, life was harder even for these ragged redskins than it had been for their forefathers after the war with Rope Thrower, when their livelihood had been deliberately burned away from them. Only Jennifer White Dove replied to his greeting, with a tight smile. They were of an age, Hawk and Jennifer, and had been close as teenagers, before Hawk joined up with the Sons of Geronimo and left the Reservation, intent on changing the world. By the time he had been through that and was ready to return, Jennifer had been married and divorced and was almost a stranger again.

The motorwagons were full of smiling, unreadable pilgrims in black, presumably joyous at being so close to their destination, Salt Lake City. The convoys had been coming through all week. Hawk still had the shakes, although they were coming under control. He had been doing road duty when the first wagons rolled past, with a US Cavalry Escort, and he had looked upon the face of the Josephite leader and known that these were the last days of the world. Nguyen Seth was his name. Hawk had read about him in the newsfax, but rarely watched teevee, and so had never seen his face before. That is, not in the flesh.

From his childhood, he had known the face, had seen it in paintings and had drawn it himself. It was the bone-white, dark-hole-eyed – sunglasses, he realized – face of the Summoner. Two-Dogs had not always been a whisky Navaho, and he had taught his son the stories his father had taught to him. The stories of the Last Days, when the Summoner would open up the Dark Reaches of the Spirit Lands and call down the worst of the manitous to lay waste the worlds of the white man and the red.

Since he had caught sight of the Summoner, he had not liked to watch the resettlers pouring through into Utah, knowing what it was they were really following. He had talked with a plastic young couple in the Reservation Diner, listened to them enthusing about their new-found life and the dictates of their faith, but had seen the deadness in their hearts. Some of the Reservation Indians had gone with them when they left, eager for a chance at something better. The Navaho Jospehites were all young, as young as he had been when he joined the Sons and painted his face to strike a blow at the heart of the white man's world. That had been a futile crusade, he knew now, but it was better than the lie Seth offered, the lie that concealed the end of all things.

The Indians of the Plains – Apache and Comanche – that he had known in the Sons of Geronimo had sworn that the white man's time was nearing an end, and that the buffalo would return. But he knew these were dreams of sand. The buffalo could do nothing against the deadweight of the Europeans.

He had been waiting for the spirit warrior his father had told him of in infancy, the One-Eyed White Girl. If the Summoner was abroad, then he would soon be followed. It was revealed in the series of pictures, drawn and redrawn in his family for generations. Two-Dogs said the One-Eyed White Girl would have steel in her muscles and fire in her empty eye, and that she would come to the Navaho – to the family of Armijas – or her education. It was the duty of the medicine man of the line of Armijas to tutor the spirit warrior through the Seven Levels, to prepare her for the final battle, in which she would stand with the other spirit warriors – the Holy Woman From Across the Great Water, the Man With Music in His Heart, the Red-Handed One, the Yellowlegs Who Has Lost Much, the Great Father in White, the Man Who Rides Alone – against the army of the manitous and the story would end.

Hawk had seen it told as a series of pictures on buffalo hides. The last pictures were just darkness. Much had been foretold, but the ultimate outcome was unknown, unknowable. "I envy you, my son," Two-Dogs had told him yesterday, "you will see the last pictures." Two-Dogs claimed his time was almost up, and was drinking even more heavily than usual. He had foreseen his death so many times that Hawk no longer bothered much with such presentiments, but, this time, things were different...

The Sons of Geronimo had been a wash-out in the end. Lots of fiery meetings and grand gestures, plenty of petitions to Washington and protests outside John Wayne movies, but in the end they had just been a bunch of dumb redskins battering their heads against the white man's bricks. Their political campaign had been as ineffectual as their terrorist "outrages," which had harmed no one but the odd insurance firm. Chata, their chief, had been shot dead by a bank guard in Wyoming during an attempted hold-up. The Sons had been running short of funds. Then Ulzana, the Apple Apache in his Gucci Ghost Shirt, would-be heir to the eagle-feathers, graduated from Berkeley, and set up a computer software firm. Hawk had sent him a parcel containing a bisected apple: red outside, white inside. The trickle of money raised by the tribes had dried up, the teevee crews stopped coming round, and the white girls all drifted away, with or without their pale-skinned babies, petitioning to rejoin the master race. Hawk didn't know where the others were. What had happened to Sacheen Littlefeather? Sky Buffalo? William Silverheels? Two-Dogs-Fucking had shrugged, and gone back to waiting for his monthly security cheques. Only Hawk-That-Settles was there to carry the dream forward, to pass it on – if need be – to his son.

Now, there would be no son.

The motorwagons were gone, and everyone was drifting away. Jennifer White Dove smiled at him again, almost soliciting his interest. On the Reservation, being a medicine man meant literally that these days. He was in charge of the drugstore, and Jennifer's husband had left her with a habit or two. Sometimes, he knew, she would bruise herself with a rock to get morph-plus out of him. There were a lot of Indians like that, so used to the cycle of hurt and deadening that it was a snowballing addiction. He didn't meet her eyes, and she drifted away with the others.

"Father?"

Two-Dogs looked up, eyes not focusing.

"Father, I must leave."

Two-Dogs nodded his head, yes. "The Holy-Place-From-Over-the-Great-Water?"

"Yes, father." It was the title of one of the pictures. Two-Dogs had long ago found the real place, an abandoned monastery in the desert. It was far south, near the Mexican border.

"She will come to you there, the One-Eyed White Girl."

"So you have said."

"And so my father said before me. So we have all said, back to the times of the peach trees."

There was an embarassing pause. Hawk always felt ill at ease in these conversations, as if he were forced to read the lines of a savage redskin in a Hollywood film. He did not talk like this with anyone else, but his father would not laugh at talk of the Holy-Place-From-Over-the-Great-Water or the Yellowlegs Who Has Lost Much.

Beyond the road, Hawk saw the table mountains lumped against the sky. They had made many Hollywood films here. As a young man, Two-Dogs had fought with many armies of extras, firing off pretend guns at John Wayne in *Stagecoach*, *Fort Apache*, *She Wore a Yellow Ribbon* and *The Searchers*. Once, Hawk had found a faded snapshot of Two-Dogs dressed in the beads and paint of an Apache standing proudly between a smiling John Wayne and a one-eyed Irishman he guessed was the movie director John Ford. Later, ashamed, Two-Dogs would picket screenings of the films he had appeared in, although he admitted in private that many times as a young man he had eaten well at a movie commissary when he would otherwise have starved. Once, a message had been sent to Ford in Hollywood, entreating aid for the Navahos after a hard winter, and the director had found a Western script to make in Monument Valley simply to bring some money to the tribe.

Still, Hollywood had done an irreparable harm to the Indian, perpetuating the lies of the Manifest Destiny, the Savage Redskin and the Noble Bluecoats.

Two-Dogs took a swig on his bottle. Hawk would never grow old like this.

"Goodbye, father."

Two-Dogs nodded, and Hawk turned. He had a long walk before him.

V

THE FIGURE STABBED at the empty air.

Naked and wet, Jazzbeaux leaped out of the tub at the knife-wielder. She didn't need this, but she was prepared. She hadn't lived through the hell of Spanish Fork to be carved up by some common-or-garden psychopath.

The knife raked her side, but she ignored the pain and struck out with the flat of her hand at the psycho's chin.

As the knife darted towards her like a hawk's beak, she glimpsed iron grey hair in a bun, and saw the swish of the long, faded dress. It was the old woman, she assumed.

Her blow connected, and Ma Katz staggered backwards, blade scraping the flower-pattern wallpaper. Jazzbeaux half-turned and launched a kick, punching with the side of her foot into the old woman's stomach.

The knife came again, and she chopped with both hands at Ma Katz's wrist, satisfied by the crunch of breaking bones.

Ma Katz shrieked like a wounded eagle, and the knife clattered to the floor. The old woman's fingers curved into talons and she scratched at Jazzbeaux's face.

There wasn't much more Ma Katz could do to her face that Elder Seth hadn't, but lines of pain opened up, and Jazzbeaux felt her vision distorting. She was used to having one eye, but now she knew she wasn't seeing what she should.

Ma Katz's face, twisted by hatred, was that of her son.

Jazzbeaux made a point with the fingers of her left hand, and jabbed it into the old woman's throat, twice.

Ma Katz coughed and spluttered, yellow tears coursing down her face. Jazzbeaux grabbed the old woman's hair, and it came away in her hand.

Sobbing, Herman Katz sank to the floor, drawing in his arms and legs as he assumed a foetal ball, trying to return to the safety of his mother's womb.

Jazzbeaux threw the wig into the toilet, and reached for a towel. She didn't fully understand the set-up at the Katz Motel, but she had been through the fires, and was surviving.

Bruno Bonney had been fond of quoting Nietszche. That which does not kill me makes me stronger. Of course, that was before she had killed him.

Herman? – Ma Katz? – whoever – had not killed her. She was stronger.

Now, she wanted breakfast.

VI

In the deserted city, Roger Duroc waited for Nguyen Seth and the resettlers. His prep crew had coptered in a few days ago, but it was psychologically important for the movement that the first arrivals turn up in the old way, like the Mormon pioneers who had first built by the Salt Lake and made the desert bloom.

Duroc's team had got the power on, and he had sent exterminator packs into the streets to begin the task of clearing out the vermin that still clung to the ruins. He had picked up a group of experienced hunter-killers from the Phoenix NoGo, and turned them loose on the remaining sandrats. There were less in Salt Lake than in most ghost cities, because of the lack of water. For the first few years, that would be the big problem for the resettlers too, but a pipeline was being built that would bring a supply down from Canada.

Seth had it all worked out.

With the backing of President Estevez, the Josephite Church was building its sanctuary in the former state of Utah. Now, it was renamed Deseret, and was only technically a part of the United States of America. It would have its own flag, its own judicial system, its own state religion, its own Great and Secret Purpose.

Duroc looked over the reports from the engineers he had sent down into the dry sewers. Their casualties had been acceptable, and the cynogen had put an end to the indigenous subterraneans. Tunnel-fighting. That took him back to Kandahar, where he had joined up with the Summoner and later fought with Al Qaeda against the Great Satan.

The lights flickered. The power was still variable, but it was a start. He had made his headquarters in what had been the presidential suite of the Hilton hotel. A portrait of Trickydick Nixon glowered down at him. Someone had shot its eyes out, perhaps a Comanche hoping to condemn the ex-President's incomplete spirit to an eternity of wandering between the winds.

He had come a long way with the Elder, as had his family from time immemorial. He remembered the day in Paris, all those years ago, when his uncle had introduced him to the tall, quiet man to whom his life would be dedicated. Nguyen Seth hadn't changed since then, Duroc knew. But then again, the Elder was older than he looked. Sometimes, he assumed the Elder had been around since the Creation. Once, tens of thousands of years ago, he might have been remotely human.

Now, so close to the Last Days for which he had been prepared, Seth was what he was, and nothing less.

Sometimes, Duroc missed his uncle. But the succession had had to take place. Duroc had had to come of age and replace the older Duroc in the service of Nguyen Seth.

Blevins Barricune, the ex-Op Duroc had put in charge of the city limits, came through on the intercom.

"We have a sighting, sir."

Duroc lit up a Gauloise. "Good."

"Twenty or thirty ve-hickles, moving slowly."

"The wagon train?"

"Affirmative."

Duroc blew a smoke ring. "Well, get the brass band out. The Elder will need a welcome. You know the hymns they must play."

"It will be done, sir. By the way, we've found some children in the old tabernacle. Five, between the ages of eight and twelve. They have no speech beyond grunts, but they've been surviving out here."

"Children?"

"Yes, sir."

"How remarkable. They must have endured many hardships to keep going out here."

"Yes. They overpowered Vercoe and Wood."

"Vercoe and Wood? What's their status?"

"Both casualties, sir."

"The children?"

"Unharmed, mostly. Pouncey was Vercoe's squeeze, and so he cut loose a bit with the cattle prod."

"That's understandable."

Duroc picked up his broad-brimmed black hat, and set it upon his head. He examined himself in the mirror. He looked very clerical.

"I'll be down directly. Have a car ready to take me to the city limits. I'll want to see the Elder arrive. The moment must be marked with all due ceremony. The vid team will record it for posterity."

That was a lie. There would be no posterity.

"And the children?"

"Oh, you know what to do. Hang them."

"Fine, sir."

"Let Pouncey do it. The man deserves something for his loss."

"Very well, sir."

Humming "All Things Bright and Beautiful" Duroc left his suite.

VII

WITH HER WOUNDS dressed and bound and clean clothes on, Jazzbeaux felt approximately like a human being. That was dangerous, she knew. Ever since she had looked through Seth's shades, she had been more than human. Or perhaps less. She felt an odd detachment that she would have to get used to. Her humanity was something useless to her, something that came from the Denver NoGo and which should have died in Spanish Fork with Andrew Jean and the others. She was still carrying it about, like a Mexican mother in a warzone still toting a dead baby at her breast. Membership in the human race was a psychological crutch she knew she could do without, but wasn't quite ready to throw away yet. There would be time.

She had left Herman Katz in the bathroom. He was verging on catatonia. Yesterday, she would have casually killed him. Now, she didn't see the point. She was saving herself for Elder Seth.

There was no food in the chalet, so she went up to the house. If there was no real Ma Katz to bother her, the place should be empty and Herman ought to have the makings of a breakfast. She wanted a pint of recaff and a toasted cheese sandwich. Perhaps a bowlful of Wally's Whale Food, and a jujube or two to give it a buzz. Perhaps not. Perhaps she didn't need drugs any more, didn't want the buzz. There were enough new things going on in her mind.

She climbed the rickety steps set into the hillside and got up to the porch of the Katz house. The door was open. Inside, the hallway was musty and dark. She saw an old French dresser with faded photographs in gilt frames under a bed of cobweb. An embroidered sampler hung on the wall, A BOY'S BEST FRIEND IS HIS MOTHER. Three identical aprons hung on a crooked coatstand. A buzzard, wings outstretched, posed stiffly over the kitchen door, its glass eyes thickly dusted-over.

The kitchen was what she had expected, dominated by an antique cooker and a fridge the size of a Buick. She found some reconstituted milk and some no-brand krill, which gave her a bowlful of mush to eat while the old kettle boiled. There was a plastic model of Redd Harvest's G-Mek V12 'Nola Gay in the packet of krill, but the wheels fell off when she ran it across the table.

It occurred to her that most people, her former self included, would not walk away from an attack by a homicidal transvestite and sit down to a healthy breakfast. She knew she was changing inside.

It was something to do with Seth's magic mirrorshades.

She hadn't slept, but she felt rested, calm, perfectly balanced. It was as if the fight with Herman had had the effect she would have expected from eight hours on a contoured mattress and a course of Doc Threadneedle's pick-me-up shots.

The kettle whistled, and she made herself some recaff. Her father always swore while he drank the stuff, claiming to have been raised on real coffee before the CAC stopped exporting from Nicaragua, but she never understood his complaints. She had had real coffee once or twice on the 'Pomps' raids down into Mexico, but it hadn't seemed special. She preferred recaff. This morning, she could barely taste anything. It was important to fill her stomach, and the warm liquid was nice in her throat, but that was it. There was no pleasure in the old sensations.

On the kitchen table, there was an old, leather-bound book. It had KATZ FAMILY ALBUM embossed on it in gold. She flipped it open. There was a plump baby with Herman Katz's shining eyes, trussed up in a blue nightie, perched unsteadily on the lap of a haggard young woman. Herman and his mother. The couple recurred over the next few pages, with Herman becoming a child, then a young man, but never losing his startled look, as if the camera flash were a slap in the face. No one else intruded in the pictures, although someone must have been there to point the camera.

The book was half-full of perfectly mounted, perfectly posed snapshots. Then, between two pages, she found about thirty polaroids loose. They were of different people, all women, but from the same view, from behind the mirror in the bathroom of one of the chalets. Women bathed, showered, brushed their teeth, sat on the toilet, peered at the mirror. They were all naked, or nearly so. The latest was no more than two days old. It was Cheeks – dead Cheeks – squatting nude, snorting a line of zooper-blast from her pocket mirror, talking to someone in the bedroom. It had been Jazzbeaux. She remembered the moment. She had been talking about the rumble with the Daughters of the American Revolution, playing with Seth's glasses, putting them on and taking them off. At the time, with the glasses on, she had imagined she could faintly discern the shape of a skull under Cheeks' plump face. The memory made her shudder.

She had seen too many ghost skulls, and all under the faces of people who were now dead. For a moment, she vowed never to look in a mirror again, in case she should be able to trace the outlines of her own durium-laced bones. Somewhere along the road, she had picked up a few extra senses, and she would have to learn to live with them.

This book, for instance, turned her stomach. She could see beyond the snapshots, and feel the gradual destruction of little Herman's personality as his mother became ever more dominant, ever more demanding. No wonder the kid had snapped.

Where was the real Ma Katz?

Jazzbeaux finished her recaff, and pushed the album away. She left the kitchen, and looked up the stairs. There was something up there beyond the landing, in one of the shuttered rooms. She knew it for a fact. It was calling to her, calling inside her head.

"Jessa-myn," it hissed. It was a woman's voice, but it reminded her of her father's whining. "Jessa-myn. Come upstairs, come upstairs."

She found she was halfway up already, unconsciously obeying the voice. She moved as if she were in a dream, wading through viscous liquid. Nothing mattered, but the voice.

"Jessa-myn, cain't you be sociable?"

Her headache was back, and her vision was disrupted. With her right eye, she saw the staircase before her, and the landing above, but with the left side of her sight, she was seeing her past replayed. There was her father, bleeding from the throat. There was Andrew Jean, face close to hers, tongue flicking. And there was Elder Seth, baring his teeth as he pushed her face into the asphalt. She shook her head, and tried to rub out the impossible visions. Her broken optic shifted painfully, and she realized she had been seeing out of her empty left eyesocket.

She had lost her eye when she was fifteen, in a brawl with the Gaschuggers outside Welcome, Arizona. She had never missed it until now.

She grabbed the banister and dragged herself upwards. She was under some kind of attack. Nothing new there.

In the darkness inside, Elder Seth laughed silently, his eyes blazing through his mirrorshades. Her face was in his eyes, distorted and shimmering.

She was on the landing now, and it spun around her. She assumed a fighting stance, but couldn't remain balanced.

The door opposite hung ajar. It creaked as it swung open. The room beyond was mainly dark, but lines of pale daylight stabbed through the slats of battered shutters. The creaking continued when the door was open. Jazzbeaux recognized the noise. It was a rocking chair, its weight shifting from the person in it.

"Mrs Katz?" she asked. There was no reply.

Reflections flashed in the darkness. Suddenly, Jazzbeaux knew whom she was about to face. Elder Seth. In the dark, Seth would be his true self, his human face off but his dark glasses still on.

The rocking carried on. Things scuttled. Rats. The house was filthy, she realized, practically falling to pieces. How could Herman and his mother stand it?

Jazzbeaux held onto the guardrail of the landing, and struggled to control her equilibrium. When she first lost her eye, she had had trouble keeping her balance, but she had thought she had overcome that. Obviously, any knock could send her mind spinning like a top.

She let go of the rail and stepped across the landing. She tottered through the open door. The smell hit her first. It was overpowering. Many things had died in this room and left their stink behind. There was a powerful chemical stench, and a psychic residue of pain and cruelty that was like a punch in the gut.

In the darkness, Ma Katz rocked. Jazzbeaux saw grey hair as the figure's head passed through the knives of light, and a dress like the one Herman had been wearing in the bathroom.

"Mrs Katz?"

She knew the woman had been dead for a long time. She stepped around the rocking mummy, and pulled the shutters open. Light streamed into the room, and caught the corpse.

It wasn't so bad, not after the things Jazzbeaux had seen back in Spanish Fork. Herman's taxidermy was inexpert, but Ma Katz was desiccated rather than rotten.

The dead woman was wearing a pair of sunglasses. They weren't anything like Seth's. Pink, heart-shaped Lolita frames and pale blue lenses.

Jazzbeaux turned away and looked out of the window. On the horizon, she could see Spanish Fork still burning. Columns of smoke were drifting up into the sky. That would attract the Road Cavalry soon. She would do well to get out of the area before they turned up. Some of the patrol who had been in the Feelgood could have radioed in a report before things started blowing up, or maybe even got away. She had only seen one corpse in union blue. There had been four in the cruiser.

The creaking behind her stopped, and Jazzbeaux spun around. Ma Katz was shakily standing, impossibly animated. Her glasses shone with reflected sunlight. The creature which should not have been came for her, clawhands jerking.

"Jessa-myn!" it shouted from its dry mouth. It had her father's voice. It had Elder Seth's voice.

She cleared her holster, and put a shot into the thing's chest. A puff of ancient dust came out as the slug went in. Her bullet tore through Ma Katz and spent itself against the wall. The thing kept coming. She shot again, trying for the head. The glasses went wonky as the upper left quarter of the head flew apart. The hair came off like Herman's wig, and the papery flesh flaked away from the exploded skull. A glass eye rolled out of its socket.

Something gurgled in Ma Katz's throat, and the dead woman collapsed in a bony heap.

In her head, the echoes of Seth's laughter died away.

"Mama," said a high-pitched voice from the landing.

Herman staggered in, his apron on again, a tray of breakfast things in his hand. He shook, but didn't spill the milk.

"Mama..."

Jazzbeaux looked at the long-gone creature on the floor, and across to her son. Herman had no adequate response in his emotional repertoire. He set the tray down gently by the bedside, and picked up what was left of the mummy. It came apart in his arms, but he bundled it onto the bed.

"You've hurt mother," he said.

Jazzbeaux tried not to look him in the eye.

"Once I tried to hurt mother, but she got better. She'll get better this time, won't she?"

"Yes, Herman," Jazzbeaux lied. "Everything will get better."

She left him there, and went out into the desert, not knowing where she was headed, or what she was going through. Inside her head, the lights went out one by one, systems shut down. She walked towards the west, towards the point where the moon had just set. The sand began at the edge of the property. She walked out onto it, her boots sinking in with each step, and left the Katz Motel behind her.

Dead women didn't walk. Dead women didn't talk with the voice of Elder Seth. She knew that. But Ma Katz had got out of her rocking chair, and the preacherman had stared at her through the mummy's glass eyes.

Jazzbeaux walked, trying to reconcile what she knew with what she had seen, what she had felt. As the sun rose higher into the morning sky, circuits went inside her greymass, flaring up and dwindling to ash. She ignored her hurts, and kept walking, dragging her feet a little, but still walking…

In Spanish Fork, the fires began to burn themselves out.

part two
the sandrat

I

IN HIS ISOLATION *tank in the Salt Lake City Tabernacle of Joseph, naked but for his mirrorshades, Nguyen Seth sampled Jazzbeaux's memories. He had access to portions of her mind she herself was losing. He could not tell why he was fascinated with this girl. It had happened before, down through the centuries. He would join in battle or in love so closely with a human that a link was established that worked both ways. Usually, it was a woman or a very young man. Sikander the Greek, Kleopatra, the Maid of Orleans, Aphra Behn, Emily of Haworth, Lizzie B, Rupert Brooke... It took a peculiar collection of qualities to catch his mental eye. It was a weakness, he supposed, but not one he could do anything about. Especially vivid was the period in Jessamyn Bonney's life between her first meeting with the Josephite motorwagons and the burning of Spanish Fork, when she had worn his spectacles. She had left her imprint upon them, and now her mind overlapped with his whenever he wore the sacred lenses. He felt himself sinking into one of the familiar vignettes...*

The Daughters of the American Revolution had been racking up a heavy rep in the past few months. They had total-stumped some US Cav in the Painted Desert, and some were saying they had scratched a Maniax Chapter in the Rockies. But after tonight, their time in the sun was Capital-O Over. And the Psychopomps would rule!

Jazzbeaux pushed a wing of hair back out of her eye, and clipped it into a topknot-tail. She took off the snazzy shades she had taken from the preacherman they'd jump-rammed this morning, and passed them back to Andrew Jean. No sense getting your scav smashed before it was fenced. She beckoned the Daughter forward with her razorfingered glove, and gave the traditional high-pitched 'Pomp giggle.

The others behind her joined in, and the giggle sounded throughout the ghost town. Moroni it was called. The War Councils of the gangs had chosen it at random. It was some jerkwater zeroville in Utah nobody gave a byte about.

The Daughter didn't seem concerned. She was young, maybe seventeen, and obviously blooded. There were fight-marks on her flat face, and she had a figure that owed more to steroids and implants than nature. Her hair was dyed grey and drawn up in a bun, with two needles crossed through it. She wore a pale blue suit, skirt slit up the thigh for combat, and a white blouse. She had a cameo with a picture of George Washington at her throat, and sensible shoes with concealed switchblades. Her acne hadn't cleared up and she was trying to look like a dowager.

More than one panzer boy had mistaken the Daughters of the American Revolution for solid citizens, tried the old mug-and-snatch routine, and wound up messily dead. The DAR were very snazz at what they did, which was remembering the founding fathers, upholding the traditional American way of life and torturing and killing people. Personally, Jazzbeaux wasn't into politics. She called a gangcult a gangcult, but the Daughters tried to sell themselves as a Conservative Pressure Group. They had a male adjunct, the Minutemen, but they were wimpo faghags. It was the Daughters you had to be conce with.

"Come for it, switch-bitch," Jazzbeaux hissed, "come for my knifey-knives!"

The Daughter walked forward, as calm as you please, and with a samurai movement drew the needles out of her hair. They glinted in the torchlight. They were clearly not ornamental. She grinned. Her teeth had been filed and capped with steel. Expensive dental work.

"Just you and me, babe," Jazzbeaux said, "just you and me."

The rest of the DAR cadre stood back, humming "America the Beautiful". The other Psychopomps were silent. This was a formal combat to settle a territorial dispute. Utah and Nevada were up for grabs since the Turner-Harvest-Ramirez and US Cav joint action put the Western Maniax out of business, and Jazzbeaux thought the 'Pomps could gain something from a quick fight rather than a long war.

This was not a funfight. This was Serious Business. Jazzbeaux heard they did much the same thing in Jap corp boardrooms.

The Daughter drew signs in the air with her needles. They were dripping something. Psychoactive venom of some sort, Jazzbeaux had heard. Hell, her system had absorbed just about every ju-ju the GenTech labs could leak illegally onto the market, and she was still kicking. And punching, and scratching, and biting.

"You know, pretty-pretty, I hear they're talkin' about settlin' the Miss America pageant like this next anno. You get to do evenin' dress, and swimwear, and combat fatigues."

The Daughter growled.

"I wouldn't give much for your chances of winning the crown, though. You just plain ain't got the personality."

Behind her patch, the implant buzzed open, and circuitry lit up. She might need her optic burner. It always made for a grand fightfinisher.

Jazzbeaux held up her ungloved hand, knuckles out, and shimmered the red metal stars implanted in her knucks. Kid-stuff. The sign of The Samovar Seven, her fave Russian musickies when she was a kid. She didn't freak much to the Moscow Beat these days, but she knew Sove Stuff really got to the DAR.

"You commie slit," sneered the Daughter.

"Who preps your dialogue, sister? John Wayne?"

Jazzbeaux hummed in the back of her throat. "Unbreakable Union of Soviet Republics..." The 'Pomps caught the tune, and joined it. The Daughter's eyes narrowed. She had stars on one cheek, and stripes on the other. The President of their chapter wore a Miss Liberty spiked hat, and carried a killing torch.

"Take the fuckin' slag down, Jazz-babe," shrilled Andrew Jean, her lieutenant, always the encouraging soul.

The DAR switched to "My Country 'tis of Thee". The 'Pomps segued to "Long-Haired Lover From Leningrad," popularized by Vania Vanianova and the Kulture Kossacks.

The Daughter clicked her heels, and made a pass, lunging forwards. Jazzbeaux bent to one side, letting the needle pass over her shoulder, and slammed the Daughter's midriff with her knee. The spiked pad ripped through the Daughter's blouse, and grated on the armoured contour-girdle underneath. The Daughter grabbed Jazzbeaux's neck, and pulled her off her feet.

Jazzbeaux recognized the move. Her Daddy had tried it on her back in the Denver NoGo.

She bunched her fingers into a sharp cone and stabbed above the Daughter's girdle-line, aiming for the throat, but the Daughter was too fast, and chopped her wrist, deflecting the blow.

Just what her Dad used to do. "Jessa-myn, cain't you be sociable?!" The low-rent ratskag. Of course, one time his reflexes had been off, and now he was recycled organs.

She danced round the bigger girl, getting a few scratches down the back of her suit, even drawing some blood. The Daughter swung round and Jazzbeaux had to take a fall to avoid the needles.

The 'Pomps were chanting and shouting now, while the DAR had fallen silent. That didn't mean anything.

She was down in the dirt, rolling away from the sharp-toed kicks. The DAR had good intelligence contacts, obviously. The girl had struck her three times on the right thigh, just where the once-broken bone was, and had taken care to stay out of the field of her optic burner. Of course, she had also cut Jazzbeaux's forehead below the hairline, making her bleed into her regular eye. Anyone would have done that.

But Jazzbeaux was getting her licks in. The Daughter's left wrist was either broken or sprained, and she couldn't get a proper grip on her needle. There were spots of her own blood on her suit, so some of Jazzbeaux's licks must have missed the armour plate. The hagwitch was getting tired, breathing badly, sweating like a sow.

She used her feet, dancing away and flying back, anchoring herself to the broken lamp-post as she launched four rapid kicks to the Daughter's torso. The girl was shaken. She had dropped both her needles. Jazzbeaux caught her behind the head with a steelheel, and dropped her to the ground. She reared up, but Jazzbeaux was riding her now, knees pressed in tight. She got a full nelson, and sank her claws into the back of her neck, pressing the Daughter's face to the hard-beaten earth of the street.

Finally, the Daughter stopped moving, and Jazzbeaux stood up. Andrew Jean rushed out, and grabbed her wrist, holding her hand up in victory.

"The winnnnerrrr," Andrew Jean shouted, sloppily kissing Jazzbeaux.

She pulled her eyepatch away, and looked at the DAR.

They stood impassive as the optic burner angled across them, glinting red but not yet activated.

"Is it decided?" Jazzbeaux asked, wiping the blood out of her eye.

Miss Liberty came forward and stood over her sister. The girl on the ground moaned and tried to get up on her elbows. The veiled Daughter kicked her in the side. The poison blade sank in. The fallen Daughter spasmed briefly, and slumped again, foam leaking from her mouth.

"It is decided," said Miss Liberty.

The DAR picked up the dead girl, and faded away into the darkness.

The Psychopomps pressed around her, kissing, hugging, groping, shouting.

"Jazz-beaux! Jazz-beaux! Jazz-beaux!"

The Psychopomps howled in the desert.

"Come on, let's hit Spanish Fork," Jazzbeaux shouted above the din, "I'm thirsty, and I could use some real party action tonight!"

Nguyen Seth smiled. He remembered that party himself. That was when he had been joined with Jazzbeaux. It was a shame. She was so interesting. Too few human beings were. But there was nothing for it, she would have to be killed. He was too near the Accomplishment of the Purpose to brook any distractions. Jazzbeaux would resist, of course. She was growing since Spanish Fork. She wouldn't be as easy to vanquish as she had been outside the Feelgood Saloon.

He would have Roger Duroc handle it.

II

DUROC HAD SPENT the last three months in France, dealing with the business of the Violent Tendency for Freedom. Operating out of a tiny flat on the Left Bank, the cell had succeeded in spreading some interesting biochemical havoc across half of the United European Community. They were only one of many small groups Nguyen Seth took an interest in, but Duroc knew the Elder saw Paris as an important flashpoint in the coming deluge and so they required more personal attention than similar factions in Johannesburg, Puerto Belgrano, Tehran, Shanghai, Mexico City, Malmo, Berlin, Belfast, Genoa or Nottingham. In the time Duroc had spent with the group, Biron, their leader, had revised the Violent Tendency manifesto countless times, while the scientific wing of the movement, Neumann and Alix, had developed some intriguing ramifications on recombinant DNA which, when injected into a shamburger, would cause the meatoid pulp to meld with the enzymes of any given stomach and expand its mass one hundredfold. Their attack on the Centre LePen hadn't been an unqualified success, but Duroc was pleased with the loss of life. And, of course, time spent in Paris meant that he could buy a new wardrobe, visit his mother and put flowers on his uncle's grave. Also, he had picked up some rare Vanessa Paradis and Johnny Halliday musichips.

Now, after thirty-seven hours in the air, he was touching down in Salt Lake City. It had proved expedient to fly from Orly to Casablanca, from Casablanca to Lisbon, from Lisbon to Montenegro, from Montenegro to Sacramento, and, by carrier-copter, from Sacramento to Salt Lake, with changes of passport at each stopover. He was used to such things, and he had been able to pass the time by fulfilling an old ambition, to read Edward Gibbon's *Decline and Fall of the Roman Empire* in the original English. He was less concerned with the fate of the customs official in Uruguay whose spine he had had to snap than he was with the course of the ancient empire on its long, slow descent into barbarism. Elder Seth had known Gibbon, and apparently given the Englishman a few insights into the fragility of civilization. Occasionally, a sentence or a phrase would leap out, and Duroc could hear it issuing from the Elder's lips. "History, which is, indeed, little more than the register of the crimes, follies and misfortunes of mankind", for instance; or, "corruption, the most infallible symptom of constitutional liberty", and, most chillingly, "all that is human must be retrograde if it does not advance". Setting aside the final volume as the copter's blades slowed, Duroc mused that Gibbon was sending a message to the beginnning of the Twenty-first Century, a message he had never realized was implicit in his text. These were the Last Days, and soon would come the cleansing fire. When civilization was no better than barbarism, the whole experiment of humanity was at an end, and it was time to clean the slate. And afterwards... ah, afterwards, there would be such wonders...

The pilot flipped up the door, and Duroc bent to avoid the still slowly circling blades as he stepped down onto the tarmac.

Elder Beach and Elder Wiggs were waiting for him. They were of the inner circle of the Josephite Temple, and knew more than most of the True Purpose of Deseret.

"Blessed be," said Beach.

Wiggs nodded. Duroc grinned, and shook their hands in turn.

Every time he came back to Salt Lake, things had changed. More buildings were reclaimed from dereliction, more dormitories built for the resettlers flooding in daily, more facilities provided.

As they walked to the terminal, Wiggs ran through the latest developments. The television station was up and broadcasting locally, and the church was buying airtime on one of the national nets. The computer interface was secretly operational, sorting through the Mormons' old listings of everybody who had ever left a record of his or her life on earth. The water pipeline was functioning properly, and three attempts to destroy it – two by the Montana gangcults, one by Jesuits – had been thwarted. The security set-up Duroc had designed was working perfectly.

They were dedicating a new runway at the airport. Duroc took the time to watch as a stout, middle-aged man walked out onto the freshly-hardened tarmac, stripped to the waist and beaming a beatific smile. The heat haze rose from the ground as he flagellated himself with a cat o' nine chains. He had to be assisted as he flayed himself, but he got most of the skin off as easily as a cardigan, and the minister only had to help him with the last few strips. He collapsed in ecstasy, and leaked blood as seven angelic Josephite children joined their voices in "The Path of Joseph".

Beach nodded his approval. "It was well done," he said. "Brother Duroc, things proceed apace. As thou canst see, the flock are dedicated, and willing."

The honoured sacrifice was loaded onto a baggage-carrying cart and pulled away for disposal. His shape was outlined on the runway like a shadow. The choir finished the hymn, and each child in turn drew his letter in the blood. J. O. S. E. P. H.

Old Joseph Shatner, founder of the church, would have been amused.

"Joseph's work will be done," said Beach.

"Yes, indeed."

The three caught the shuttle bus from the terminal, and were driven into the city. Duroc gave a brief account of his doings in Paris, and of his important visit to Berlin. Wiggs smiled, and Beach nodded. His news was digested.

"How are things at the tabernacle?" Duroc asked.

"All is well," said Beach. "Elder Seth is under a great strain, of course. The Dark Ones are demanding, but he has been bearing up remarkably. He is much involved with the rituals these days. Miracles and wonderments."

Duroc knew what that meant. He had lived with miracles and wonderments all his life, ever since his uncle had told him something about the family's history and the eternal presence of Seth in their lives. He had made his first apport as a teenager. He didn't like the demon stuff, was happier with a phosphor grenade than a geas, but he had to know his business. Gateways were opening up here in Salt Lake, and things would be coming through the like of which had not been seen for thousands of years. They were dealing with events of Biblical proportion.

Inside the tabernacle grounds stood an X-shaped cross, and upon that hung a ragged figure that had once been a man.

"Jesuits," Wiggs snorted. "As thou canst see, Rome sends them out by the dozen. If Seth could be bothered to use his influence in Washington, we should have the Prez protest to Papa Georgi. The priests are becoming a nuisance."

They got off the shuttle, and stood at the base of the crucifix. There was a small gaggle of onlookers, mostly bored.

The crucified spy shifted, gargling from his crushed throat.

"Three days he has been up there," said Beach. "His name is Rafferty. Irish, of course. Three days, and he has not died. Jesus Christ himself did not last so long, I think."

"Jesuits are notoriously stubborn," Duroc mused.

An attendant from the tabernacle came along with a bucket and a sponge on a stick. He first used it to wipe some of the filth from the priest, then lifted the sponge to Rafferty's mouth, forcing it in.

"We can't have him dying of thirst before his flesh has been mortified enough to appease the Dark Ones," said Wiggs.

"Indeed not," agreed Beach.

Rafferty tried to spit, but swallowing was involuntary. He groaned, knowing each drop of water meant an hour or more of life. Duroc was intrigued by the man's predicament. Forbidden suicide by his religion, he could not induce death by, for instance, agitating his pierced hands and feet until loss of blood carried him away. He could only await starvation, suffocation, exposure, simple fatigue or a merciful bolt of lightning.

Wiggs and Beach chortled, making some joke about the Jesuit. Duroc considered reprimanding them. One had to respect an enemy like this. He was dying as well as the man at the airport. That could not be denied. Once, trying to resist his Destiny, Duroc had studied for the priesthood, but the vocation of his family had outweighed the call of Rome.

Duroc looked up at Rafferty, and the priest turned his head, meeting his gaze with pained, still-clear eyes. Duroc saluted the Jesuit, and the dying spy turned his eyes skyward.

"Come," said Beach, "Elder Seth is waiting."

III

There was sand in front of her, sand behind her, sand to the left and sand to the right. That's the way it had been for longer than she could remember. It was dusk, and the cold was falling. The murdering sun had dipped below the horizon, and this was the time when she could forage for food. Alert, she stalked the jackrabbit, her stiletto poised for a deft jab. There was plenty of game in the desert if you looked. Small animals could live off the whisps of yellow grass that persisted in growing, and large animals could live off the small animals. She was a large animal, a sandrat. She had been a regular person once, but that had been before the voices started up in her head, before the dead woman got out of her rocking chair, before the preacherman reached into her mind and gave it a sharp twist...

The Sandrat had more names than she could remember, and different people to go with each one. She recalled her father's name. Bonney. It was a good name. People who bore it came to her in her rare sleeping periods, and she learned from them.

There was Anne, in thigh-length leather boots, her ruffled shirt open to show a deep cleavage, a blood-greased cutlass in her hand, a rolling deck under her, warpaint on her face. Billy, a smoking Colt in his left hand, a toothy grin on his face, dwarfed by his oversized chaps, a battered hat on his long, ratty hair. And Bruno, sections of his undershirt cut away to emphasize his carefully-nurtured musculature – the result of long hours pumping iron, not expensive bio-implants – a cigar between his teeth, the flexible aluminium whip in his hand. The Bonneys were a dangerous breed.

She found the rabbit, chewing on a stubby cactus, and stabbed it in the neck. It kicked twice, and died. She wiped the stiletto off on its fur and slipped it into the sheath in her boot, then sucked the warm, salty blood from the puncture she had made. The meat she would dry out in the sun tomorrow. Chewed steadily, it should last her for days. As for water, that would come in minute drops from the cactus.

Sandside was only a desert if you were too used to concrete under your boots. She didn't use her gun much any more – ammunition only came her way very occasionally – but she was skilled at knife-hunting. Last night, she had taken one of the wolfdogs that had been following her for weeks. The rest of the pack had turned away. She considered tracking them, but didn't feel the need to make any particular point of it. There was honour among predators.

Strange voices had been talking inside her head forever. Not just the the Bonneys. Andrew Jean was back, beehive still in place, and chattering away like the old days. The days before the sand. And Mrs Katz, a gentle soul who held no grudge for the loss of her skull. And all the voices of Spanish Fork. The drawl of Judge Thomas Longhorne Colpeper, pompously expounding points of law; the gentle Detroit brogue of Trooper Washington Burnside, whose gun she still carried; the primal shriek of Cheeks, who had been maddened by the D.I.V.O.R.C.E. from her body; comments about the weather from Chollie Jenevein, the gasman; chemical tips from pharmacist Ferd Sunderland, who knew the Latin name of every cactus, root and fungus in the sand, plus the effects it would produce if chewed, smoked or swallowed; too many others to distinguish individually.

She had seen the world as it really was, once. Now, she was stripped down to the bare essentials of her person, trying to deal with her knowledge. She was forgetting everything else – the sub-language she spoke, things she knew, chunks of her past, people she had killed – but she had a clear memory of the way the world really looked. That was important.

By night, she walked, hunted, and fed. By day, she put up a shelter against the sun and listened to the cacophony inside her. One day in every seven or eight, she slept. It was a good, clean life. When she first came to the sand, a long time ago, she had had a pocketful of pills and squeezers, but she had lost interest in them. They rattled as she stalked, sometimes alarming her prey, and so she scattered them into the sand, to be ingested by the things that lived below the dunes. Her hair she had hacked short with her knife. She kept clean by washing in sand, and buried her stools well away from her nest of the moment. She was a good animal.

She thought she might be in Nevada, but it was hard to tell. It was just sand and rocks. It could have been Colorado, Arizona, New Mexico, California, or Deseret. It was all the same, the Big Empty. In her head, Burnside remembered someone calling America the United States of Sand and Rocks.

Sometimes she found things stranded surreally, left by God-knows-who. The original pioneers had been forced to lighten the loads on their wagons by strewing all manner of excess baggage across the western half of the continent. Bookcases, iron safes, furniture from the Old World, a diving bell. And the new resettlers were no different. They left their goods behind as they strove to find their Canaan.

Days ago, the Sandrat had found a huge jukebox, with a selection of hits from Sove musickies. Petya Tcherkassoff's "The Girl in Gorki Park", Tasha's "Love, Sex, Love", Vania Vanianova's "Long-Haired Lover From Leningrad", Andrei Tarkovsky's "Happiness". She had pressed buttons, but nothing happened. She polished the chrome, and wiped sand away from the stained-glass frontage, but it was finally useless, just another piece of garbage from a past that could have happened to someone else for all the trace it had left on her.

She had examined her curved reflection in the chrome mirror. Her cheekbones were prominent, and the ridges of her eyesockets. She saw a skull beneath her skin, but the image meant nothing, although somehow she thought it should. Her hair was growing out again, black and clean. She had been badly hurt some time ago, but her body was dealing with that. She had bruises, but no fleshrot.

The moon shone overhead like a new dime. The sand turned silver-grey, and the Sandrat wandered across it. She had been moving in large ellipses, crossing and recrossing her path in a complicated pattern. The moon called to her, she thought, pulling her this way and that. She went where it directed her, tracing a design on the face of the Earth.

The problem was the other Voice in her head, the one that could silence all the rest, the one that brought its pictures with it, the one that poured memories into her mind until she thought she would burst.

There was a face to go with the voice. A face that wore dark glasses and was shadowed by the wide brim of a flat black hat.

A face that was white, but was often split by a red smile. Red needlepoints glinted behind the shades. When she left the desert, and the Sandrat knew she would eventually come to the end of the sand, the face would be waiting for her.

She knew too much about him to let him live.

His name was Nguyen Seth, and he was older than the United States of America, older than the Black Plague, older than the written word, older than cultivated grain, older than the wheel, older than human language…

Nguyen Seth was as old as Death.

Something came to her, a graffito she had seen on the wall of a burned-out Josephite temple in Denver, back when she was with the girlie gangcult. "Within strange aeons, even Death may die…"

She hadn't known what it meant then, but now she knew it had been inscribed there just for her. The moon was pulling at her even before Spanish Fork, leading her to her destiny. Her whole life had been directed towards this one task.

The strange aeons were over, and it was nearly time for the Sandrat to kill Death.

In the distance, predators howled, wolf to coyote, mutant to mongrel. The Sandrat opened her throat, and howled too, joining in their song of the chase.

With the taste of blood still hot on her tongue, she sang in a long, keening cry of the joys of the kill…

Dropping to all fours, she bounded across the sand.

IV

ZEEBEECEE, THE STATION *That's Got It All, feels it imperative to interrupt Screwing For Dollars, with Voluptua Whoopee for this important newsflash. Here, direct from the Capitol Building, is luscious Lola Stechkin…*

"Hi, America! It's April the 3rd, 2022, and this is Lola. Here's some news we hope you can handle.

"Ms Redd Harvest of the Turner-Harvest-Ramirez Agency has just announced that the suspect apprehended in Nome, Alaska, last week in connection with the thirty-eight-state murder spree of the serial killer known as 'The

Tasmanian Devil' has been definitely connected with four hundred and eighteen of the Devil's six hundred and forty-two confirmed kills to date. However, Washington has been rocked by the further revelation that the alleged killer is Dr Ottokar Proctor, the respected economist and adviser to President Estevez, the man often referred to by the electronic media as 'the architect of the Big Bonus'.

"The president's office is keeping a silence on this one, although we are assured that a statement is being prepared. Sources close to President Estevez indicate that he is deeply shaken by the arrest of Dr Proctor, who has been a frequent guest at the White House and is known to be a close friend of the Estevezs, and was godfather to little Joey and Charlie Jr. It has been suggested that the President will instruct the Attorney General to appear for the defence in any trial of Dr Proctor, so important is the doctor's contribution to the administration considered to be. 'He's the only one who really understands the economy,' President Estevez said in a speech three weeks ago, 'and I figure it's safe with him.' Opponents of the Big Bonus have been issuing handbills and vidmail shots featuring T-H-R scene-of-the-crime photographs from the horrific quadruple cheerleader-slaying in Columbus, Ohio, of last December. The handbills bear the slogan, 'He did this to Mary Lou, Betty Jo, Crissie Leigh, Rachael-Rose and the United States of America'.

"Sonny Pigg, lead singer of the Mothers of Violence, who last month released a successful solo album dedicated to 'The Tasmanian Devil', has issued a press statement in which he claims that 'the Devil is a real gone guy, and we should go with the groove for him when the bloodtide comes round. Doc Proc should be made fuckin' Prez immediamente 'fore we lose this great country o' ours to godless commies, camel-fuckin' ragheads, vegetarian homosexuals and sovrock faghags.' By a bizarre coincidence, Dr Proctor's last television appearance was on the popular Musichip Jury show, during which he described Pigg's 'Tasmanian Devil' as 'the worst piece of ordure ever'.

"Dr Ottokar Proctor, forty-two, was born in Venice, California, and graduated first in his class from Yale at the age of fifteen. He is a world-renowned expert in Side-Demand Financing, post-Jungian psychology, American-made animated cinema, the history of Italian opera and medieval European history. His publications include *Giving It All Away: Modern Money Matters*, *Sylvester P Pussycat: A Psycho-Sexual Case Study*, *After Puccini* and *The Euro: Paper Money or Solid Brass?* He has been a popular guest in numerous network talkshows, and introduced ZeeBeeCee's Emmy-award-winning *How to Get Rich in 80 Days* last year. Through a series of influential papers and reports, Dr Proctor was in the forefront of modern economic theory. 'America has a lot of assets', he claimed in his last speech to congress, 'we should cash in on them.' The Estevez administration has reduced personal income tax to virtually nothing, while raising finance through hefty duties on imported items – as you know, a cup of real Nicaraguan coffee now costs $150 – and such daring schemes as the leasing-out of America's armed forces to Canada during the Quebecois uprising.

"Dr Proctor has been kept in seclusion temporarily in the time-locked underground strongroom of the Anchorage branch of the GenTech Nomura Agricultural Loan and Trust Co, and has not as yet been able to confer with his lawyers or issue a public statement. Ms Redd Harvest has made available to this network a volume of evidence that is still being sifted by our experts. However, there would appear to be no chance at this time that the T-H-R conclusion will be proved wrong. As Ms Harvest has said to us over a satellite link, 'Dr Proctor... he was the Devil all right.' We'll bring you more on this upsetting story as it develops. In the meantime, this is Lola, handing you back to the scheduled program."

But before we get back to Voluptua and the gas jockey from Bixby, Mississippi, here's a message from GenTech...

V

THROUGH THE SAND, there was a road. One day, Bonney decided it was time to return to the world of cars and concrete and people. She had learned all that the moon and the sand could teach her, and she must search elsewhere. Eventually, she would kill Seth, but in the meantime she had to change herself. She was a walking weapon already, but Seth had only made her into a rough flint axe. She must hone herself into the likeness of her beloved stiletto. She would only have one shot, and she had to be ready to make it count.

She sat by the road and waited, for three days. The sun and the moon passed overhead, the one beating, the other whispering. She heard the motorsickle coming from twenty miles away, and had time to prepare herself. She stood up on her two legs, and purged the animal from her soul. She must be a human person again. Her face was still crooked, but her body was fully healed now, lithe and strong. She set her torso at a provocative angle on her hips, arched her knee a little, and stuck out her thumb.

The cykesound became a speck on the road, and grew bigger as it approached. From the engine noise, she recognized an Electraglide. Out here, that meant the Maniax were back, or perhaps one of the minor biker gangcults, Satan's Stormtroopers, the Apple Valley Pigfuckers. She knew what to expect from the cykeman, but she was counting on his not knowing what to expect from her.

The sickle slowed as it approached, and she imagined the biker licking his lips inside his helmet, anticipating a tasty morsel. He was a Maniak all right, flying colours, with a pair of sawn-off pumpguns crossed on his back, and a long braided pigtail whipping out like an epileptic snake from under his horned skidlid.

She was wrong about the biker. He was smarter than most. When he got within twenty yards of her, something spooked him and he gunned the hog, speeding past her. A shower of pebbles fell short of her shin. He punched the air and yelled something as he weaved from side to side across the road, zig-zagging into the distance.

She realized he was expecting to be dodging gunfire. She had been relying on her blade, her teeth and her hands for too long. She had forgotten the sidearm, which she had kept sand-free but not discharged in months.

The next one, she swore, she would shoot for his ve-hickle and leave alive for the predators.

She had to wait four more days. And this time, there was more than one rider…

VI

DUROC HAD NEVER seen Nguyen Seth like this. Usually, his face was as unreadable as a mummy's bandage mask. Now, he seemed to be in pain, and the lines on his cheeks were almost cracks. He took off his dark glasses, and Duroc could see points of blood in the Elder's ancient eyes.

They were in the private library, where Seth kept his books. It was a unique collection of the forbidden, the outré, and the mystical. Duroc thought the library was something very near to Seth's autobiography. Through the pages of hundreds of books, many famous and some unknown, the undying one could trace his passage down the years. Not since the fire at Alexandria had there been such a concentration of the world's True Knowledge in one building. Here were the secret histories, the stories behind the stories, the truths so terrible they could only be written as fiction, the chronicles of the insane, the lives of the damned.

Somewhere here were the contributions of Duroc's ancestors: a series of articles co-written by Pierre Henri Duroc and Donatien Alphonse Francois, Marquis de Sade, speculating on the limits of the human mind when confronted with endless pain; some transcripts from the meetings of Robespierre's Committee of Public Safety, in which the fates of some of the first families of France were decided on a whim; a suppressed account of certain discoveries in a pre-human city that came to light in Nineteenth-century French Equatorial Africa before the cyclopean stones mysteriously sank into the soft jungle earth; Cauchemar et Fils, Maitres des Mondes Perdues, an unpublished novel by M Jules Verne that was purchased from the author by a Great-Great-Great-Uncle and consigned to obscurity because it described a steam-driven engine to open up a gateway to a world of dreams that bore a remarkable similarity to a device that the Duroc of the time had indeed developed.

Sitting at his huge desk, surrounded by his books, Seth wore a Chinese robe, embroidered with dragon gods, and a black skullcap. His hands were those of a week-old corpse.

"The girl," he said, his voice uncommonly thin. "Jessamyn Bonney."

Duroc remembered. Elder Wiggs had told him all about Spanish Fork. "Jazzbeaux? She must be dead, surely. You took her out into the road and... uh... battered her fatally. That must be an end to it."

"No," Seth said, raising a long-nailed finger, "she is not dead. She is in the desert, changing."

He pressed his finger to his forehead. "And she is in here. She wore the spectacles, and now some fragment of her is inside my mind, just as some fragment of me is lodged in hers. Tick-tock, tick-tock."

Duroc was perturbed. Seth rarely talked about the things that set him apart from the rest of mankind.

"And is that serious?"

"Roger, it could jeopardize all we have worked for... everything."

Duroc remembered the files he had accessed from Bruyce-Hoare in Denver. He made a point of checking up on people who got in the way of the Path of Joseph.

"Jessamyn Bonney. She's just a girl, a juvenile delinquent."

Seth's thin lips assumed a configuration that might have passed for a smile. "She was, Roger, she was. Now, she is turning into something else. Through me, she has been extended. I believe that she may be the focal point through which the Ancient Adversary will try to thwart the designs of the Dark Ones."

Duroc had barely heard of the Ancient Adversary, but he knew this entity was one of the few Great Unseen Powers that stood in opposition to the Dark Ones, the extra-dimensional masters to whom Nguyen Seth had dedicated his long life. The Ancient Adversary had other names: Harry Half-Moon, Puitsikkakaa, The Dawn Reptile.

"I made her, Roger. Each man makes the sword which will kill him, and I made Jessamyn Bonney."

There was something disturbing in all this, beyond the threat to the Great Work. Duroc got the impression that Nguyen Seth was almost proud of the girl he feared. For centuries, no one had come along who could make him afraid. Perhaps the old man found that... stimulating? Exciting? Underneath it all, Seth was still at least partially a man. Duroc could never hope to understand his master fully. That was one of the challenges of his life.

Seth was paging through a book. It was not what Duroc would expect, not the *Necronomicon* or some volume by Undercliffe or Karswell. It was *Peter Pan in Kensington Gardens*, with illustrations by Arthur Rackham. Duroc remembered the story. His uncle had taken him to see the Walt Disney film when he was a child. Could Nguyen Seth be identifying with the boy who never grew up?

"I knew JM Barrie, you know. I was there in 1912, when he unveiled the statue of Peter Pan that still stands in a London park."

Suddenly, it clicked. "Tick-tock, tick-tock! It's part of the story, isn't it?"

"Yes, Roger. One of the prophecies. I am Captain Hook and she, the crocodile. She has a part of me inside her, and I know she will come for me some day. I can hear her. She too has a clock ticking inside her."

"Tick-tock, tick-tock, tick-tock."

Seth's smile soured, and he shut the book.

"Bring me the head of the crocodile, Roger."

"I'll see to it personally."

"No, you are too important to the Great Work to get sidetracked on this thing. Just make sure you secure the services of some capable people. The longer we wait, the stronger she gets."

Duroc left Seth in his library. In among the books, there was a long-case clock. As its pendulum swung, it ticked.

Second by second, the world crept towards its End.

VII

It was a convoy. An arvee and ten or twelve outriders. The Sandrat recognized the set-up. She had herself travelled with groups like this. It was a gangcult war party. There was a ninety-five percent probability they would be hostile. Gangcults were in the hostility business, after all.

She dredged up her past, recalling the girl who had been Jazzbeaux, who had been a War Chief. The Sandrat assumed the chapter was finished. The business at Spanish Fork had left them dead or gone. That would nullify all the treaties that protected them. There would be an open season on scattered singletons.

She had none of her 'Pomp colours left, but she knew she was still recognizable. The eyepatch was a give-away.

They were bearing down fast. There wasn't time to find a sandhole and hide. She would have to take her chances.

She unflapped her holster, and shifted it round so it hung behind her waist, out of sight.

Maybe they would want a girl for recreational purposes. She could put up with that if it got her to a city, or within reach of a ve-hickle she could scav. It would be no worse than she had lived through before.

The outriders were almost on her. She stuck out her thumb.

It was worse than she could have imagined. The arvee was painted red, white and blue, and had a Statue of Liberty hood ornament. An ice cream truck musichip played "Yankee Doodle". The point rider wore tight white-and-blue striped pants, a red tailcoat, a dyed white beard and a stars-and-stripes stovepipe hat. On his cyketank was a bright legend, AMERICA? DON'T FUCK WITH IT!

It was the Daughters of the American Revolution, with a few Minutemen thrown in. And they remembered only too well who she was.

The pointrider turned and skidded to a stop, signing to the rest of the convoy to follow suit.

"Well, looky-looky-looky," said Uncle Sam, "if it ain't that commie ratskag Jazzbeaux Bonney, late of the Psychopomps, late of the human race. You look like somethin' the goat wouldn't rut with..."

The Sandrat stood stiffly, wondering whether she had a chance.

The arvee doors opened up, and the DAR piled out. Miss Liberty was there. She tucked her unlit torch under her arm, and smiled. She had more teeth than a game-show hostess on ZeeBeeCee, and breasts like udders.

"My deah," she cooed, croaking like Katharine Hepburn, "it's been sempleah ages..."

The Sandrat didn't give them any resistance as they took her weapons away from her.

Miss Liberty raised her veil and kissed the Sandrat on the cheeks. The President of the DAR chapter was old for the gangcult game, twenty-three or -four. It must be the politics.

It was late afternoon. The light would be going soon. A couple of Minutemen were binding together two cloth-padded lengths of wood. They got their cross put together and planted in the sand.

"Such a shame about President Estevez's Big Bonus, wasn't it?" said Miss Liberty. The Sandrat had no idea what she was talking about. "Well, I've always said that Mee-lee-oh was just a tad too radical to hold high office in these heah United States."

A teenage matron squirted gasoline on the cross with a flyspray. Uncle Sam brought out a box of marshmallows and some skewers. Three blonde-haired, freckle-faced children in immaculate overalls, with Old Glory on one tit and the swastika on the other, sang "Row, Row, Row Your Boat."

"I think we're gonna have us a regular patriotic cook-out here, Madame Prezz," said Uncle Sam.

Miss Liberty put her arm around the Sandrat. "My deah," she said. "You wouldn't happen to have a light, would you?"

The Sandrat spat in her face.

Miss Liberty smiled, and wiped the spittle away with a lace-edged hankie she produced from her sleeve.

"Oh well, nevah mind."

She took out her torch and twisted it. A jet of flame shot out and fell upon the cross, which caught light immediately.

"It warms your heart, doesn't it? This used to be a hell of a country, before we started letting red slits like you run loose in the streets frightening the children with their hammers and sickles."

The children joined hands with Uncle Sam and danced around the burning cross.

The Sandrat was shoved roughly towards the cross. She felt the heat wafting across the evening air towards her.

"I guess what we've got here, Jazzbeaux," Miss Liberty said, "is a triumph for Truth, Justice and the American Way..."

VIII

IN THE OUTER *Darkness, the Ancient Adversary waited while the Dark Ones swarmed towards the light. It had long since ceased to define itself except in terms of its enemies. The game that was being played out in the shadows around the planet Earth was old beyond even its understanding. For an eternity, it had been alone against the Dark, unsupported even by the fragile hopes of humanity. Now, it was reaching out, spiralling its essence down towards the wormhole in the fabric of the Dark, ready to feed itself into the earthly plane, to become one with the Vessel. It had observed the Vessel from afar, peering through the lens in the moon, tracking the human dot through the sandscape.*

Without knowing why, it assumed a ghostshape. Dimensions meant nothing in the Darkness, but it stretched its tail across the shadows, and thrust its snout towards the light. Sharp teeth grew in rows, rough ridges raised across its back. Flat toadlike eyes blinked, watering. There was nothing to see yet, but that would come.

Clawing at the substance of the dark, it wriggled towards the Gateway, squeezing its eternal purpose into the elongated bulb of its lizard brain.

Without knowing why, it talked to itself.

"Tick-tock, tick-tock, tick-tock..."

Down on the Earth, the Vessel was waiting, and so was the Prey...

IX

MISS LIBERTY MARCHED her towards the cross.

"I just want to ask you one question," the leaderene said.

"Go on," said the Sandrat.

"Are you now, or have you evah been, a member of the Communist Party?"

Flames licked the darkening sky. The DAR stood around, waiting for the entertainment. The children had stopped singing, and were lighting cross-shaped sparklers. They waved them around, chanting "burn the commie, burn the commie" until Uncle Sam cuffed one of them around the ear.

The Sandrat felt the old skills coming back. Human speech returned, and her brain raced. "Like the man said in the song, 'you have nothing to lose but your chains.'"

She twisted out of Miss Liberty's grip, and sank a foot into the woman's midriff. The leaderene went down with a satisfying thump, her spiked coronet falling off.

The Sandrat darted back in time to avoid the spear of flame from the torch, and flung a handful of sand at Miss Liberty. The Daughter dropped the still-burning torch and a pool of fire spread around her. Her robes went up. That put her out of the fight for the moment.

There were only twenty-five or thirty more of them. Not easy, but she could do it. After all, she had been given a brain to think with while these patriots were being force-fed *The Thoughts of Spiro Agnew, The World According to William F Buckley* and *Killing Commies for God and Country.*

"We hold these truths to be self-evident..." she recited.

Uncle Sam came at her, long arms outstretched. She kicked him in the face with her boot-heel, and he got a grip on her knee.

"Indivisible under God, with Liberty..."

Other hands grabbed her, and she was dragged towards the crucifix.

Miss Liberty was shrieking as she burned. The Daughters wouldn't have enough water with them to waste on her, but the children were shovelling sand at the woman, trying to smother the flames.

The Sandrat bit into the wrist of one of the Minutemen, chewing until she severed the artery. He fell away, blood gushing into her face, trying to stanch the flow with his fingers.

"And Justice for all!" She spat a bloody froth at Uncle Sam.

She got one foot in the sand, and dragged it. The patriots were having trouble holding her fast. She scratched down a face with her desert-hardened claws, and broke some ribs with an elbow.

"I'm just exercising my right to Freedom of Expression."

It was just her and Uncle Sam now. She slipped behind him, pulling his arms back until his shoulders popped, and pushed him into the dirt. He had a gun in his waistband, a long-barreled Buntline special. She relieved him of it, and made five bullets count, dropping Minutemen and Daughters where they stood.

"Who wants the last one?" she asked.

The remaining gangtypes looked at each other. A tall, well-built girl in a star-spangled bathing suit knelt by Miss Liberty, and picked up the coronet.

"No volunteers, huh?"

The Betsy Ross Bimbo settled the coronet on her Annette Funicello hairdo.

"So you've just elected yourself Boss of the Beach, huh?"

The new leaderene tottered forwards on five-inch spike heels – not the ideal sandwear – rolling her hips. She had a pair of batons with wickedly barbed ends. She twirled them like a majorette, and did a few ninja moves.

"Back off, prom queen!"

Damn, she needed her last bullet. She would have to fight. She slid the gun into her holster, and spread her hands in a sign of peace.

"Can't we settle this constitutionally, with a debate and a referendum?"

The Beach Bunny swung her batons in a deadly arc.

"Just you and me, commie," the Daughter said. "Miss Liberty was my den mother."

"It's always somebody's den mother, or sister, or brother, or pet rattlesnake, huh? Why can't people just be dead and forgotten?"

A baton shot out, piercing the air where the Sandrat's shoulder had just been. The Daughter dodged an elbow thrust, and brought the majorette rod down on the Sandrat's back. It was a good hit, and she had to use all of her concentration not to go down.

The Daughter was a Champion Twirl Tootsie. To get around that, she would have to get in close, and go for some serious cat-fighting. The Sandrat hugged the girl, and pulled her close. The Daughter's face crinkled up in disgust. The Sandrat knew she had an edge. She licked the girl's mouth, tasting strawberry lipstick, and flicked her lightly freckled cheerleader's nose with the pointed end of her tongue.

The Daughter looked as if she were ready to give out with the old Technicolor Yawn. "What's the matter, saph? Worried that you'd like it too much?"

The Daughter wriggled, trying to get a knee up into the Sandrat's stomach. Her rock-hard hair was shaking.

"Maybe you don't kiss on a first fight, huh?"

The Daughter grabbed a handful of hair, and yanked hard. It hurt, but the Sandrat could handle it.

"Hey, no fair! Tammy's cheating!"

The Sandrat lifted the majorette up, and tossed her away. She landed badly, and crawled away.

"Nobody loves a sore loser, Gidget."

The other Daughters were in a semi-circle around the Sandrat. She drew her gun. "Remember the last bullet, everyone? Good, there'll be a pop quiz after recess."

She took aim, and shot the arvee in the gastank. Uncle Sam was loaded with ScumStoppers. The bullet punched through armour plate, the tank exploded, and the arvee rose up into the air in a whirl of flame. The DAR must keep all their ammo in the bus, the Sandrat thought. There was quite a fireworks display. A flying wheel knocked the crucifix over, and chunks of wreckage rained down on a fifty-foot circle. Two or three of the cykes blew up in sympathy. Miss Liberty wasn't the only one on fire now. Patriots were running all over the place, periwigs ablaze, screaming for help, burrowing into the sand and rolling.

"See, whoever has the biggest gun gets to kick the crap out of everybody else. It's the American Way."

The Sandrat was untouched in the eye of the hurricane. She knew the fire wouldn't hurt her. It was destiny.

She picked up a few more guns from corpses, and didn't feel naked any more. One or two still felt like fighting, and she shot them.

She left the children alone. They would make good sandrat material. Along with the majorette, whom she saw being helped away from the fire by the kids.

"You'll be able to work on your tan tomorrow, surf sweetie," she shouted after the Daughter, "but don't hold your breath waiting for the tide to come in."

She found an unburned six-by-three stars and stripes in the sand. She picked it up and draped it over Miss Liberty's still-smoking remains. She shot a salute at the cooked corpse.

"Like I said, the American Way, sister."

She found a cyke parked out of range of the explosion, and straddled it. It was strange having a sickle between her legs after all these months, but the reactions came back. You never forget. She took a helmet from the handlebars. It was starred and striped, but it would do. She kick-started the machine, and drove away from the fires. Someone took a shot at her, but missed. She searched through the pannier for a musichip to put into the helmet's sound system, but only found *Selections from John Phillip Sousa*, *The Best of Kate Smith*, and *John Wayne's America*. She threw the chips into the sand for the predators, and upped the speed. In the panniers, she did find a supply of Good Ole Home Cooking – Oreos, Hershey Bars, Babe Ruths, Wrigley's Gum, Pork Popsicles. She was back in civilization, at last.

Her hair flew out behind her, and the clean air struck her face. She would have to do something about her face now. Once she got her bearings, she could head for Dead Rat and get Doc Threadneedle to sort out her skullplates. Maybe she should invest in a few more elaborate bio-amendments. Her credit should be good.

Her wilderness years were over.

She wasn't hallucinating any more, she knew. The voices were under control. She wouldn't be seeing any dead women getting out of their rocking chairs. Things were clear again.

She smiled, and her heart beat away the seconds, tick-tock, tick-tock, tick-tock.

part three
jessamyn

I

IT HAD TAKEN Duroc at least three quarters of an hour to get through the Holderness-Manolo security system. They had X-Rayed, palm-printed and eyeball-photographed him, then handed him over to a pair of clean-cut young men, name-tagged Lawrence and Skipper, for a friendly cross-interrogation. While waiting for his stats to be confirmed, he was offered the services of a barbie doll "recreational secretary". He politely turned the girl down and waited to be admitted to Bronson Manolo's office. They had never met before, but as soon as Duroc was inside the Agency's inner sanctum, the Chief Op looked up from his blondwood desk, flashed a monied piranha grin, and acted as if his visitor were an old college buddy who had happened to have walked in off the street.

"Rog-babe, hi, can I have Kandi fix you some coffee?" The Op produced a Mickey Mouse snuffbox full of white powder. "You want some toot-sweet?"

Duroc was dressed in the black conservative suit and pilgrim hat of a Josephite Elder.

"No thank you, Mr Manolo. I have abjured stimulants."

Manolo showed the even, white teeth again.

"Take me out and shoot me down like a dog, old buddy, I was forgetting. Grab some chairleather. I hope you don't mind us weaker souls indulging the vices?"

"No, of course not."

"Cosmic." He pressed a button on his desk-console, absent-mindedly dipping his pinkie in the cocaine and running it across his gums. "Kandi-cutie, decant me some Nicaraguan and pump it through. Oh, I'll be brainstorming with Rog for a couple of tick-tocks, so hold all calls up to and including state government. And have a nice day."

In his business, Manolo was the coolest of the snazz. He hadn't said "real coffee", but he made damn sure you got the message. This office was expensive in a subtly ostentatious way, minimalist but designed to impress the discerning. The undiscerning probably never got further than Lawrence and Skipper. One wall was a picture window affording a pastoral view of Lower Los Angeles right down to the beach. On the wall behind Manolo was a David Hockney original. Mounted above the painting was a six-foot narwhal horn. On the desk was an incomprehensible executive toy that buzzed and flashed occasionally, displaying chrome tubes, jewels and crystal lumps. In the corner there was a discreet datalink terminal got up to look like a Thirties radiogram.

Manolo leaned back in his chair, and patted his thousand-dollar blow-waved haircut. His hairstyle consultant must throw in a Tom Selleck moustache twirl for free. He was wearing a silvery Italian suit over a T-shirt which read HONK IF YOU LIKE HUNKS.

Duroc remembered why he tried, wherever possible, to avoid Californians.

A bust-enhanced beauty queen in a goldthread string bikini wandered in with Manolo's Nicaraguan, which steamed in an authentic 1919 World Series Commemorative Mug, and wandered out again. Manolo's eyes followed her jiggle from the door to the desk and back. Kandi took the time to flash a smile at Duroc; he supposed the company must have a charge account with the same high-flying Beverly Hills dentist. Or maybe it was all the fluoride in the water.

"Great ass, huh?" said Manolo, licking his moustache. "Oh, I'm sorry, reverend, I was forgetting."

"Elder. My title is Elder."

"Cheezus, what a maroon I am. Elder. I'll get it. Say, are you French?"

"Originally, yes. I have been with the church for ten years now."

"Heyy, cosmic, man, cosmic. I'm very spiritual myself. I attend the Pyramid down at the Surfside Mall. Gari – that's my Guru – says it's important to get in touch with your inner being. I always take the time to meditate between my squishball practice and the tanning parlour."

Sunshine three hundred and fifty days a year, and Californians fry themselves under microwaves. There was a sign up at the airport – Schwarzenegger Airport, naturally – that read CALIFORNIA: WE'VE HAD THE TWENTY-FIRST CENTURY HERE FOR TWENTY-TWO YEARS. Duroc had had to smile at that. As a succession of paycops, stewardesses, diplomatics, immigration officials, armourcabbies, narcotics relay expeditors, hotel functionaries, arms dealers and hookers told him to "have a snazz day" and shoved his credit card through their machines, he wondered whether they would like what the rest of the Twenty-first century held for them when Nguyen Seth rained it down on them.

"Your agency comes highly recommended," he said.

"Yeah. Me and Bob Holderness are the most on the coast. At least, Bob was until the Surf Nazis got him. You don't see that gangcult much these days, because we genocided them. It got personal. Nasty work, but the karma was right for it. City cops looked the other way, and the Cal State Angels loaned us hardware. Bob was a great buddy, and a great guy... He had a lot of friends, no matter what you read in the trades."

There was a framed picture on the desk. Duroc had assumed it was a father and son shot. There was the younger Manolo, plus an older man with the same teeth, hair and moustache. They were standing either side of a surfboard, and there were some Kandi clones in the picture.

"Twenty years ago, he worked with all the topster Ops – Matt Houston, Cannon, Banacek, Mannix, Lance White. Those were the great days of the business in La-La Land, before we closed the state borders and tossed the immigrant filthos back into the desert."

"An impressive record, indeed."

"And could he surf! We're talking radical in a tubular way!"

Manolo took a couple of hits of coffee, and picked up a wrist-exerciser that probably doubled as some kind of sex aid.

Squeezing away so that his biceps shifted in his sleeve, he asked, "So, Rog, what's going down the chute?"

"I beg your pardon?"

"What's the beef? The case?"

"Ah yes, the case."

He put his briefcase on the desk.

"Not that kind of case, pilgrim."

"I know what you mean. I have some documentation for you."

"Zero-degree cool."

Duroc took out the file on Jessamyn Bonney, and slipped off the electronic seal.

"We want this woman."

Manolo showed his dazzling choppers again, and took the file. He flipped it to the photographs, and werewolf-whistled.

"Okay if you like the type. I'm a 3-B man myself, blonde bimbos with boobs. Kid must want to be a Disney cartoon villainess when she grows up. Look at that black eye make-up and the suspenders. Is that hair for real?"

"She's killed perhaps forty or fifty people."

"Ouch. Antisocial lady."

"Among them, several Elders of the Josephite Church. She attacked a wagon train two years ago. We have been compiling this dossier ever since."

"The church don't forget, huh?" A beady glint appeared in Manolo's clear blue eyes as he got his first scent of blood money and began to turn into a shark.

"Something like that. We are prepared to meet your regular fee. On top of that, you will note that there are seventeen outstanding warrants filed by various state and federal authorities against her. Should you be successful, you will be able to pick up a bounty on each of them."

"How much is this kid worth?" He licked his moustache again. Duroc wondered whether it was an implant.

"It's in the file."

Manolo flipped the pages until he came to the accounts. He ran his eyes down the column of figures as if he were taking a good look at Voluptua Whoopee in a no-piece swimsuit and whistled "Dixie."

"A prize package. You have us on the case, padrone. And we never give up. We'll have this… uh… Jessamyn Bonney… behind electro-bars at Tehachapi just as soon as the schedule allows."

He continued to page through the file absent-mindedly, fiddling as he did so with the snuffbox, making sure that the gold inlay buttons on Mickey's rompers caught the light.

"No, you misunderstand."

"Run that round the block again, Rog, and see if you can sneak it by under the limbo-line this time."

"We in the church are not interested in the apprehension of Ms Bonney. In Deseret, we adhere to a Biblical code rather than to the laws and statutes of the United States."

"Heyy, the Bible, man. Heavy book. I keep it right here in my desk with the I Ching, Illuminatus and my Castenadas."

"Then you are familiar with the saying 'an eye for an eye'?"

"Absolutamente, Rog."

"Then, you will work it out. Jessamyn Bonney has killed members of the Church. In turn, we would like you..."

A real smile crept onto Manolo's face. It didn't show off his teeth, but it told Duroc a lot more about the Op's character.

"to shut down the ratskag's terminal with massive overinvestment?"

Duroc nodded. He knew Manolo would be taping this meeting, and he didn't want to say it out loud in words.

"So, it's liquidation not incarceration that's your bag. Fine. We can handle that consignment. Mucho extra dinero, of course, but if that's what you want..."

"The Tabernacle of Joseph is not poor."

"I can tell where you're coming from, Rog."

"You accept the commission."

Manolo stuck out a hairy hand, and Duroc shook it. Gold bracelets rattled.

"She's somewhere in Arizona, we believe. You might try to look up a Dr Simon Threadneedle in a township called Dead Rat."

"Dead Rat? Downer of a handle. Those vibes are negatory, Rog."

"I'm sure you can get on top of it."

"That's a charlie A-One breeze-from-the-freeze affirmative-to-the-max topside positive situation in the black column roger, Roger," Manolo chirruped.

"You mean 'yes'?"

Manolo looked hurt. "Yes."

II

THIS IS ZEEBEECEE, *the Station That's Got It All, and here with the Bathroom Break Bulletin is luscious Lola Stechkin...*

"Hi, America. It's November the 9th, 2022, only forty-seven shopping days to Christmas, and this is Lola, inviting you to share a shower. Here it is, folks, all the news you can handle...

"Sunnydales, Iowa. Dr Ottokar Proctor, 'The Tasmanian Devil', today took up residence in the high-security wing of this semi-private mental hospital. Experts remain divided on the question of Dr Proctor's state of mind during the period when he is confirmed to have been responsible for seven hundred and fifty-three homicides, but the Supreme Court has ruled him insane and irresponsible. It has been suggested that President Estevez intervened in the judicial progress with a plea for clemency on the grounds that Dr Proctor is too essential to the shaky economy of the United States to be executed. Dr Proctor, already a wealthy man, has received an eight figure sum for the movie rights to his forthcoming autobiography *What's Cookin', Doc?,* and director Kim Newman has already announced his intention to cast either Ashton Kutchner or Jim Carrey in the leading role.

"The Sea of Okhotsk. The sinking last week of the GenTech exploratory submersible Yukio Mishima remains a source of controversy. The craft, designed to scan the seabed for mineral deposits, was raised today by a joint Soviet-GenTech team and brought ashore at Kitashiretoko Misaki, Sakhalin. Premier Abramovic himself has announced that he intends to cooperate fully with the GenTech experts in an effort 'to get to the bottom of this tragedy.' Kentaru 'Barracuda' Ishii, GenTech's deepsea disaster specialist, has not as yet ruled out the possibility that the Mishima went down due to 'hostile action'. The Blood Banner Society, the shadowy Japanese ultra-nationalist group, have issued a declaration to the effect that the Mishima, coincidentally named after one of the heroes of the movement, was lost through an unprovoked sneak attack, and that it would be avenged. The 102nd Russian submarine fleet at Petropavlovsk has been alert ever since the international courts overruled the Soviet appeals and gave GenTech the right to conduct its surveys in the area.

"Cloudbase, Earth Orbit. Daniel Digby, provost of the G-Mek Orbital, has issued a formal denial to allegations by Ayatollah Bakhtiar that fugitive graphic novelist Neil Gaiman has been in hiding in the facility, and has requested that the Pan-Islamic congress stand down the Inter-Satellite Ballistic Missiles currently targeted on them. 'You can come up and look around,' Digby has said in a personal message to the Ayatollah, 'he's not here. I don't even like comic books.'

"On a lighter note, the Battle of the Bands in Fairport, Rhode Island, during which heavy metal groups Deathtongue and the Mothers of Violence played simultaneous sets in the same auditorium for thirty-eight straight hours has been resolved in single combat between the rival lead singers. Fuh-Q Charlie of Deathtongue and Sonny Pigg of the Mothers are expected to be out of the Reconstruction Wing of Cedars of Lebanon Hospital in time for their big Christmas 'Fuck the World' concert at the Hollywood Bowl next month.

"This has been Lola Stechkin at ZeeBeeCee, soaping my back and signing off. If it's all right with you, it's all right with us..."

Next, we go live to the Nikita Kruschev Ballrooms in Moscow for the semi-finals of The 2022 Warrior Chess Tourney, with a special guest appearance by the Samovar Seven. But first, here's a message from GenTech...

III

Jessamyn lay flat on the contoured table as the Doc sliced away the facial bandages, still relaxed from the morph-plus shots she had been taking every day. Doc Threadneedle was humming "The Girl in Gorki Park" as he wielded his scalpel. He was an artist with the knife, she had heard, and had apprenticed with the great Zarathustra at GenTech BioDiv before his "suspension". His field was bio-improvements engineering, and he had been placed in charge of some hush-hush military project that had racked him up a rep as the Frankenstein of his generation. She had never heard the whole story, but apparently some of his ideas were considered a little too daring for the traditionalists in Tokyo, and he found the rug pulled from under him. A few years ago, he had replaced her squished left eye with her first optic implant. At that time, he had offered to give her more extensive treatments – apparently, he found her a promising subject but she hadn't had the cold kish to lay out. After some shrewd scavving and a touch of inventive accountancy, she had more than the price of the pudding.

She had been undergoing treatment for over six months. She wondered how much of what she had been born with was left. She probably wasn't even legally the same person any more. A few weeks ago, she had spent her eighteenth birthday in a drug-induced coma, with her back opened up as durium shieldlinks were laid around her spine. She had even let Doc Threadneedle into her greymass to plug a few loops, although she didn't want too much done in there. She didn't hear voices much anymore, but Seth was still whispering dangerously, and sometimes she would dream his memories, vividly recalling some trivial incident from the remote past.

In a mud hut on an endless plain, she sorted through the bones of unrecognizable animals. Shackled to an oar, she strained in a galley as an oiled mountain of flesh beat a huge drum. In the depths of a monastery, she toiled by candlelight, laboriously copying out a crumbling manuscript, translating from one unrecognizable language to another. In a jungle whose oppressive steam-heat made sweat run inside her steel breastplate, she cut the throats of three befeathered priests. On a battlefield, she robbed a dead general of a leatherbound book grasped so tightly in his frozen fingers that two of them came away with it. In a shelter under London, while bombs exploded overhead, she coupled in a frenzy with a dead-faced young woman.

But that wasn't her. That was him. Nguyen Seth, the Summoner. Elder Seth, the Unspeakable. The more she picked up about his past, the more she realized how inadequate her vision of the world had been. She had been born to a life of violence, desperation and death, but she had never believed corpses could walk, manshaped creatures could endure for thousands of years, or that another person's mind could leak into your own.

"Don't open your eye yet," said the Doc. "I have the lights on."

The bandages were lifted from her face. Free at last, she wriggled her nose.

The Doc whistled through his teeth.

"Hmmnn, even if I do say so myself, that is quite some job. You could pass for a musickie model."

Jessamyn raised her hand, and felt her face. The dents in her forehead were gone, and her nose was reset. There was some flesh over her cheekbones again. Her chin was straight. And the improved optic was a solid lump under her left eyelid.

"It's not just a burner," Doc Threadneedle had told her as he unwrapped it from its tissue like a sugared almond. "Gen-Tech have upgraded the product to include a kind of bat-sonar, and a heat sensor. You won't be able to see through it, but it will increase your field of perception. One model contains a micro-camera for surveillance, and the DeLuxe Tripball can filter light patterns and transmit them to the brain as psychoactive impulses. At last, a high with no side-effects. You can trip on Christmas Tree Lights."

She had picked out the combat model. Psychedelics didn't interest her these days. She had long since grown out of her disco dingbat phase.

"'Kay, I've dimmed the lights. Ready."

She opened her eye, and blinked in the gloom. She saw the Doc hovering by the table, and sat up. Her spinesheath buzzed slightly as the bioservos went along with her nerve impulses. Eventually, she wouldn't be aware of the hum, Doc told her. She would accept it just as she accepted her heart-beat and her pulses.

"Try the optic."

She closed her real eye, and opened the other. Her image of the room was clearer, like a line drawing. Doc Threadneedle was a man-sized conglomeration of hotspots. The blobs went from deep orange to bright yellow. The radiator elements shone like the bars of an electric fire. She could even see the faint heat pattern of the cat in the next room.

"Interesting, huh?"

"Snazz, Doc."

Doc Threadneedle laughed.

"What is it?"

"Snazz. You haven't talked like that since you got here."

"I suppose not. You have to grow up sometime."

"Not if you can afford the Zarathustra Treatment."

She eased her legs off the table. Her blastic-augmented kneejoints were smooth.

She touched the floor, and pushed herself away from the table. She was a little unsteady. A touch of dizziness. The Doc supported her with an arm around her waist.

"Wait a moment. The optic cyberfeed will kick in. Your brain's been told what to expect. It's just warming up."

He walked her to the centre of the room, and let her go. She tottered, and put her arms out. The Doc pushed the wheeled table back against the wall, giving her some space.

It was like a click inside her. The dizziness went away.

"Try it," the Doc encouraged her. "The flamingo position."

She tucked one foot into her crotch, sticking out her knee, and lifted her heel from the floor. Finally, she was balanced in perfect comfort on the ball of her big toe.

"How does it feel?"

"Wonderful. There's no strain."

"You should be able to stand like that for a week before the nerve implants get tired. Here, catch..."

He tossed a book at her. She reached out and caught it without so much as wobbling.

"You could take up ballet."

She balanced the book on her head, and laughed, turning in a slow pirouette on her toe.

Doc Threadneedle slowly turned up the lights. The line drawing faded, and she saw the colours as well as the warmths.

She looked down at herself. Below her hospital gown, her legs were still as she remembered – although her reinforced thigh and shin bones made them two and a half inches longer. She still had the faint white scar on her ankle, although the cross-hatch of scratches on her right knee was gone.

She dropped her other foot to the floor, and turned around. She felt good. The Doc's patented micro-organisms were beavering away inside, keeping her at the peak of perfection. She was hungry, not with a need for food but with a desire for tastes.

"Makes you feel kinda sexy, doesn't it?"

She smiled. "Well… yes."

"Everything will be better, Jessamyn. Food, sex, exercise. You should develop an ear for good music. Forget sovrock and get into Mozart and Bach. You've got the greymass for it now."

"Doc, have you?"

He grinned. She realized she didn't know, couldn't imagine, how old he really was.

"Yes, of course. You don't think I'd do anything to a patient I wouldn't have done to myself?"

He put his hands out and fell to the floor, as if to do fingertip push-ups. Tipping himself forwards, he touched his forehead to the tile and kicked into the air. He straightened out, feet extended towards the ceiling, and rose into a handstand. Then, balanced on the fingers of his left hand, he put his right into the pocket of his labcoat and brought out a packet of sweets. He poured one into his mouth and offered the pack to her.

"Showoff," she said.

He pushed the floor, and flipped over in the air, landing on his feet. Straightening up, he was a middle-aged, rangy black guy again.

"Yes, of course. I don't get much chance to, you know, out here in the sand."

"Couldn't you…?"

"Go back?" Wrinkles appeared on his forehead. The fun sapped out of him. "No. GenTech doesn't forget. Zarathustra won't forget. One day, he'll try to take me out, you know. That's the real reason for all these 'improvements'. One slip, and you're excommunicated. He's not like he seems on the talkshows. They called me a Frankenstein, but his ambitions go further. He's a Faust, a Prometheus… and, in the end, I'm afraid he's a Pandora."

"You've lost me. Frankenstein I know from the videoshockers, but who are the others?"

"It doesn't matter, Jessamyn. I'm not like him. I've changed your body, and I tried to rewire a few of your neurons, but I've left you alone where it counts."

"And Zarathustra?"

"He doesn't want to improve the quality of an individual life. He wants to recreate the human race in the image of his ideal. Zarathustra isn't his real name, you know. It's something German, really."

"He's a… what was that old gangcult called… Nazti?"

"Nazi. Maybe. There are still a few left. The Mayor of Berlin, for instance, Rudolf Hess. Zarathustra has certainly dosed himself on some of his own miracle rejuvenators."

They left the surgery, and Doc Threadneedle locked up that part of the house. He had a large place, with as many modern conveniences as a sandhole like Dead Rat could offer, but it wasn't what someone with his skills could rate in a PZ.

He didn't seem to miss the gadgets and gizmos, though. His house was full of things she had only ever seen in old films with Rock Hudson and Doris Day: a vacuum cleaner, which did the work of a suckerdrone; a gramophone, which played unwieldy round black musidiscs with added scratch and hiss as part of the music; an electric kettle that took ages, maybe two minutes, to heat up enough water for a cup of recaff, and didn't do anything about the impurities and pollutants.

Buzzsaw, the cat, curled around Jessamyn's legs.

"I've got you some clothes," said the Doc. "Your desert gear was more holes than hide. Magda ze Schluderpacheru had something surplus down at the Silver Shuriken."

He indicated a neat pile of drab-coloured garments.

"The Silver Shuriken?"

"It's the local saloon. A yakuza operation, naturally. They're the only people who can keep anything open out in the sand, and not be closed down by the gangcults. Magda is a honey. You should meet her."

"I'd like to. It's been so long since…"

The Doc grinned. "Since you saw anything but my ugly mug, I understand. It's time you got out of the house. You must be stir crazy."

She wandered over to the chicken-wired window, and looked out. It was a clear night. The constellations twinkled.

"You should be with young people your own age, get yourself back into the swing of society."

"Uhh?" She had been distracted, looking out the chicken-wired windows at the half-disc of the moon. "I'm sorry. You're right. I need to… to do something."

She felt funny, as if things were happening inside her.

"I meant to tell you about that. Your body is like an engine. If you don't turn it over regularly, it will complain. With all the alterations you've had, you'll need to take vigorous exercise for several hours a day. I'd prescribe running, dancing, fighting, healthy eating and athletic sex."

"You could get to be very popular back in the city-states, Doc."

Doc Threadneedle smiled sadly. "Yes, but not with the right people."

Jessamyn picked up Buzzsaw, and felt the tingle of static from the cat's fur. It was like a mini-rush in itself. She realized she was down from the morph-plus, and that her senses were sharper than they had ever been before.

"Suck your finger and stick it in a light-socket sometime," the Doc said. "You'll be surprised."

She stroked the cat. It squealed and struggled from her grip. It disappeared upstairs.

"You don't know your own strength yet. You'll have to be careful. Here, try one of these."

He tossed her a thick yellow-covered book. She held it between her forefingers and thumbs and neatly tore it in half.

"I lose more telephone directories that way..."

IV

DEAD RAT, ARIZONA. What a place for an Englishman to end up, don't ch'know? Bloody buggering ha-ha-ha, eh what? Of course, Sarn't Major James Graham Biggleswade couldn't exactly go back to Blighty and expect them to hang out the welcome mat in Fulham, not after that tricky bit of bloody buggering business down in the Falklands – oh, excuuuuse meeee, the Mal-bloody-buggering-vinas – back in '11. Bit of a blooming sodding disgrace really, in actual fact, eh? These fakenham days, nobody hupped, frupped and trupped when the older Mastsarge yelled. Fact was, nobody knew who James Graham Buggered-to-bejaizus Biggleswade was. The sandrats just called him Jitters. His hands sometimes stopped shaking long enough for him to light a fag or give his teeth the once-over with Pepsodent, but that was every other Scumday in a month with a zed in it.

He sat in the corner of the Silver Shuriken, as far away from the bleeding video jukebox and bleeping zapper games as possible, sipping the foul antifreeze that passed for beer in the U S of Bloody A. He would have cut off his left dough-nut and sold it to Johnny Maradona for a pint of Six X Wadsworth, two bacon-and-cheddar sarnies and a packet of crisps with a blue twist of salt in them.

Mrs ze Schluderpacheru had taken pity on him, and gave him some sweeping-up chores in return for room and board and the occasional session with Fat Juanita. The old lady was like that, big-bloody-hearted. Jitters knew she was doing two people a favour, because Fat Juanita got depressed when the johnny-passing-throughs left her downstairs in the parlour with her knitting and gave all the custom to Gretchen, Connie Calzone, Margaret Running Deer and the Games Mistress. Fat Juanita was too bloody old, fat and stinky for the Game really. Not exactly prime camp-follower material. Bloody buggering lovely personality, though. If Jitters didn't have a wife and kids back in the old country – which, come to think of it, he probably didn't these days – he might just have dragged Fat Old Stinky Juanita up before the padre and tied the old knot. A soldier should be married, gave him a sense of what he was fighting for. Difficult to get the old fire up for the Greater Glory of flag, Empire and Prime Minister Peter Mandelson, but hearth, home and humping still meant something in this godrotten hellhole khazipit of a world.

Just now, the Silver Shuriken was pretty quiet. Mrs ze Schluderpacheru was doing the accounts on her musical wrist-calculator, working how out much of her take would have to go to the yaks this quarter. Gretchen, the new girl, was putting up the Christmas decorations, replacing the black crepe around the crush velvet portrait of Wally the Whale with sparkly tinsel. The rest of the professional ladies were slumped around the telly in see-through armchairs, watching some kids' show called Cyclopaths, about a bunch of motorsickle chappies who went around slaughtering people they didn't think much of. That was one thing about America, the telly was crap.

Jitters missed the good old BBC, with the Light Programme and the Home Service. It might not be in strain-on-your-meat-pies Trideocolor or go on all night like America's bloody buggering 11623 channels, but at least some nice bint like his old French teacher came on at ten-thirty and said good night as you drank your bloody buggering Ovaltine and waited for the shipping forecast. He missed the classic serials, with Great British actors in adaptations of the works of Great British writers like G A Henty, Dornford Yates, Sapper, Dennis Wheatley and John Buchan. They were on the Home Service, along with all the programmes about how to make do in the kitchen what with the rationing, and the fireside chats from the Prime Minister. That had been old Kenneth Clarke last time he was in the old country, but he had popped his clogs of apoplexy while explaining the Fall of Port Stanley to Natasha Kaplinsky on *Nationwide* and it was that upstart Peter Mandelson now. And on the Light Programme there was *The Black and White Minstrel Show*, where Benny Elton and Ricky Mayall had got their big break; *The Archers*, with Julian Clary and Caroline Quentin as Dan and Doris, saving the Ambridge enclave from gypsies and travellers; *Doctor Who*, with Stephen Fry visiting Great Moments of British History; *The Muffin the Mule Hour*... Most of all, he missed Dale Winton as the old-fashioned robocopper in *Dixon of Dock Green*, zapping the Frenchies with his bio-implant bazookas.

Should have had PC George Dixon at Port Stanley back in '11, Jitters thought. Johnny Argie wouldn't have seen off the task force so bloody buggering easy if the old "evenin' all" had been on the South Atlantic beat.

Gretchen was up a ladder now, sticking Bethlehem stars over the bulletholes on the ceiling. She was wearing a mesh-foil microskirt, a Miss Piggy wig and strawberry pasties, her usual uniform.

The swing-doors swung open, and Curtius Kenne ambled in, chewing tobacco. He looked up at Gretchen, and spanged the spittoon with a jet of brown filth.

"Nice view," he drawled. "Haw haw haw!"

Curtius was a cowboy builder. His van was painted up with pictures of Gene Autry and Hopalong Cassidy, and he called his firm the Boot Hill and Laredo Double Glazing Company. He guaranteed his windows against everything up to a BlastMaster minimissile, but you were usually too dead to complain if he supplied you with defective merch. He loped across the bar, swinging his hips to show off his twin Colts, and got his polished pseudoleather boot up on the bar.

"Any chance of a belt of Shochaiku Double-Blend, Magda?" he asked Mrs ze Schluderpacheru.

The owner looked up from her calculations and raised an eyebrow. Her feathered hat bobbed.

"Now, Curtius, honey, you know I keep that stuff only for my special customers."

Magda ze Schluderpacheru was Romanian, originally. Like Jitters, she had knocked around the world a bit and wound up in Dead Rat. Bloody buggering shame if you asked him. Nice people ending up clogging this plughole when the PZs were full of undeserving wankers, wallies, wasters and wooftahs.

"Ain't I one of your special customers?"

"Hell, not since you gave Hot Pants Hannah that dose of the Cincinatti Pox you ain't."

"That weren't me."

"You goddam prove it, and then maybe I'll dig out that bottle."

"Any time, Magda, any time." Curtius started unbuckling his gunbelt.

"Hold on there, cowpoke. I don't mean like that. I mean with a medical certificate."

"Ah shee-it, I ain't going to no mad doctor and gettin' mah pecker all X-rayed. Probably shrivel up like a cactus in a microwave. Haw haw haw."

Curtius Kenne thought he was funny.

"Then, cowpoke, you better get used to having nothing but cows to poke for a while."

"Whisky, straight."

Mrs ze Schluderpacheru poured Curtius a shot. Even her sumpstuff was okay by Big Empty standards. If you poured it on the table, it probably wouldn't even eat half-way through.

"Thank you kindly ma'am. That's a real nice dead bird you got on your hat. You kiss it to death yerself? Haw haw haw."

Curtius Kenn was a bloody nuisance, and sooner or later someone would put a ScumStopper under his heart and get himself free drinks on the house for a month.

The cowboy turned around, and surveyed the bar. He looked at Connie and licked his nose. She ignored him, and turned up the sound on the telly. Disappointed, Curtius looked for amusement elsewhere.

"Has anybody heard the one about the Maniak Chieftain and the six-weeks-dead camel corpse?"

"You told us yesterday," said Margaret Running Deer.

"Yeah, and the day before that," said Connie, touching up her lipstick with a finger to cover the razorscar under her nose.

"And it wasn't funny then," said the Indian Girl, picking her nails with her scalping stiletto.

Having had no luck with the girls, Curtius finally noticed Jitters in the corner. A mean look crept into his eyes.

"Hey Jitters, you limey bastid, last Thursday I saw me some Argentinian fellers marching down Main Street with Gen-Tech weapons. You still runnin' away from that there South Atlantic battle?"

Jitters hadn't run away. He had been ordered to make a tactical withdrawal. It had been a rout, but that hadn't been his fault. Nobody had known how well equipped the bloody buggering Argies would be the second time around.

He didn't say anything. Curtius took his drink and carried it over to the corner. He sat down.

"Hell, you limeys are yellower'n a cat's pee on a canary. We've bailed you out of two fuckin' world wars, and you're still whinin' about it. You oughtta get yourselves some backbone. Get yourselves some real men, you know, maybe you could buy some of John Wayne's frozen sperm and impregnate some of your frigid women with it. Get yourselves a generation with cojones the size of key limes, eh?"

Jitters just smiled, and sipped his drink.

"Leave him alone, zeroid," shouted Mrs ze Schluderpacheru. "Jitters is all right. He never gave nobody no venereable diseases."

Curtius grinned, showing off the diamond inset into his front tooth.

"Me and old Jitters is just having a sociable little drink, Magda. Chatting over old times. He was like a war hero, y'know. Got his ass peppered at Goose Green."

Jitters had been wounded in the first landing, in the shoulder. It hadn't been what they'd been told to expect by the Daily Mail. They didn't know that the Argies had GenTech and G-Mek hardware. They'd all gone over the side, singing Johnny Lydon's hit "Who Do You Think You Are Kidding, Mr Galtieri" and 98% of them hadn't made it to the beaches. In five minutes, everyone he had been with on the long voyage over from Pompey was dead. Jitters had been wounded early, and washed back to the landing craft. They'd piled him in with the dead, and it was only later a naval ensign noticed him twitching. That was when they started calling him Jitters. He still twitched.

"You're a blister on the behind, Curtius," Mrs ze Schluderpacheru shouted, "leave him alone or you're barred for life."

Curtius took his drink, smiled slowly, and backed away.

"So long, hero. Hey, I heard me a new one. What's red, white and blue and got piss all over it? A British flag in Buenos Aires, haw haw haw! Good 'un, ain't it?"

Jitters drank his drink.

* * *

V

SHE RAN THE five miles from Doc Threadneedle's place in twenty minutes. Not a world record, but acceptable. She wasn't sweating, but there was a pleasurable sense of exertion. Some time, she would have to push herself, to find out exactly how improved she was. For a real work-out, she'd need an opponent. She experimented with her new optic, shifting her patch to her right eye and perceiving the world through heat patterns. She saw the sands cooling as the temperature fell.

She was wearing a black karate suit. It was loose, but felt good. She ran on bare feet.

Her heightened senses were working overtime. She would have to get used to that. She was sensing far more people and ve-hickles in the area than could possibly be there. For a while, she would have to downscale her first impressions. Doc Threadneedle had warned her about it.

He bicycled alongside her, keeping level, occasionally asking questions and nodding to himself.

"No prob here," he kept saying.

He set her tasks, and she accomplished them. "That rock, vault over it", or "the old fence, run through it." It was easy.

"When do I get to squeeze a lump of coal into a diamond?"

Doc Threadneedle laughed. "When I can stop a speeding locomotive with one bound."

"It's a deal."

The town was just coming alive, as she got to the Silver Shuriken. Sandrats were pouring in to fence their weekly scav. A Maniak chapter had been through last week, and one or two of them were still around, enjoying the yakuza hospitality at the ze Schluderpacheru place. The gaudy girls were being kept busy.

Doc Threadneedle parked his bike next to two Maniak sickles, and chained it to the hitching post, setting the boobycharges in the padlock to blow if anybody tried to tamper with it.

They went into the saloon.

"Doc, honey," said a large woman behind the bar. Doc Threadneedle leaned over and kissed her. Her mainly exposed bosoms wobbled over the top of her black corset. Looking at her heat patterns, Jessamyn saw the cold outlines of the wavy dagger and the pepperpot charge-gun stashed in her garterbelt stark against the warmth.

"Jessamyn, this is Magda. She's a friend."

"Ohayu, sweetheart," said the woman. "Welcome to the Shuriken. First drink is on the house. Sake?"

Jessamyn thought a moment. "Scotch and Canada."

Doc Threadneedle was startled. "Not yet, Jessamyn. You'll burn out your greymass. Try a perrier."

"Okay, mineral water."

Magda took a green bottle from the cooler and poured a tall glass of sparkling liquid. Jessamyn took a swallow. Her altered tastebuds tingled, and she felt a spasm of pleasure in her stomach.

"Whew! That's a kick!"

"Get used to it."

Magda fished out a bottle of Shochaiku, and gave Doc Threadneedle a shot. He sipped it.

Jessamyn thought it out. "I get it. It wasn't the alcohol you thought would hit me..."

"Of course not, your greymass could shrug off a concentrated squirt of pure smacksynth."

"It was the taste."

"Right. You've got a touch of extrasensitivity. Work up to the extremes."

She drank some more water. It was beyond anything she had ever experienced. "I feel like a new girl."

"Jessamyn, you are a new girl."

She began to relax. This was fun. She hadn't expected to have fun ever again. (In the back of her mind, the moonface tick-tocked, tugging her towards her responsibilities.) She looked around the bar. It was typical of the places she had been in during her Psychopomp days. Half Oldstyle-Western, half Scavsurplus-High Tech. The customers drank and drugged peacefully, trying not to make contact with each other, and the gaudy girls plied their trade quietly.

There was a cowboy song on the juke, "I Dreamed of a Hillbilly Heaven", and the two Maniax were practicing their fast draws against a GenTech Amusements Machine that zapped you insensible with a light voltage if the computer-generated gunslinger cleared leather faster than you did. One of them lost a showdown, and slumped on the shockplate, dropping the gamegun. His gangbuddy pulled out a real gun, and cocked it.

"Whoa there, big fella," said Magda. "Them things are expensive."

Jessamyn thought the Maniak might start a fight – she needed some action just now, her muscles tingled – but the heavy-set panzerboy backed down, and hauled his pal off.

"Just natural high spirits," Magda said. "Them boys skinned a solo Op out in the sand last week, fenced his hide to the yakmen. Well off his trail, this feller was. Some fancy-pants search-and-destroy customer from Los Angeles, California."

"Which agency?" Doc asked.

"Holderness-Manolo."

"I've heard of them. Glamour boys. Industrial warfare, mostly. The occasional movie star divorce. High flyers. They don't come in-country often."

Jessamyn sipped her drink. There must still be warrants out on her. But it didn't mean anything. There would be paper out on nine-tenths of the people in the room, including the gaudy girls and the town drunk. This was a townload of fugitives. Buzzsaw the cat was probably high on the FBI's Most Wanted Felines list.

"Any idea who the solo was gunning for?"

"Nahh, could've been anybody? The Red Baron was through a month or two back, racking up his score. And an esperado by the name of Al Amogordo took Buck Standish out on Main Street Wednesday last. Crossed his eyes and exploded Old Buck's head in some quarrel over a high yaller lady, then hit the trail in Buck's G-Mek convertible."

"There'd be a price on him."

"Yeah. The solo was probably after Al."

Doc Threadneedle ordered another drink, and tipped a few drops into Jessamyn's water. "Try that."

It was astonishing. "This is better than sex."

"Have sex, and then see what you think."

Jessamyn cooled out her mouth.

A cowboy sauntered over to the bar, and sidled up next to them.

"Hey, beaut, you in the market for some home-baked Western-style lovin'?"

She looked him over. "Come on, Wyatt Earp" she said, "do I look like a hog-tied sheep to you?"

The cowboy pushed his stetson back onto the crown of his head. He had thick-oiled hair, and old acne scars.

"Well, hell, lady, if that's your attitude, perhaps you'd better just sew it up, sister, cause there ain't no better stud bull than Curtius Kenne in the whole territory."

Magda laughed. "Ignore him, Jessamyn. He just won the election. The town hasn't had an Official Asshole for too long."

Curtius smiled, and a gem sparkled. "Jessamyn? That's a real purty name. Is that for real?"

"Yes. Excuse me."

She grabbed him by the back of his neck, and scraped her empty glass across his smile. He screeched, and she let him go.

He was bleeding from the mouth. She looked at her glass. It was not scratched.

"Paste, huh? I thought synthetic stones were getting better these days."

"Why you..."

He drew his hand back, and she reached out to stop the punch. It was as simple as catching a falling cup. She pushed a little too hard, and Curtius shouted.

"My shoulder."

Doc Threadneedle stepped in, and gave the cowboy's arm a wrench, setting the joint back in true.

"Sorry. Don't know my own strength."

Kenne was mad now. Everyone in the bar was looking.

"You're... you're one of them things, ain't you?"

There was fear and hatred in his voice. "What do you mean?"

"One of the Doc's monsters. You ain't human. Hell, Doc, your packagin' gets better and better, but what you put inside stinks to high heaven, you know. It's gettin' so a fella don't know where he's dippin' it. I take it all back, sister. You're just a sexclone with steel teeth, and I ain't interested."

The drunk in the corner, who wore what was left of some kind of camouflage outfit, came over, pulling a revolver out of his britches pocket. Jessamyn tensed, ready to shear his head off his neck with a karate move.

Magda shook her head, and Jessamyn relaxed. The drunk plonked his gun down on the bar.

"You've got a quarrel, settle it this way. Best of seven."

"This is Jitters," Magda said. "He's British."

The drunk saluted smartly. His hand vibrated. She didn't need to be Sherlock Holmes to know how he had picked up his nick-name. Jessamyn hefted his gun. It was a seven-shot model, a Webley and Scott .38 Bulldog, standard British Army Issue. A toy next to a ScumStopper Magnum, but it could do the job. She broke it, and slid five slugs out, leaving two consecutive bullets chambered. She sighted down the barrel. It was off, but it would do for a round of roulette.

"You game, cowboy?"

Kenne gulped, and looked around for a way out. "Guess I am, Mizz Frankenstein, guess I am."

"Ladies first?" She pointed the gun to her temple.

"Toss you for it."

Magda dropped a one-armed bandit token on the bar. Kenne guessed lemon, and won the first pull.

Click.

He sighed with relief, and passed the gun over. Then, he took a shot of whisky. Magda refilled his glass. It vanished down his throat, by-passed his stomach and stood out on his forehead as droplets of 90% proof sweat.

"The good stuff, huh?"

"Fella deserves Shochaiku if it's gonna be his last drink."

Jessamyn slipped the barrel into her mouth, and sucked it like a lollipop, fluttering her eyelashes at Kenne. His eyes popped.

Click.

"Your move."

"Good thing it's Curtius," Magda said, "if'n he blows his brains out, at least we won't be all day scraping them off the floor. Just my dainty little hankie will be enough to clean up that kind of a smeared speck."

Kenne's adam's apple was bobbing up and down. Jessamyn looked him in the face, smiling pleasantly. Shutting his eyes tight, he jammed the gun against his skull, and...

Click.

"Give it here." He was reluctant to let it go. She raised the gun, and pulled the trigger.

Click. "Bang," she said. Everybody jumped. Kenne spilled his drink. "No, really, just joking."

Kenne took the gun.

"Have you worked it out, cowboy? Three chambers, two bullets. Short odds."

They'd turned the music off now. Jitters was sucking at a bottle. Only Doc Threadneedle was apparently uninterested in the game.

Kenne looked at the saloon door. The Maniax were standing between him and it. That was his bad luck. The gangboys were in the entertainment mood tonight, and nothing appealed to them more than watching some asshole respray the ceiling with greymass. He looked down at the gun, which must be feeling pretty heavy.

"Two chances out of three, cowboy."

He did it quickly. Up to his head. Pull. Click.

He let out a whoop, and slammed the gun down onto the bar, breaking glasses.

"Whooo-eee, I thought I was gonna fill my britches fer sure, sister. Looks like I win, eh? Unless you want to play on, Mizz Frankie Stein?"

Jessamyn picked up the gun.

"You can go home now, sister. It's all over. Buy us all drinks, and it'll be forgotten. Ain't nobody gonna hold it against you."

She put the barrel to her temple.

"You don't have to do it," said Magda. "That would be crazy. Even Curtius ain't that big an asshole."

Her finger tightened.

"Hold on there," Kenne pleaded. "Two out of two, remember. Them's crazy person's odds."

"Jessamyn..." said the Doc. "Stop it."

Everyone in the saloon was looking at her. Their heat-patterns flared, as if they were blushing all over.

She pulled the trigger.

* * *

VI

COCOONED INSIDE THE air-cooled cockpit of his DeLorean "Snowbird" SandMaster, Bronson Manolo checked the dispositions of the Holderness-Manolo forces surrounding Dead Rat. Within five minutes, they should all be in place.

Once the spotman reported back that Jessamyn Amanda Bonney was in Dead Rat, Manolo had called in Holm Rodriguez from Denver and Susie Terhune from Phoenix. Terhune was an assault specialist solo who had sub-contracted for H-M on several occasions, and Rodriguez was their top Colorado Op, further qualified because he came from the quarry's home turf. When he was with the Denver paycops, he had busted little Jessamyn on some juvie beefs. Truancy, stealing lollipops, pulling PZ brats' pigtails, whistling commie songs in church, assault with a deadly weapon: kid-stuff like that.

"One good thing about this action," Terhune claimed, "at least nobody in Dead Rat could possibly be classed as an 'innocent bystander'."

H-M had enough field Ops to handle the sanction, but Manolo recognized his limitations, and had had Rodriguez and Terhune augment his forces with some local soldiers who knew the sand. Most of his full-scale skirmishes had been in NoGos or Urban Blight areas. Out here in the Big Empty, the situation was quite different. Less cover, more miles. This was sandrat heaven. He was quite willing to delegate field command to Terhune until the objective was obtained.

He checked his GenTech digital chronometer against the dashdial. He was synchronized with the machine.

"Ommm," he said to himself, shifting his level of psychic awareness, "ommm."

Gari the Guru had given his blessing on this sanction down at the Pyramid. "You can't destroy, Bronson, you can only convert a thing's form." That was true, converting forms was Manolo's business. He took nasty live people, and turned them into nice dead ones. Bob Holderness would have been proud of him.

When this take-out was over, he was looking forward to a session in the hot-tub with Kandi, maybe a few snorts of cocoa, and some radical waves to ride out in the bay. The pollution didn't kill the ripple, and couldn't get through to you in a skin-tight SCE unit.

Manolo didn't groove to the Big Empty. He was a cityguy. He didn't like to breathe anything he couldn't see.

"In place, Bronson," said Terhune. Her light blinked green on the mapscreen. "Mortars ready to ride. Let's nuke the spook."

"Rodriguez?"

Manolo tapped the screen, and Rodriguez's light flared. "Okay for sound, chief. We're in place."

"The quarry?"

"We tracked her from the Threadneedle site. She's in the Silver Shuriken now. We've given her enough time to get blasted out of her skull."

"Excellent. Judicious. Righteous."

"Thanks, bro."

Manolo pulled his seatbelt across his lap, and plugged it in. The console lit up, and he flicked some buttons. The inboard computer flashed stats at him. The weapons systems gave him some readiness read-outs.

"Okay José, let's spread some karma..."

VII

THE BULLET FLATTENED against her temple. She felt as if someone had taken a swing at her with a sledgehammer, but didn't fall off her stool. Her arm flew out, wrenching her shoulder, but she kept a grip on the gun. She shook her head, and the spent slug fell to the saloon floor.

"Let's look at that," said the Doc, prodding her sore spot with his fingers. "Hmmnn, more bruising than there ought to be. Your steel-mesh underflesh hasn't quite knitted properly. The durium platelocks are fine, though. You might have done something less drastic to test my handiwork, but everything seems to be holding up properly."

Curtius Kenne was staring at Jessamyn as if Jesus H Christ himself had ridden into town on a donkey, walked into the bar looking for trouble, and kicked him in the gonads with steel-spiked sandals.

"Fuck me," he said, almost in reverential tones.

Jessamyn handed him the still-smoking gun. "Didn't I mention that I had a bullet-proof skull?"

He took the weapon and looked at it. The barrel was blackened at the end.

"Silly me."

One bullet, one chamber.

"Your turn," she said.

He held the gun as if he didn't know what it was, and looked at her.

She smiled pleasantly. "You heard me, cowboy. It's your shot."

Jitters laughed and clapped his hands, then slapped Kenne on the back. "Yessir, now it's time to see some bloody buggering Yankee guts and glory spread out all over this pub, eh what? That do-or-die Davy Blooming Crockett spirit. Come on, Ragtime Cowboy Joe, take your medicine. The bint did her bit, now it's up to you to show us what you're made of..."

Kenne swallowed his spit. Tears leaked out of his eyes.

Jessamyn knew what the cowboy was made of. Flesh and blood and bone, just like everyone else. No blastic, no durium, no implants, no steel, no diamond-chips. Just chemicals and 78% water.

They weren't even the same species, Kenne and her. She couldn't feel anything for him. But she helped him.

She took the gun, and put it into his hand properly, wrapping his fingers around the butt, shoving his forefinger through the trigger-guard, and held the barrel to his ear. She thumb-cocked the piece, and stood back, admiring her handiwork. Kenne stood like a statue, Rodin's Old Cowhand Blowing Brains Out.

"The game ain't over till the whistle's blown."

The cowboy was sobbing now, the gunbarrel shaking against his flesh.

"That cracker-ass pussy ain't gonna do it," said one of the Maniax, turning away in disgust. "Never no good entertainment out in the sand."

Kenne was shaking all over. He lowered the gun, and it hung limp in his hand, barrel to the floor.

"Just a bloody buggering knee-trembler, eh what?" Jitters jumped up and down, face red with excitement.

Jessamyn picked up her perrier and finished it. The moment was over. Magda poured her another drink. Later, she would pick up the misshapen bullet from the floor. It would make a nice souvenir for her charm bracelet.

Kenne turned, and staggered towards the door, his chest heaving as he cried. A dark stain was spreading from the crotch of his Levis.

"Got your arses whipped in Nicaragua, and now you've lost it all in bloody buggering Arizona," Jitters shouted, keeping up with the broken American.

"Oh, say can you see, by the dawn's bleeding light, what so proudly we turn into spineless gibbering jellyfish with no dicks at the twilight's last gleaming..."

Kenne struck out at the drunk, but Jitters stepped back.

"Whose broad bums and shite cars through the perilous night, as on the ramparts we cowered in abject and pathetic fear was so chicken-shit streaming..."

The cowboy was nearly out of the door now. People were back to their drinking, drugging and whoring. Tcherkassoff was on the video-juke, with "Siberian Sayonara".

"Oh the rockets' red glare, the bombs bursting in the air made us manufacture chocolate in our underpants through the night though our god-rotted yellowstain rag was still there..."

Kenne sagged against the doors.

"Oh, say does that star-strangled banner yet flap..."

Jitters leaned close and spat at the cowboy.

"O'er the land of the Yanks, with their heads full of..."

Then, the explosions started.

VIII

As the mortar-flashes lit up Dead Rat, Holm Rodriguez signalled to his soldiers to move in. They were all people he could trust, unlike that Angelino pendejo Manolo. This wasn't a surgical strike, this was a massacre. All well and good, and he had no real objection to anything that rid the world of a townful of sandrat trash, but it was a pretty inelegant manoeuvre.

He sent Mostyn out on point, giving him Lucy Cheadle as back-up. Mostyn's M-29 spat, and somebody rolled down the dunes. The soldier gave Rodriguez the thumbs-up. First kill. That gave him dibs on the scav, not that there would be much worth looting in this sandhole.

Susie Terhune's crew laid down some heavy fire. Buildings started burning. The incendiary charges Manolo's experts had set up earlier in the day went up on schedule. By the time they got to town, most of the heavy stuff should be over.

Despite his bulky Kevlar Hell-and-Back suit, Rodriguez moved fast. He jogged every morning with lead weights slung on his chest, back and thighs to get him used to the extra poundage of the armour. The IR visor of his helmet showed him the desert as if by the light of an overcast day.

His team looked like a gang of astronauts in desert-camouflage kit.

"Ve-hickle coming," Lucy Cheadle's voice crackled in his earchip. "Cyke, two riders. Can't be our girl. The reading's wrong."

"Take them."

"Done, sir."

The cyke came up over a dune, and Mostyn and Cheadle caught it in a crossfire. It exploded in mid-air, and the two riders somersaulted to the sand. Haggett got in there with his bayonet, and speared the two as if they were straw figures.

"Down and out," Haggett shouted.

That had lost them precious moments.

"Come on, team," Rodriguez ordered, "let's move it. We're expected at the Silver Shuriken in 78 seconds. Manolo will ream our asses if we're off-schedule."

The soldiers jogged at full speed, M-29s jiggling in their arms. Rodriguez thought they must all look like big, hairless teddy-bears romping over the dunes.

They tore in formation down the main street, firing at anyone in sight. The gas station was an inferno. Someone dashed out of an alleyway, pumping a shotgun. Haggett's sandy expanse of chest was splattered red. "I'm hit, I'm hit," he said, sinking to his knees, his communicator crackling as he faded. Mostyn reacted, and brought the sumpsucker with the shotgun down with a burst of fire. It had been an old-timer, with a long white beard and a Gabby Hayes hat.

They jogged round a corner, and found themselves in what passed for the town square of Dead Rat, Arizona. There was a disused town hall, an abandoned Sheriff's office, and a still-operational five-customer gallows. And the saloon.

"Make the play," Rodriguez shouted. "Now!"

Mostyn and Cheadle humped themselves up the stairs, and crashed into the Silver Shuriken, guns discharging.

IX

She would have to learn to trust her new senses. There had been people out in the desert. And now they were in town, and she had to assume they were after her. It was just like the good old days. Cops and Ops and Soce Workers, all after her pretty little head.

Part of the ceiling had come down, and everyone was panicking.

"Magda," she said, "give me a gun."

"Sure thing, honey, take your pick."

The older woman pulled out a tray of handguns, and used it to push the glasses and drinks off the bar. Jessamyn picked a Smith & Wesson semi-automatic pistol, and jammed a couple of extra clips into her waistband.

"Good choice," said Magda, taking a Colt Python police special.

Some of the sandrats were milling around. Some of them weren't, because they were dead.

"Guns on the house," Magda shouted. "Come and get 'em."

Jitters and Curtius Kenne had been knocked flat by the first blast. They stumbled to their feet. Kenne had a proper grip on Jitters's gun now. One chamber, one bullet.

Doc Threadneedle tugged her sleeve. "Remember, don't be too confident. Jitters' revolver was just a pop-gun. Your underflesh won't stand up to depleted uranium or armour-piercing rockets, and you still burn and bleed like the rest of us."

Magda ze Schluderpacheru was unslinging a rocket-launcher from under the bar, and passing it across to the Maniax. Jitters was trying to wrestle his gun out of Kenne's grip.

"You got your Colts, yankee bloody doodle. Give me my gun back."

Two hefty figures in combat suits thundered through the doors, spraying the saloon with fire. The pointman steadied and looked around.

He saw Jessamyn and took aim. She was right. This was all for her benefit.

The pointman pulled the trigger, but his shot went wide. The Maniax had the launcher readied, and put an anti-tank missile into his stomach.

He was torn backwards, his hands flailing, and he got a grip on the doorjamb. He was completely impaled, his combat suit stoved in, the trefoils of the missile sticking out of his gut. The rocket fizzled, and shot through him, exploding against the gallows on the other side of the square.

Jessamyn could see right through the hole in the dead man. His sidekick froze, and was cut down by fire from all quarters.

A phosphorus grenade rolled in through the door, and everyone dived for cover.

She could see the explosion through closed eyelids. Her heat sensor sent pain signals to her greymass.

"Fuck," she swore. "You realize, of course, that this means WAR!"

X

MANOLO WAS PLEASED. It was all according to the plan. Casualties so far were acceptable. As far as he was concerned, the loss of all personnel in the field with the exception of Bronson Manolo could be classed as an acceptable casualty rate if it got the job done. Not that he was callous. H-M had a hefty policy with General Disaster to provide for the dependents of those lost or handicapped in the service of the Agency.

His mapscreen was lighting up all over. Terhune had laid down all the fire they needed, and Rodriguez's team was in town, cutting loose.

"Gas station, saloon, hotel, town hall..." He checked off the targets as they flared.

He flicked the counter. 0347. Within a five mile radius of the town square of Dead Rat, there were 0347 warm people, excluding the H-M personnel in their combat gear.

Ooops, 0345. No, 0341. The number fell, as the people cooled.

He dug a brew out from the cooler under his chair, and flipped the ringtop.

This was proving to be a stroll.

As balls of fire filled the interior of the Silver Shuriken, Jessamyn dived for a window. She crashed through a tinsel and spray-snow Christmas decoration and, curled up tight, turned head over end through the air, landing neatly on her feet in the street.

One of the soldiers stood in front of her, presumably awestruck behind his or her faceplate. She shot through the helmet, and the soldier sagged to the dirt.

Two more of the space invaders skidded around the building, bringing up their guns. She got them both with a single burst, and sprinted away, zig-zagging down a side-street.

It was a clear night. The half-moon shone down placidly.

0326.

Jitters had his gun back, with just one bloody buggering round left in it, so he would jolly well have to put it to bloody good use, wouldn't he, by jove.

Curtius Kenne was cut in half by a falling beam, worse luck, so he couldn't use his one shot to spread the cowboy's greymass on the wall. There was no place like the thick of battle for settling an old score. So many people were dying that no one would notice a few more.

Jitters had been splashed with some of the liquid fire from the grenade, but he was lucky enough to have been blown through a hole in the wall by the blast. He rolled in the sand, until most of the flames were out.

There were troops yomping down the main street of Dead Rat. It was like being back at Goose Green. But he wasn't going to withdraw tactically this bloody buggering time, no sir, not with brass knobs on...

He held his gun up in readiness. His hands weren't shaking now.

0318.

GRETCHEN TURNER KNEW she should never have left Des Moines with Barry, the electrofence salesman. Her mama had said as much, but D-M was such a zeroville. Barry had been a rat, all right. He'd left her in a town just like Dead Rat. Since then, those had been all the places she'd known. But Magda ze Schluderpacheru was better than the other madams, the Silver Shuriken could have been a nice place with a little work. The girls were nice. They had a nice team. Gretchen couldn't feel anything below her chin, and she knew that wasn't good. She couldn't see either. There was fire all around. As she blacked out, she thought it was a pity she hadn't gotten round to finishing the Christmas decorations.

0317.

AN ARMOURED VE-HICKLE trundled slowly through the town, searchlights revolving on the roof. That would be some kind of command module, Jessamyn knew. That gave it a high spot on her list of things to put out of commission.

0314.

★ ★ ★

Simon Threadneedle, late of GenTech, switched off his pain with the circuitbreaker he had inserted into his own greymass. The combat unit had sprayed napalm or some napalm analogue into the Silver Shuriken, and he was clothed in fire. Nothing would get the stuff off him until it burned itself out. This was the sort of juice that burned even underwater.

It was amazing what modern technology could accomplish. The GenTech labs couldn't do anything about the common cold and no government had been able to develop a workable public transport system, but when it came to deathware, why, there were wonderful new toys on the market every fall, just in time for Christmas.

His plastic-laced flesh melted away, and the durium bonesheaths heated up. He didn't know how high a temperature they could take before they went into shut-down, and he supposed he wouldn't get a chance to record his findings if he did pursue the experiment to the end. His clothes had burned away instantly, as had all his bodily hair and most of his skin. Tarnished metal shone through his musculature as he walked through the fire. He stepped out of the wall of flame onto the steps of the saloon, and strode, still burning, into the street.

A soldier tried to shove a bayonet into his throat, but the steel buckled against his adam's apple superconductor. With fiery hands, he lifted the besuited killer off the ground, and bent his back until it snapped. Gunfire rattled against his pectoral shields, and he staggered backwards from the blast. He was holding up even better than he had hoped.

0307.

"Large concentration of bodies coming our way," said Danny Riegert from the monitor. "Looks like a lynch mob."

"Get ready to rock and roll," Susie Terhune snapped, taking the controls of the chainguns. The command unit was in its strategic position in the town square. The roofguns swivelled.

"Forty or fifty, armed and angry."

"Wait till you can distinguish their heartbeats on the sensor."

"Yes, ma'am."

Her husband had left her the year before for some Tex-Mex bitch, claiming that she was too boring to live with. Chuck and Benny, her kids, whined that she was never home. She had just had painful surgery to remove an ovarian cyst that had turned out to be benign. And she had never seen the Pacific Ocean.

She tapped keys, and flicked switches.

"A hundred yards, and closing..."

"Tell me when they get to fifty."

"Yes, ma'am."

The computers hummed, as the smart bullets picked their targets. Once locked on to a heartbeat pattern, they would whizz around like fireflies until they found the precise biosignal that would allow them to explode. What do you know, these babies really did have your name written on them.

"Fifty."

She turned on the maxiscreamers, and the riot-control noise boomed through the town, shaking teeth loose, bursting eardrums, bringing rickety buildings down.

"Spot on. They're running around like chickens at a geek convention."

The smartguns locked, and flashed READY at her.

When she was out of this, she'd check out a sexclone with a moustache like Bronson Manolo and a body like Pitt, rent herself some clean water and a whirlpool bath, and have herself a party and a half.

She initiated the firing sequence.

"They're about to scatter, ma'am."

"So much the better."

The guns started spitting intelligent death into the night.

0235.

JESSAMYN SAW A crowd going down, those damned smugslugs spinning through the air like midges.

GenTech had developed the little bastards. But once they were on the market, the corp had spent a lot of R and D money coming up with a way to beat them. And Doc Threadneedle had access to that technology.

She took a deep breath, and a tiny sponge inside her heart – a bioengine – inflated, changing her heart's signature. It was peculiarly like having the hiccoughs. Thanks to the little organism, her life signal would change every twenty seconds for anything up to half an hour.

People she didn't know died around her, but she was untouched.

0199.

BRONSON MANOLO HUMMED a Butthole Surfers number to himself, and touched up his hair, using the rearview mirror as he patted his coiffeur. He wanted another beer, but Gari had him on one-a-day for as long as his organic rice diet was holding up. Dammit, he deserved another brew. He was working hard. Let the Pyramid Pooper take a hike just this once, eh?

0196.

What the hell, people in Africa were gasping for a beer, and he had a whole case stashed here. He reached for a can.

0188.

"You can be a success," he chanted to himself, "your mind is a chisel, your will is a hammer, and life is a rock."

He focused on the miniature plastic pyramid on the dashboard, and willed this mission to succeed.

0179.

RODRIGUEZ TOOK UP a command position in the old jailhouse. It must have closed down when the state police pulled out, abandoning these backwaters to the gangcults.

His crew were in pairs, going on a house-to-house, and he was ticking off the cleared locations on his streetmap. He had taken off his helmet and gloves for the job, and was stabbing with a stub of lightpencil at the screenmap Manolo had given him. Half the town was down by now.

But still no Jessamyn.

He remembered their girl as she had been when he first had her through the system in Denver. She could have been hardly eleven then. But with a clown-white face and fetish-chains, she looked older than sin.

"Livery stable clear," Baldrey barked in his ear. He checked the building off.

He also remembered Jessamyn's Old Man. Now, there was a seriously disturbed individual. No wonder his precious had ripped his throat out.

"Any sightings of Jessamyn?" he asked on the open channel.

"Don't worry," Terhune said. "She hasn't got a chance."

She had had big, sad, green eyes. Two of them, then.

"No, Susie. You're right. She's never had a chance."

0156.

THE ARGIES WERE coming for him, bloody buggering bastards of dagoes that they were. He could hear the grease on their hair frying from ten miles away.

Sarn't Major Biggleswade signalled for his troops to follow, and made a dash across the burning street.

"Forever England," he shouted, "the Falklands are Forever England."

Teddy-bear shaped Argies rushed at him, firing ineptly. He was over the top like PC Dixon taking out a French terrorist cell.

"Come on lads, we can whip 'em. Corned beefeaters! Pansy Sanchos! Gaucho gauleiters!"

He was hit in the legs, but he backed out of the line of fire. Where was the Union Jack? Someone was supposed to be carrying it.

"For England, God and St George!"

0134.

JESSAMYN FELL TO a crouch, and clambered across the square on all fours, recalling her sandrat days. She was a good animal again.

A soldier loomed over her, and she rolled, firing upwards in an arc. The suit punctured and bled, the faceplate cracking.

Wriggling her shoulders and pushing with her feet, she covered the last ten yards. Her karate jacket ripped, but the skin of her back was unabraded.

She got to the command ve-hickle, and spread herself against its treads, firing across the square at some stray killers.

0086.

SIMON THREADNEEDLE WAS almost burned out now. His eyes had popped, but the sensors inside his skull fed him heat patterns that were clearer than any visual input. Most of the tissue was gone, but the bio-implants still functioned. And he still had his greymass.

Magda ze Schluderpacheru was dead, had died near the beginning of it. That was a shame. She had been soft and warm, the last of his meatform's attachments.

Curtius Kenne was dead too, and most of the other citizens. He hadn't kept track, but he thought he had sensed Jitters going down.

Where was Jessamyn? She should survive. She had been a walking ruin when she came to him, and he had made her better.

Better than anyone. Better, even, than he had made himself.

Should he have told her, he wondered? Should he have mentioned the strange symptoms and side-effects he had been observing in his own case?

The detachment. The languor. His feelings were heightened, but his drives had been running down. He could barely relate to people. Before Jessamyn had come to him, he had sometimes spent days at a time sitting in front of the windows in his bedroom, looking at the unchanging, unmoving desert as the sun and the moon did their daily dance.

The moon...

0050.

MANOLO BELCHED, AND excused himself. 0049. 0048. 0047. 0045. 0043. 0039.

"MA'AM," SAID DANNY Riegert, "we've got a weird reading, close to the ve-hickle."

Susie Terhune slipped the lase to automatic, and let it continue slicing up the rooftops.

"Specify."

"Down low, by the treads, in actual contact with the module."

"Our girl?"

"Hard to say. The heartbeat doesn't match, but it also keeps changing. I think it's some kind of systems error."

"Idiot, don't you read *Guns and Killing*? She's had a heart-sponge implant. Let me think, let me think..."

Terhune's fingers flew over the keyboard, pulling a close-range weapons menu out of the memory.

1: MINISCREAMER

2: CLOSE-RANGE SMARTGUN

3: ELECTROCHARGE

4: GAS GRENADE

She punched in a Code 3, and a Confirm.

The ve-hickle buzzed, as it discharged.

"See how you like that, bitch!"

0036.

JESSAMYN FELT HER body arch as the electricity hit. She sucked in a double-lungful of air and screamed, but not in pain. It was her predator's howl of triumph.

She remembered Doc Threadneedle suggesting she try sucking her finger and sticking it in an electric socket.

Every nerve in her body came alive. She had never felt stronger. How long would this last?

She scrambled up onto the top of the ve-hickle, still feeling the hyperbuzz.

Sex could not be better than this.

She came to the smartgun mounting, and ripped the multi-barrelled weapon out at the roots. It came away as easily as a dead treebranch. Metal tore. Wires shorted out.

The screamers started again, and she let the durium shields up inside her ears.

There was a battened hatch on top of the ve-hickle. This was going to be like opening a can.

0029.

* * *

Biggleswade saw the British heroine climb up onto the Argie tank, and cheered. He dragged his dead legs behind him, and pulled himself towards the battle. The girl was bloody buggering Victoria Cross material, and he wanted to be there to see her run the Union Jack up the flagpole at Port Stanley. Puerto bloody buggering Galtieri in-bloody-buggering-deed! The girl got a good grip on the hatch, and pulled it away, tossing it across the square like a dustbin lid.

0027.

The girl-thing was in the command centre. Susie Terhune scrabbled under her seat for the handgun stashed there.

Riegert was gone, out the hatch, screaming. He had made a dash when the quarry had dropped through.

Terhune got a shot off, but the quarry leaned to one side and the slug missed. It ricocheted off a bulkhead, impossibly loud in the confined space, and buried itself in the fleshy part of Terhune's thigh.

Blood filled her lap. She was strapped into her seat.

She tried to raise her hands, tried to surrender, but she couldn't move, words wouldn't shake loose of her mouth.

The quarry came for her. Jessamyn Bonney looked so young.

The screen flashed up a weapons menu, requesting operator input.

The quarry took her by the scruff of her neck, and shoved her face into the screen.

The glass cracked, and Terhune felt something go inside her skull. Sparks showered out of the ruptured system.

The quarry rammed her into the screen again. Terhune's face pushed through the window into the workings of the command module. Currents crackled around her, and she smelled her hair burning.

She continued to twitch like a headless chicken long after she was dead.

0019.

MANOLO PULLED ANOTHER tab, and sucked the beertube. He sensed the pyramid vibrating.

THE ARGIE CAME flying out of the tank, running from the British heroine. Jitters took careful aim, and got him with a headshot. The foreigner stumbled on a few steps, his brains leaking out around his earphones, and collapsed in a heap.

Bloody buggering serve him right!

He tried to sing "God Save the Queen," but blood came up from his chest. He realized he was due for shipping home to Blighty. With these scratches, he was out of the rest of the war. Bloody shame. He hoped the rest of the lads would do him proud.

There'd be free drinks for him for years in the Wise Serpent in Micklethwaite Road, Fulham.

The burning building behind him settled, and a triangular slice of wall slid out of place. Bricks rained around him, crushing him into the street.

"God Save..."

0018.

MANOLO FLICKED A switch and brought up the other figure. 0012. There had been 75 Holderness-Manolo personnel at the outset of this engagement. Now there were 12.

He thought about that. He had expected losses, but this was above even his guestimate.

Terhune wasn't answering. "Rodriguez, do you copy?"

"Yes, sir."

"Your position?"

"The jailhouse. It's pretty hairy down here."

"Have you terminated the quarry?"

"I cannot confirm or deny that."

0017-0012.

"There are seventeen hostiles left alive. Do you have reason to suspect that Jessamyn Bonney is among their number?"

There was a pause. "No reason, sir. But she is. I know she is. She'll be the last."

0017-0011.

H-M had just lost another man. The reparations on this were going to be cosmic. General Disaster would be upping the Agency's premiums next year for sure. The accountants would shit themselves at that one.

"Don't pull out until you've taken her down, Rodriguez."

"I don't intend to."

"Good man."

0016-0011.

Manolo decided to ride the vibes for the moment.

JESSAMYN LEFT THE dead woman with her face in her terminal, and climbed onto the top of the command module. There was less gunfire now, but the whole town was on fire. The streets were littered with the dead. It was like Spanish Fork all over again. Like too many towns.

A crazy man, someone she had never seen before, took a shot at her from a rooftop. The slug rang against the armourplate of the ve-hickle. She took aim at the sniper, but his roof collapsed under him, dropping him into the fire.

The only thing still standing in town was the gallows. There wouldn't be much use for that in the morning.

0011-0010.

They nearly had parity.

0010-0010.

That was a comfort. One H-M combat Op in full kit should equal four or five sandrats.

0010-0008.

Maybe desperation brought out survival instincts in the gangscum.

Rodriguez was still in place.

Nevertheless, it was time to take a little precautionary measure. Manolo pulled the security systems keyboard out of the dash, and entered the lock-down programs.

Durium shields slid down the windows, blanking out the moonlight. The interior lights flickered, and came on.

The wheels retracted, and the shutters closed their apertures. The DeLorean settled on the sand like a beached powerboat. Multiple locks slid into place, sealing the vehickle tighter than the Bank of Tokyo.

Explosive bolts sealed shut the cardkeyholes in the doorhandles. The only way in now was through the computer palm-recognition slab, and that was programmed only to reverse the lock-down upon the authority of executive-level Holderness-Manolo personnel.

0007-0004.

It was quiet in the DeLorean now. The LED figures blinked in silence. Manolo heard his own breathing.

0006-0003.

SIMON THREADNEEDLE WALKED down the main street. He knew he must look barely human, a robotic skeleton with a few charred scarecrow tatters hanging from the steel.

"Jessamyn," he called.

She looked round. She did not register any shock.

"Doc?"

"Yes. I'm in here somewhere."

"Doc..."

"I know."

They stood, looking at each other. She was bearing up well, a few bruises but nothing serious. Her clothes were torn, and her hair was a mess, but there was no damage. He could feel proud of himself.

"Is this over?" he asked.

"Nearly. No one's shot at me for a minute."

"So, we won?"

She made a gesture, indicating the scatter of bodies. "If you call this winning."

"You're here. That's what's important."

"It doesn't feel important."

0002-0002.

Manolo had the cast of characters worked out. H-M still had Rodriguez, and himself. The others would be Jessamyn Bonney and the doctor, Threadneedle. That would be the last of it. They were the improved humans.

0002-0002.

THE DOC WAS in bad shape. Only now did Jessamyn realize just how completely he had transformed himself. His face was a melted-tar smear, with durium highlights. She saw the wires threaded through his limbs.

"Jessamyn, there are things you have to know about the treatment."

His voice was still the same, although she could see the silver ball in his throat where it was generated.

"Zarathustra closed down the project for good reasons, by his lights. There are... side-effects. Psychological, I think."

A cold hand caressed Jessamyn's metal-sheathed spine.

"You'll have to work at it, work at remaining human inside... I'm not sure that I've managed it all that well, myself. Sometimes, I just sit and stare, forgetting... for weeks, Jessamyn, for weeks. I can do almost anything with this improved body, but my mind has got blasé about it. When you're superhuman, so little seems worth the bother. You must resist that. You must..."

"Doc?" She was almost pleading with him. Don't die, don't die!

The servos in his cheeks made a smile, although there was no flesh to pull. His teeth grinned perpetually.

"You're crying. That's good."

Jessamyn put a hand to her face. There was moisture around her optic.

"Biofluid."

"No, I gave you back some tearducts when I inserted the new model. I had some to spare."

The town hall collapsed, sending a cloud of ash and sparks across the square.

0002-0002.

RODRIGUEZ WATCHED FROM the jailhouse. Jessamyn was talking to the tall thing. He hadn't been able to raise Manolo for minutes. It was down to him. The house-to-house had been called off. He didn't think he had any soldiers left, but himself.

He pulled on his gauntlets, and picked up his helmet. It locked into place.

He picked up his M-29, and silently slipped a new clip into the magazine.

0002-0002.

HIS LEFT ARM hadn't moved since he walked out of the Silver Shuriken. He detached it, and dropped it in the street.

"Let this be a lesson to you, Jesse Frankenstein's-Daughter. You are not invincible."

He didn't know how long he could live like this. His skullplates were leaking biofluid. That meant his greymass would be affected.

There was always the Donovan Treatment, but he didn't think much of the idea of being a disembodied brain in a jar.

"Jessamyn, you have things to do. You'll know, when the time comes, what they are."

He looked up at the half-moon.

"I don't understand myself, but I've been dreaming again. We don't dream, you know. Us improved humans. We use up all that brain capacity that's left dark in normals, and there isn't any room for dreaming. But I've dreamed since you came here, since I began work on you. I've dreamed of the moon, and of a plain of salt. I don't know what that means, but it's important."

There was dismay on her face, now. For the first time, she looked her age.

"Doc?"

"Goodbye, Jessamyn."

He had built a suicide switch into his brain. Blinking in a pattern initiated the shut-down sequence. A vial opened, and a biospunge filled with mercury, then burst...

0001-0002.

HOORAY FOR OUR *side. Rodriguez must have scragged one of the things!*

Jessamyn looked down at the smoking remains. The Doc was gone. She hadn't understood everything he had tried to tell her. Again, she was all alone, as she had been after her father's death, and after Spanish Fork. Alone with the dead. He had called her Jesse Frankenstein's-Daughter.

She was not alone. A soldier came out of the old jailhouse, rifle held lightly in one hand, barrel pointed down.

"Jessamyn," his voice was amplified by something inside his helmet. "Do you remember me?"

She laughed. "In that get-up, I wouldn't know you if you were my father."

"I'm sorry. It's Rodriguez. Holm Rodriguez. From Denver."

She did remember him. He was with the Bruyce-Hoare Agency. After she had killed her father, he had been one of the interrogating officers. And before that, she had seen him several times. He had raided the downtown warehouse arena the night she defeated Melanie Squid in the Kumite. As cops go, he had been okay. She tried to recall his face, but got it mixed up with the actor, Edward James Olmos. Swarthy, Hispanic, sharp eyes.

"I know you, Rodriguez. You're a Juvie Op. In case you hadn't heard, I turned eighteen last month. I'm grown-up now."

"I'm not with Bruyce-Hoare any more. I accepted a position in the private sector. Holderness-Manolo."

"Fancy."

He was edging towards her, slowly.

"Look," she said, stopping him in his tracks. "You gave me a break over Daddy. I'll return the favour. Just turn around and walk out of here. You don't have to die."

She wished she could see his face.

"No, really. You can live to an old age, have kids, rent a house on the beach, get into politics."

The rifle wavered. She knew he wasn't going to bite on it.

"Rodriguez, you don't have to be an asshole. It's not a contractual obligation."

The gun jumped, but she wasn't in front of it when it went off.

She extended the forefingers of her right hand in a V, and jabbed at Rodriguez's faceplate. The reinforced darkglass shattered, and she felt warmth around her hand as her durium-laced fingerbones stabbed through the man's skull.

Wiping her fingers off on her trousers, she told him, "You didn't have to die. You didn't have to."

0001-0001.

She knew the procedure. There would be some top cat out there in the desert, sealed up tight in his High Performance Auto, sitting out the slaughter and counting the expenses. Mr Holderness or Mr Manolo, she expected.

There was supposed to be no way to get at the bastard. But she felt she had to try. She needed some leverage to help her attack the Op's ve-hickle. She looked around for a tool, and found a soldier's dropped bayonet. It still had a good edge.

It would have to do.

0001-0001.

Manolo stabbed the dashbuttons, intending to blank the reading. Only one figure disappeared.

0001.

It was 0001 in blue. His own reading. As long as the number was there on the dashscreen, he was alive.

He would have to sit it out, but he would live. He'd spend hours down at the Pyramid talking through his emotions on this one. There would be untold anguish to purge in the group sessions. But Gari would help him cope with it. Guilt was no good, he knew. He had to quash that, and learn to feel good about himself again. That was the main thing, to feel good about yourself.

He wished he hadn't blasted so many beers. His bladder was full to straining, and there was no catheter-tube in the DeLorean. He would have to piss in the backseat, and that was imported Argentine leather hand-tooled by a specialist flown in from Tijuana.

He should never have taken on this penny-ante bounty hunt. Bob Holderness wouldn't have touched it. He had wanted the Agency to specialize in political cases. That was probably why he wasn't around any more. Manolo had always known there were men in suits behind the Surf Nazis, but he'd never carried the vendetta to them.

When he got out of here, he would make that up. He would track down the boardroom where the orders were issued, and he would declare all-out war on whichever Jap-corp or state authority had been behind the singe.

The car shifted, and something clanged. She was out there. Jessamyn Bonney.

She couldn't get in, but she was out there. The ve-hickle rang with her blows. She would get frustrated soon, and go away. Bronson Manolo could wait her out.

He had chewed his moustache ragged. His teeth were clogged with hair. That wasn't supposed to happen. His barber-surgeon had guaranteed the attachments against all eventualities.

The banging continued.

0001.

Manolo muttered to himself. "Home freeee, you can't get meee…"

She would have to be an H-M exec to get through the DeLorean's brain, and unseal the system.

The banging stopped, and there was peace for a moment. She must be giving up, walking away. Manolo had pressed his bleep-alert. The Insurance people would be here within minutes.

There was a hum of machinery, and a hiss of expelling air.

It wasn't possible. The car was rolling over and kicking its legs for her. The doorseals receded, the shutters vanished.

Manolo squirmed, pushing himself back against the seat. He didn't even have a gun.

A breeze passed through, as the doors raised like beetle-wings.

"Ommmmm," Manolo said, trying to attune his thoughts. Positive thinking could make this go away. "Ommmmm."

She was a dark silhouette outside. She threw something onto the seat beside him.

It was a human hand, raggedly severed at the wrist.

"Open sesame," she said, slipping into the car.

0001.

0000.

0000.

0000.

part four
jesse frankenstein's daughter

I

THE MONASTERY OF Santa de Nogueira had been imported stone by stone from Portugal to the Gila Desert, Arizona, in 1819, and abandoned after the Mexican-American War. Parts of it were eight hundred years old, the basements were half-filled with fine sand and whatever lived there, lived alone. When the heart of America dried up and blew away, things didn't change much in the Gila Desert. But the sand was thinning: the bones of dead monks were drifting to the surface of the pit that had once been a graveyard, while the headstones sank slowly towards the bedrock.

This was the Holy-Place-From-Over-the-Great-Water. It was exactly as it had been drawn in the family for generations. Hawk-That-Settles knew it at once. He was struck by the way that the buffalo hide pictures from the last century, drawn by his great-great grandfathers, showed the monastery as it was now, in 2023. This was not only the place, this was the Time.

He had walked the length of the state, his waterskin slung over his shoulder, keeping away from the roads and the gangcults. The Navaho had long since learned that the best way to live was to stick to the land no white man would want to take from him. Taking his direction from the moon and the stars, he had kept on course. By day, under his sunshade, he had Dreamwalked ahead, learning where the sandrat nests were, divining which waterholes were safe.

Once, he had sensed a presence following him on the trail. A man on a horse. Perhaps a ghost, perhaps not. For two full days, Hawk and the horseman travelled the same course, just out of each other's sight, but then, one evening, the presence was gone. Hawk almost missed the stranger. They had been a match, an Indian and a cowboy. There had been no Darkness in the stranger, and Hawk recalled that one of the spirit warriors who would stand with the One-Eyed White Girl in the last battle was called the Man Who Rides Alone.

Otherwise, it was an uneventful trek. Hawk slept with his guards up, and was not much bothered by spirits. Of course, there was great agitation in the spirit world as the Last Days drew nearer. He half-expected to be set upon by demons – the God of the Razor, Tartu or Misquamacus – but his part in the developing story was ignored. Once, a wendigo, straying far from its Northern haunts, brushed by riding a freak wind, but it took no interest in the lone Indian.

Everywhere he went, he felt traces of the One-Eyed White Girl. She was fighting her battles elsewhere, hauling herself out of the rut of common humanity to the point when she would be ready to accept the training the medicine man of the line of Armijah was destined to give her.

He arrived at Santa de Nogueira three days before the spirit warrior. He passed the time Dreamwalking. He travelled, sensing the works of the Dark Ones everywhere. Wars raged, famines spread, diseases ran unchecked. Death enveloped the world, seeping from boardrooms to battlefields. Those who could commit suicide, directly or indirectly, were doing so; in this War, suicide was the only way to resist the call-up. Everyone alive was being influenced, Hawk knew. Everyone would have to take sides. He was very much afraid that the side he had chosen would be outnumbered forty to one by the minions of Darkness.

Then, at nightfall, she came out of the desert in a sleek automobile with bloody upholstery. He saw her dust devil from a long way away, and knew that she had been led here by her own dreams, by the pull of the moon. Her picture was titled the Moon and the Crocodile. She would be confused, but he would have to deal with that.

The machine slid to a halt inside the courtyard, and Hawk stepped out of the shadows. The car's door raised, and the One-Eyed White Girl emerged. Her hair was long and black as a raven's feather, untied so one wing partially covered her patch-covered missing eye. She wore loose black pyjamas, moccasins and a black brassiere. She wasn't tall, she wasn't obviously muscled, and she was young, a girl not a woman.

She didn't look like a great warrior, but Hawk sensed her strength immediately. He knew some of her past, and he would learn more. Her eyepatch apart, she bore no obvious scars, but she had fought many battles, vanquished many foes. He opened his mouth, and sang the song of the One-Eyed White Girl, the song his father had taught him.

Her hand went to the holstered gun slung on her thigh. She had polished black fingernails, a single touch of ornamentation.

He spread his empty hands to show her he meant no harm. His song continued, echoing through the monastery as once the chanting of the monks must have done. The devout were long gone, but the Sacred Purpose remained.

The girl's hand relaxed, and fell away from her weapon. The moon rose, and her pale face glowed.

* * *

II

THIS IS ZEEBEECEE, *The Station That's Got It All, bringing you What You Want twenty-four hours a day, sponsored by GenTech, the bioproducts division that really cares...*

And now, as part of our public service program, we hand you over live to Lynne Cramer and Brunt Hardacre in our Beverly Hills Studios...

"Hello, America. It's June 16th, 2023, and it's Lynne again, welcoming you to SnitchWatch USA, the program in which you, the viewer at home, can help fight crime for cash money and prizes by interfacing with our datanet on your home peecee. Remember, GenTech is offering goods or the credit up to the value of ten million dollars for any and all information leading to the arrest of ever-so-desperate felons. Now, over to our Op from the Top, Brunt Hardacre..."

"Thank you, Lynne. Last week, you'll remember, we put a bounty out on the head of that scuzzbo, Jimmie Joe Jackson, South-Western Sector Venerated Warthog of the Maniax. Well, we've sorted through the heads that were sent in to the studio, and we're real pleased to report that Jackson's was indeed among them. He's positively been identified by F X Wicking of the T-H-R agency and by Colonel Younger of the United States Cavalry, and those bio-implanted replacement lungs are winging their way to a viewer in Phoenix who has asked us, for reasons we fully understand, not to reveal his name. Thank you, public-spirited do-gooder, whoever you are, and good luck with your tar-free windsacks..."

"Say, Brunt, what do you think? Would someone with terminal cancer have a better life expectancy than someone who was publicly known to have ratted on the Maniax?"

"That's a good question, Lynne. Of course, we'll never know the answer because ZeeBeeCee absolutely guarantees the confidentiality of all our informants. Not one has ever fallen victim to a gangland-style hit after coming forward with solid information. Some other stations don't have such good security, you know, and their crime-fighting shows rack up pretty heavy casualties. But with ZeeBeeCee, you can snitch in safety…"

"Phew! Say, I sure feel safer now that Jimmie Joe Jackson is out of business, Brunt."

"There are a lot of people who feel like that, Lynne."

"I'm sure there are. Tell me, who's the scumbag for today?"

"Well Lynne, today we're giving equal time to the ladies and throwing the spotlight on one of America's Most Wanted Femme Criminals, Ms Jessamyn Amanda Bonney, sometimes known under the aliases of Jazzbeaux or Minnie Molotov. Guns and Killing magazine currently rate her as the sixth most dangerous solo outlaw in the Americas, and she is the highest-ranked woman on the list, coming in at thirty-seven places above the Antarctic esperado Ice Kold Katie. Formerly affiliated to the Psychopomps gangcult, her chapter was broken up in 2021 during a pitched battle with the Road Cavalry in Spanish Fork, Deseret, Jessamyn is now believed to be working alone."

"What kind of a girl gets to the Most Wanted list, Brunt?"

"Jessamyn was born in 2004 in the Denver NoGo, Lynne. She got off to a bad start on the streets as the child of Bruno Bonney, convicted pimp, pusher, armed robber and bilko artist. ZeeBeeCee has gained a court order allowing access to Jessamyn Bonney's juvenile records, stored in the central infonet of the Bruyce-Hoare Agency, and we can exclusively reveal for the first time on national television that evidence which has come to light since her 2018 parricide hearing has suggested that she was indeed guilty of the murder of her father, a crime for which she was acquitted in court on the testimony of one Andrew Jean, since deceased, a gangcult associate and known perjurer."

"Well, that's just a thrilling revelation, Brunt."

"You said it, kiddo. After knocking off her old man, Jessamyn rose through the ranks in the Psychopomps, and racked up quite a score. Then, after Spanish Fork, our information gets a bit shaky. We have uncovered evidence that suggests she was working in league with famed mass murderer Herman Katz in the Spanish Fork area..."

"That's the guy who stuffed his mother?"

"You got it, Lynne. Now, sources close to the receivers of the H-M Agency of Los Angeles suggest that it has been conclusively proved that she was involved in the massacre at Dead Rat, Arizona, last year, during which a peaceful force of process-servers were murdered by members of the Maniax gangcult, who then razed the community to the ground. It will be remembered that popular Los Angelino Op Bronson Manolo lost his life in that engagement."

"I remember it well. Bronson Manolo was a personal friend of mine. We were co-worshippers at the Surfside Pyramid."

"Tough break, Lynne. It is believed that Jessamyn underwent extensive bio-engineering under the scalpel of Dr Simon Threadneedle, the disgraced GenTech surgeon who was also among the dead in the Dead Rat Incident. Details are not yet available, but it is possible that Dr Threadneedle turned her into some sort of cyborg death machine."

"That's not good news for law-abiding citizens, is it?"

"Certainly not, Lynne."

"So, is Jessamyn Bonney in fact the Most Dangerous Woman in the World?"

"Well, we asked that question to Redd Harvest of the T-H-R agency as the Op was on her way to face a cadre of the Trap Door Spiders."

"And what did Ms Harvest say?"

"I can give you the exact quote. Her reply was 'Not while I'm alive, she fucking isn't.'"

"So, what's Jessamyn up to these days?"

"Little has been heard of her since Dead Rat, but she is believed to be in the South-Western United States. Her known associates are all deceased, although a sighting which has not been discounted would put her in the company earlier this year of Hawk-That-Settles, a Navaho medicine man and dealer in controlled substances. Hawk-That-Settles left the Navaho Reservation last year and is classed by the US Cavalry as a 'renegade', having been associated in the early Twenty-first century with the militant Native American terrorist organization, The Sons of Geronimo."

"Scary people, Brunt. What does Jessamyn look like? Is she pretty?"

"You don't have anything to worry about, sweetheart."

"Flatterer."

"Well, Jessamyn's appearance has changed over the years, from her first arrests as a pre-teenager to this last photograph – please excuse the quality, it's a blow-up from a spysat picture taken from an orbital pass over Arizona last December – which shows her as we must assume she is now. She is identifiable by her missing left eye, and her green right eye. Her hair has usually been black, and worn long. She is, of course, dangerous, and should not be approached."

"And what's the damage, Brunt?"

"Rewards on her total over one million dollars, for offences that range from felony bank robbery to first degree murder. Bounties on her head have been filed by the United States Government, the Holderness-Manolo Agency, Turner-Harvest-Ramirez, GenTech, G-Mek, the Federal Bureau of Investigation, Hammond Maninski, the Winter Corporation, Westinghouse, Co-Cola, the Tabernacle of Joseph, the National Enquirer, Interpol, the Government of the Republic of Mexico, Walt Disney Enterprises, the Denver Civic Improvements Committee, the Colorado Diocese of the Roman Catholic Church, and this station, ZeeBeeCee."

"And in addition to those rewards, Brunt, we know that anyone coming forward with information leading to the apprehension or termination of Jessamyn Bonney will be entitled to one hundred thousand dollars' worth of bio-improvements supervised by Dr Zarathustra himself, a duplex apartment in the PZ of your choice, a fully-guaranteed and pirate-protected Caribbean cruise, this complete household computer hook-up and two thousand hours net-time on the interface of your choice, one of our new range of Venus-Adonis model companions, and a further one hundred thousand dollars in the currency or negotiable bond of your choice. So, viewers at home, do not hesitate, if you have even the slightest piece of useful data, hook up that modem and call, in complete confidence, our unmonitored SnitchLine on the number that is flashing at the bottom of your screen...

"The lines will remain open for three days, until the next edition of *SnitchWatch USA*. Until we next meet over the airwaves, this has been Lynne Cramer..."

"And Brunt Hardacre..."

"Saying 'Keep America Safe for Americans', and have a snazz day..."

III

THIS WAS WHERE the moon had brought her. The moon, and Hawk-That-Settles. He had explained it to her, explained that there were great forces in the universe and that she was destined to serve them. She didn't yet know how she felt about that. Serving great forces was not what she had signed up for this trip, but somehow it felt right. The gang-girl she had been seemed as remote from her as the child she had been before that. Doc Threadneedle had warned her that the alterations he had made would affect her mind, so she could be confused without realizing it. But actually, she felt her thinking was clearer now. She had been at her worst between Spanish Fork and Dead Rat, when Elder Seth and the voices of the dead were arguing inside her head. Now, she had that under control. The monastery of Santa de Nogueira was a peaceful place, and she was working through her life, straightening out the kinks in her psyche. Hawk did not look like a soce worker or a shrink, but he was getting to her in a way the juvie officials never used to.

They sat at the great wooden table, drinking a little water out of earthenware bowls, chewing cactus. She had given up meat. The taste was too strong, and brought the memories of martyred animals into her mind. She could live on water, and a little cactusflesh. She felt all the better for it. Doc Threadneedle had turned her into a human perpetual motion machine, like one of those dipping birds her father had bought her as a child. If she kept her beak wet, she could go on forever.

There were seven levels of spirituality, Hawk had told her, and she must ascend through them all before she was readied for her appointed task.

It was all new to her, but the Indian seemed to know what he was talking about, and so she had gone along with him.

The Navaho knew what the moon wanted of her. On their first night in the monastery, with a silver crescent faint in the sky, Hawk gave her a gnarled root, and told her to smear a little of the juice of it onto her tongue before sleep.

Frankenstein's Daughter though she was, she still dreamed. That night, she dreamed of the Great Crocodile in the Moon. Then, she dreamed she was the Great Crocodile in the Moon. Finally, she was herself and the crocodile at the same time. When she told Hawk of her dream, he told her she had reached the First Level.

She didn't feel any different.

By day, she exercised her body as Doc Threadneedle had advised. Hawk joined her, and, clad only in breechclouts, they ran through the sands, wrestled to a standstill – Hawk was wiry, but strong, and agile enough to compensate for her bio-improvements – and climbed the outer walls of Santa de Nogueira. She continued to surprise herself with the capabilities of her augmented flesh.

By night, they made love and shared their dreams. Doc Threadneedle had been right about the sex. At last, she realized what all the fuss was about. She could experience the pleasure of lovemaking with every nerve-ending in her body. Sometimes, she thought she disconcerted Hawk with her love, but he kept apace with her. She told him about the Elder, and of the eternity of memories he had poured unasked into her head. He taught her a position for sleeping that placed the forepart of her brain at the apex of a pyramid. Nguyen Seth's past faded, and became the memory of a memory. Without realizing it, she had reached the Second Level.

"Your body has advanced beyond the human, Jesse. Your spirit must catch up with it, or you will fail the moon."

Hawk was a Dreamwalker. That meant he could project his spirit as he slept, and wander the material world and even the spirit lands. She asked him to teach her the trick, but he said that she was not ready yet. She must keep spirit and flesh wedded. She was to be a Spirit Warrior. He showed her old pictures, drawn with pigments on hide, and she recognized scenes from her life. There she was, being battered into the roadway by Nguyen Seth, struggling with the reanimated corpse of Herman Katz's mother, wandering the desert on all fours, tossing Holm Rodriguez's severed hand into Manolo's DeLorean. All these had been drawn before she was born, and yet they were exact prophecies. The pictures of her life yet to come were as vivid, and yet she could see no meaning in them. The background of one was recognizably Santa de Nogueira, and she was locked in struggle with an ordinary-looking man about whom a dark cloud was gathering. Others were disturbingly abstract, and Hawk could give her no clue as to their exact meaning.

There were other Spirit Warriors, she was told. Even now, they were following their own destinies, being drawn towards some Last Battle in which they would stand against things Hawk called the Dark Spirits, whose front man on Earth she recognized as Elder Seth. If she survived, he said, she would eventually meet the others, but there were many possible destinies. Several of the pictures were ominously ambiguous. Jesse found it hard not to see in them versions of her death. In one, a woman with red hair and red hands – another Spirit Warrior, Hawk said – was throttling her, face turned into a mask of hate. In another, she was a small speck overwhelmed by a vast and writhing darkness that reminded her of nothing so much as pictures she had seen on the cover of Tcherkassoff's album *Black Holes and Other Singularities*.

Sometimes, Hawk was like the masters she had seen in Chinese martial arts movies, talking in parables, and drawing out his pupil's skills through subterfuge. But, at other moments, he was as lost as she was, another slave to the whims of the moon. This frightened her. She needed no doubts. She learned about Hawk's life as he learned of hers, and they became close. She had never had time to think about love before, had thought that Bruno had burned that out of her. Now, she wasn't sure whether she truly loved the Navaho, or whether he simply happened to be the only human being she had contact with. Love used to be just something she heard about in sove songs or followed in pic-strips. The songs came back to her now, and she thought of all the things she hadn't had: a junior prom, dates, valentines, flowers. All the things that Mary-Kate and Ashley had in the movies, she had missed. When the Olsen twins were arguing with their Mom whether they should wear a strapless dress to the dance, she had been carving up gang-girls in warehouse arenas, then picking out some cock-for-the-night from the stud line. She was eighteen now, and it was too late to be a teenager.

She became pregnant, but lost the baby in the fourth month. At first, she hadn't wanted it, but the miscarriage devastated her. Somehow, she knew it had been her one chance to reproduce, and that it had passed. There were other things she had to do in her life, things forces beyond the reach of her mind deemed important. That night, for the first time, she cried uncontrollably. Her tears seeped through the cotton mattress of her cot and fell onto the European stones. Hawk was gentle, and she sensed his feeling of loss was even greater than hers.

Red-eyed and hollow inside, she was appalled when he told her she had reached the Third Level. "You have found your heart, Jesse. You will bear no more children, but you can now travel into the spirit world in safety, anchored by your heart in the world of men. Now, you can be a Dreamwalker."

Her tears had been the pathway. The Doc had told her something of the sort as he died. But, once the flood was dried, she could cry no more.

A month passed. The moon swelled, filling out as her belly ceased to, and then dwindled again. She spent a lot of time thinking about her father. She was sure he had told her the story of the Moon and the Crocodile when she was a child, but she couldn't remember it. At the time, she had thought he had made it up himself. Now, she wondered whether the moon crept into his mind too, driving him to pick up his rod and mark her back. Those woundings had been steps on the path that brought her to Santa de Nogueira, she realized.

Everything in her life – all the pain, blood and death – had been pushing her onwards and into the desert.

When the time came, Hawk mixed up the blood of her menses with peyote, plain brown sugar, mescal, ground-to-flour stonechips from the oldest walls of Santa de Nogueira, water, his own seed, whisky, buffalo grease and an ampoule of smacksynth. He told her to shut her eyes, and smeared the paste over her face, leaving breathing holes over her nostrils. It hardened to a mask, and she lay under it for three days, wandering inside her body. She appreciated Doc Threadneedle's handiwork, but also she learned to love what had been done for her before the biowizard came along. He had just provided some polish for a machine that was already a miracle of design.

When the mask came off, she knew she had reached the Fourth Level.

Hawk built a fire in the courtyard, and kept it burning for a week, producing dried wood from God knows where. Jesse sat and stared into the flames, seeing faces in the patterns.

There was Seth, and Doc Threadneedle, and Hawk-That-Settles and her father. There was Mrs Katz, impossibly animated, chopping at her mind. And others she didn't recognize: a young woman from over the sea, sometimes dressed in a nun's habit, sometimes holding a clear-handled gun; a foreign man, dark-complexioned and dangerous, his hands red with blood; a beautiful young-old man with generous lips, picking up a guitar and smiling; and a man in a tropical suit, with a deathshead skull behind his smile. But, most of all, there was the crocodile, full moons in its eyes...

The faces twisted, and scenes were played out. Some, she recognized: the NoGo walk-up she had shared with her Dad, Spanish Fork, the Katz Motel, Dead Rat. Others were obscure, yet-to-come images that meant nothing to her. A gathering darkness over a white plain. Graves opening to spew the dead. An ocean as smooth as glass closing over things vast, alive and hateful.

When the fires burned down, Jesse was afraid. She had reached the Fifth Level, and she could no longer go back. She could not turn from the destiny that had been alotted to her.

She looked and looked at the place where the fire had been, searching for the future, but could only see ashes.

IV

To GET HIM from his "confinement space" to the conference room involved leading him down Monsters' Row. This was where the United States of America put the Worst of the Worst. Hector Childress, the Albuquerque Chainsaw Killer, considered so dangerous that he was welded into his cell; Spike Mizzi, the New Hampshire Ghoul; Rex Tendenter, the smiling Bachelor Boy who had butchered and cannibalized around fifty middle-aged women, and still received three sacksful of fan mail every week; Nicky Staig, the author of the Cincinnati Flamethrower Holocaust; "Alligator" McClean, the Strangler of the Swamp; LeRoy Brosnan, the Sigma Chi Slumber Party Slasher; Jason, the Cheerleader-Chopper; Colonel Reynard Pershing Fraylman, the Expressexecutioner; "Jane Doe", the grandmotherly Columbus poisoner whose boarding house rated four stars in the Guide Michelin, despite the high turn-over of clients headed for the graveyard; Herman Katz, the Arizona schizoid who stuffed his mother and stabbed women who caught his eye; "Laughing Louis" Etchison, who carved bad jokes into the flesh of blue-eyed blondes.

And somewhere in the facility, thanks to the Donovan Treatment, scientists could poke at the disembodied brains of the Great Names of the Past: Gacy, Bundy, DaSalvo, Gein, Berkowitz, Sutcliffe, Starkweather, Scorpio, Krueger. This was where they kept Dillinger's dong, too.

If there were ever a Serial Killers' Hall of Fame, it would have to be in the Sunnydales Rest Home for the Incurably Antisocial. The monsters had a name for the Home, Uncle Charlie's Summer Camp. It was officially classifed as a private research institute, and Dr Proctor knew from his government contacts that the care and upkeep of the monsters did not come from the public purse but from a corporate subsidiary with interests in mental abnormalities. It sounded high-toned in the reports, with the odd announcement that there might be a cure for homicidal mania, but Sunnydales added up to a zoo-cum-freakshow for rich scientists.

Sergeant Gilhooly's bulls had held him against the wall with the threat of cattle-prods as Officers Kerr and Bean shackled his hands, feet, knees, elbows and neck. He had about 200 pounds of chain over his dress whites. He gave them no trouble. He didn't need to. He enjoyed this monthly ritual.

Sometimes, to amuse himself, Dr Proctor would break the chains. To look at him, people could never see the Devil inside. His strength was in his brain, he knew, but he had not neglected the cultivation of his body. He needed an instrument to carry through his schemes. As they clapped the manacles around his thick wrists, he remembered the sharp snaps of the spines he had broken. It was a good, clean method. In Tulsa, he had taken out the linebackers of the local pro ball team, one after another. All it took was a little dexterity, a little pressure, and a lot of muscle. He smiled at Gilhooly, imagining how little it would take to break him.

As he was led down Monsters' Row, the chanting began. It was McClean who began it.

"Otto-kar! Otto-kar!"

Then Staig, Brosnan and Mizzi joined in.

"Otto-kar! Otto-kar! Otto-kar!"

He smiled, and did his best to take a bow.

"Otto-kar! Otto-kar!"

They were all at it, Jason in his sub-mongoloid gargle, the silent Fraylman with a nod of his usually immobile head.

"Otto-kar! Otto-kar! Otto-kar! Otto-kar! Otto-kar! Otto-kar!"

A man should be king of something, Dr Ottokar Proctor thought, even if it was only King of the Monsters.

Etchison rattled a plastic cup against the bars.

"Otto-kar! Otto-kar!"

The serial murderers punched the air. Kerr, the officer in charge of the block, snapped out an order. Guards hurried up and down the row, administering reprimands, waving cattle prods. That just encouraged them.

"Enjoying this, aren't you, Otto?" said Gilhooly. "Makes you feel like Colonel of the Nuts?"

"I don't like to be called Otto, Sergeant. My name is Ottokar."

"Otto-kar! Otto-kar! Otto-kar!"

"Shaddup, yah goddamn fuckin' looneys," yelled Officer Kerr. "No privileges, no visits, no lawyers, no nothin'!"

In his cell, Herman Katz refrained from harming a fly. He nodded to Dr Proctor as the nice man was led past. He didn't join in the chanting, but he approved.

"Otto-kar! Otto-kar! Otto-kar!"

Childress rumbled like a chainsaw as Dr Proctor was led past his cell. They didn't call them "confinement spaces" on Monsters' Row.

"If you ask me, Otto, this is where you ought to be, not in that luxury room out back. You should be with all the rest of the whackos."

"I told you, Sergeant. My name is not Otto."

"Otto-kar! Otto-kar! Otto-kar!"

Gilhooly muttered to himself, something about finding another route from Dr Proctor's quarters to the conference room.

Jason shook his bars, and the whole row vibrated. He strained against the hardcrete-rooted durium, and plaster fell from the ceiling. He had taken his machete to over a hundred teenagers before they caught him.

"Good morning, Jason," Dr Proctor said, "how's your sciatica?"

The killer roared, and Gilhooly flinched, his hand twitching towards his gun.

"I don't think shooting him would do any good, Sergeant. They tried that back in '82. They also tried drowning, stabbing, burning and electrocution. Nothing doing. It's a tribute to the endurance of the human spirit, don't you think?"

They were nearly at the end of the row.

"Miss Doe, how are you?" Dr Proctor was courteous to the poisoner.

"Very well thank you, Ottokar. When are you going to come over and try some of my home-baked apple pie? You're looking thin, you know. I'm sure you're not eating properly."

"Maybe next week, ma'am. I'm a little tied up at the moment." Apologetically, he lifted his manacled hands. "Thank you for the cinnamon cookies. They were delicious."

Incredulously, Gilhooly asked, "You ate them cookies? After what she did?"

"She's no threat to me, Sergeant."

The cell nearest the door was Tendenter's.

"Rex, good to see you..."

Tendenter flashed his million-dollar smile. "Hey, doctor, how are you doing?"

"Can't complain."

finished that book you lent me. I'd like to
about the Greater Rhodesian economy some-
had some thoughts about it I'd like to share with

That's a fascinating field, Rex. I'd like very much to confer with you, but my President calls..."

"That's okay, doctor, I understand."

"Otto-kar! Otto-kar! Otto-kar! Otto-kar! Otto-kar!"

"That's it," screamed Officer Kerr. "Lockdown in the booby hatch! No exercise periods! No teevee! No porno!"

"Otto-kar! Otto-kar! Otto-kar! Otto-kar! Otto-kar!"

The door guard opened up, and Dr Proctor was bundled through. He tried to wave goodbye to his peers, but the chain between his knees and his wrists was too short.

The door slammed shut, and the soundproofing cut out the chants. The hospital corridor was almost unnaturally quiet after Monsters' Row.

"Ahh," said Dr Proctor, "my public."

"Come on, Otto," said Gilhooly, dragging him.

"I believe you are being deliberately obtuse, Sergeant."

Gilhooly didn't reply. Dr Proctor did his best to keep up with the sergeant, rattling his chains as he jogged down the corridor on his leash, like a good dog. Bean kept up the rear, riot gun cradled like a baby in his beefy arms.

Dr Ottokar Proctor liked dogs, cartoons, Italian opera, Carl Jung, French food, Disneyworld, *The New York Times Review of Books*, pre-Columbian art, good wine, walks in the park on Sundays, horse-racing, Percy Bysshe Shelley, the romantic novels of Margaret Thatcher, and killing people.

They were waiting for him in the conference room. F X Wicking of the T-H-R Agency, Julian Russell from the Treasury, and a dark-faced man he didn't recognize.

"Good morning, gentlemen," he said.

"Dr Proctor," said Russell, "can we get you anything?"

Dr Proctor chinked as he shrugged. "My freedom would be nice."

Wicking sighed and dropped his papers. This was going to be just like all the other meetings, he was thinking. He was wrong.

Dr Proctor sank into the specially-adapted, floor-rooted chair, and Bean padlocked his chains to the spine.

A secretary came in with coffee. She did her best not to look at Dr Proctor. He was reminded of the girl in the Coupe de Ville between Coronado Beach and Chula Vista three years ago. The one who had lasted for two nights and a day. She put cups in front of the delegates, and handed Gilhooly a child's dribble-proof plastic container. The sergeant propped it on Dr Proctor's shoulder-shackles, and angled the nipple so he could suck it, snarling as he did so.

"Thank you, sergeant." He took a mouthful. "Ahh, real coffee. Nicaraguan?"

Nobody answered. Russell spooned three loads of sugar into his cup.

"Watch your blood sugar levels, Julian," cautioned Dr Proctor. "You could be cruising into heart-attack country."

Wicking pulled out his PDA, and switched it on. It hummed as the miniscreen lit up. The Op would be in contact with his home base throughout this consultation.

"How is Ms Harvest?" Dr Proctor asked. "Well, I hope." Wicking snorted. "I do wish she wouldn't take so many unnecessary risks out in the field. I've been following her stats, Francis. The odds get shorter every time she takes a solo action. She should never have come for me alone, you know."

"She got you, didn't she?" Wicking wasn't giving anything away.

"Yes, of course, but she had an unfair advantage."

"And what's that, Ottokar?"

Dr Proctor smiled sweetly. "Let me put it this way, what's the difference between Redd Harvest and, say, Jessamyn Bonney?"

The dark man reacted to the dropped name, as Dr Proctor had known he would. "Bonney? The psycho-killer?" said Wicking. "I've no idea."

"A badge, Francis. A badge."

Wicking didn't laugh. Dr Proctor drank some more coffee. Russell snapped a digestive biscuit in half, and dipped it in his cup.

"I suppose a cookie is out of the question? Ah well, we live with disappointments."

Dr Proctor gave some thought to the dark man, and smiled. He realized that this was the meeting he had been waiting for ever since the trial.

"Tell me, how are they running at Santa Anita?"

Nobody knew.

"Well, we ought perhaps to get down to business then."

Russell brought out a sheaf of papers. The dark man sat calmly, examining Dr Proctor. He was taking the man's measure at the same time. This meeting would be between the two of them. Wicking and Russell were just stooges along for the ride.

"This is Roger Duroc, Ottokar," said Russell. "He's not with the government."

"How do you do, Mr Duroc." Dr Proctor knew the Frenchman by reputation. "Pardon me," he corrected himself, "Monsieur Duroc."

Duroc nodded. "Very well thank you, Dr Proctor."

"Good. And how are you going to get me out of this place?"

There was a pause...

V

HAWK-THAT-SETTLES HAD BEEN waiting for the One-Eyed White Girl all his life. And here she was.

Looking across the abandoned chapel at Jesse, he wondered yet again. Was this really the one? She was jumping up her ladder two steps at a time, like a good little mystic, but there was still a core of confusion to her. This messiah was spending too much time in the desert. The years for wandering and contemplation were up, and it was time for the miracles.

Also, far from Two-Dogs-Fucking, he had doubts about himself. Perhaps he was fated to be just another Whisky Navaho, and all this medicine was dangerous tampering with forces beyond him.

She sat quietly, her one eye closed. He knew she saw him through the machine behind her patch. Her supple body was shot through with machinery. He could feel the lumps under her skin and muscle as they made love, and had to remind himself these were not cancers or tumours but the benefits of the white man's science. She could sit for whole periods, days sometimes, not moving, not speaking. Part of that was the meditation necessary for her education. But part of it was something else, something that she called her Frankenstein's Daughter trances.

Sometimes, as she clung to him in the nights, he was reminded of the other white girls, the rich liberals who had come to the Reservations and dressed up like Pocahontas, who had been passed from buck to buck, who had been the stuff of jokes at the councils of the Sons of Geronimo. They were all looking for something from the red man, something Hawk knew he didn't have. There was a crocodile egg inside Jesse, growing as their dead baby had grown, but the shell was still just a white girl. A one-eyed white girl.

Of course, most white girls could not break a wrestler's back or crush stone to dust with their naked hands. But strength of the body was not enough for Jesse, she would need all the strength of her spirit if she were who she seemed to be.

She was getting stronger inside. Sometimes, Hawk was frightened by her strength. He knew something of her past, knew she had been swept away by a stream of blood. One night, without being asked, she had told him about her father, about what he had done to her, and about how he had died. Hawk had heard many bad stories, but this scared him as no other had done. It was not so much the horrors she recounted that got through to him as the manner of her telling, as if these things had happened to someone else, a character in a film or a teevee soap. She claimed to have no scars any more, but Hawk thought Jesse was all scar tissue.

When she slept, her thumb crept babylike to her mouth, and he thought he could see her as she might have been had she not been born in a bad place, at a bad time to a bad father. Just another white girl. No better and no worse than the rest.

He left her, and wandered through the sand-carpeted corridors of the monastery. He heard the echoes of the prayers of the long-dead monks. They had come here to convert his forefathers to their faith, but had perished. Their faith was still here, though. Their meditations had created a channel to the spirit world that was still open. They had come to teach the Indians a lesson his people had already known for a thousand years. But he could not hate the Jesuits. They brought Bibles and statues of the Blessed Virgin with them from the Old World, not Springfield rifles and smallpox.

He looked up at an eroded statue of Jesus on the cross, its face ground away like the figurehead of a ship that had been through too many typhoons. He bowed his head to the carpenter; a powerful manitou was to be revered, were he born in a tribal hogan or a Judean stable.

His child by Jesse would have been a son. He would have named it himself, in the old way, as he had been named, by taking the first thing the child looked upon. Here, that meant he could not have much of a name: Stone-Wall-Standing perhaps, or Sand-That-Stretches-to-the-Sky. Back on the Reservation, he had known Navaho children called Three-Cars-Bumper-to-Bumper, Broken-Telephone-Booth and Maniak-Corpse-Rotting. His father, Two-Dogs-Fucking, had not been fortunate in his naming, and had determined his son should not suffer. Hawk's mother told him that Two-Dogs was the only one of the tribe who had seen the hawk for whom he was named, but that the others had gone along with him.

The pregnancy had been a part of Jesse's education that he had not understood until its messy, bloody conclusion. He resented the spirits who would give him a son and then take the child away before its birth, just to teach a one-eyed white girl a lesson. His father had never explained, had never understood, that Hawk's part in the story was merely as an attendant upon the creation of the crocodile girl. Her feelings mattered, his were as feathers in the wind. He might as well be a Wooden Indian standing outside a drugstore for all his feelings counted.

He believed that the spirits really didn't give a damn about any of them. They were just being made to jump through hoops as part of some vast pre-ordained pattern.

Walking across the courtyard, Hawk looked up at the sky. It was late afternoon, and the moon was already up. The moon was sacred for Jesse.

"Tell me what you want, moon spirit?"

The man in the moon grinned his lopsided, reptile-jawed grin down at him and did not answer.

"Sonofabitch," he spat.

Perhaps he should leave this place, leave Jesse to work out her own fate. He should look after his father. The old man drank too much, and was provocative of trouble. If he didn't kill himself soon, he would find someone else to do it for him. There wasn't much for him on the Reservation, but there was more there than sand and stone.

The one-eyed white girl could reach her Seventh Level on her own. She didn't really need him. She had many battles to fight, and he would only be in the way. He wondered if she was worried about him, if she ever even gave him any thought. Her face was in his mind constantly, the memory of her tugging at his heart like a fishhook. He was a Navaho brave, the last of the renegades, but Jesse made him weak.

He looked at the sand, and trembled. There were things out there in the world that would be coming here soon.

His battles were beginning.

VI

"THAT ISSUE IS not under discussion," the T-H-R man said. "There can be no negotiations on the question of liberty."

"Aw shucks, Francis. Not even if I promise not to do it again?"

Dr Proctor's eyes twinkled. He was like a naughty little boy who knows he cannot be sent up to his room.

So this was the Tasmanian Devil. Wrapped up like Houdini before an escape, he didn't look like much more than a good-humoured man in early middle-age. How many had he killed? It didn't matter. He was unquestionably America's leading murderer. That was what made him of interest to Nguyen Seth, and, therefore, to Roger Duroc.

"You've never stopped doing it, Ottokar. We know that. We don't know how you've done it, but since you came to Sunnydales there have been a lot of deaths. Death by violence or accident or suicide among the inmates has risen by 28%, and among the guards…"

"89%. I read the sanitarium newspaper, you know."

"It may not be your hands, Ottokar. But it's your mind. We know that."

Dr Proctor laughed a little. "Prove it, Francis."

"We will."

"And then what are you going to do? Lock me up, and throw away the key? You already did that. There's not much you can punish me with, is there Francis?"

"We can unlock your cell, chain you up like you are now, and let some of your victims' relatives visit you with blow-torches..."

Dr Proctor didn't betray anything more than mild amusement. "And is that an official promise, Francis? Because if it is, then my lawyers will be most perturbed."

"Frank," cut in Russell. "Couldn't we bring this meeting to order. The President has authorized me to..."

"Ah yes, Oliver. How is Oliver, Julian?"

"He's well."

"And the kids? Recovered from the birthday party?"

Duroc knew that the President's children played pass-the-parcel with a severed arm at a White House social event just before Dr Proctor's arrest. It had been the Devil's idea of a joke.

"The nightmares are slowly going away."

"That's good news."

Dr Proctor signalled with his head for the sergeant to take his baby-cup away.

"I don't suppose anyone has a cigarette?"

Nobody did.

"So few people smoke any more. Dreadful habit, but it passes the time. I have a lot of time, you know."

"Ottokar," said Wicking. "We are sanctioned to offer you books, videotapes, magazines, and a limited, monitored access to telephonic and written communication with the world outside."

"I have those things."

"We can increase them, sweeten the deal..."

"You could," he allowed.

"The President is very concerned, Ottokar," said Russell. "He would like you to take a look at these trade figures..."

The Treasury man held out his papers, and spread them on the table in front of Dr Proctor. The chained man ignored them. He was enjoying this, Duroc knew.

At his trial, Dr Proctor had admitted that he had deliberately encouraged the Estevez administration to follow near-suicidal economic policies in order to foster an increase of chaos in the world. When asked about his motivation, he had referred them to Jungian theory. "Our collective unconscious is becoming too ordered," he had claimed, "someone had to do something to bring back the element of surprise." Now, the government kept having to crawl to a convicted mass murderer to ask him to help them sort out the spaghetti tangle of figures he had left behind him.

Dr Proctor raised an eyebrow as he casually glanced at Russell's documents. "Tut tut tut. Those tax rebates aren't working out at all, are they? Silly me. I should have seen that loophole all the Japcorps are squirrelling through, shouldn't I? You know, national economies mean less than corporate systems these days. I might devote a monograph to the subject. Take the case of the growing conflict between GenTech East and the Soviet Union, for instance. Logically, their trade war could develop into a shooting match, and then where would we be? You should have the CIA keep a close watch on this Blood Banner Society. Nationalism and commerce make a nasty team."

"Ottokar, the President has personally asked me to convey to you his best wishes, and authorized me to offer to you any liberties up to but not including freedom from this institution if you'll only agree to work in an advisory capacity for a six-month period, just until the budget has passed."

"I'm truly sorry, Julian, but I'm not interested."

"We'll let you accept ZeeBeeCee's offer of another TV series. You can host the talk show."

"TV. It's just a toy. Close down all the television stations in the United States. Now, there's some sound economic advice for you. Cut out the admass, and decrease useless consumption. Cut out the lifebite, and throw people back on their own devices. Your friends in Deseret have the right idea, M. Duroc, bring back the pioneer spirit. When it was just a question of a man, a rifle and a horse against the savage Indians."

"This is getting us nowhere," said Wicking. "As usual. He's fucked the country, and now he's sitting back and surveying the mess."

"I really think we're close to a breakthrough," said Russell.

"You work out of New York, Francis. What's playing at the Met. Did you see Sir Oswald Osbourne in Pagliacci?"

Wicking threw up his hands, and slumped in his seat. His jacket opened, and Duroc saw he was carrying a discreet gun. Dr Proctor saw it, too.

Time passed, and everyone in the room looked at each other.

Finally, Dr Proctor broke the deadlock. "M. Duroc, talk to me. Tell me what you can offer. Tell me about Jessamyn Bonney and the Josephites."

Duroc was impressed. The man might be as crazy as a backstreet Bonaparte, but he was sharp, and he had sources of information nobody knew about. He hadn't tested ESP-positive in his medicals, but there were ways round the examination.

"Well?"

Duroc drew in a breath. "Dr Proctor, I do not represent the government. Unlike Mr Wicking and Mr Russell, I have no legal authority here. I am not even an American citizen.

I am French by birth, but my current passport lists me as a resident of Deseret – you know what that means?"

"Oh yes, an interesting geopolitical experiment, Deseret. Oliver should never have gone along with it. A bad precedent. Within seven years, Missouri, Arkansas and Kentucky will petition for secession from the Union. And perhaps Tennessee. You heard it here first. It will come. Oliver should send reinforcements to Fort Sumter. I'm sorry. I digress. Academic footnotes, it's a bad habit."

"That's quite all right. The Church of Joseph would like to employ you as a consultant in the case of Jessamyn Bonney. You know her?"

"I know of her. We haven't moved in the same circles."

Duroc brought out his file. It had been amended a little since the death of Bronson Manolo.

"This is ridiculous," Dr Proctor said. "Please may I have a hand? The left will do."

Wicking chewed his lip, and signalled to the sergeant. Gilhooly drew his pistol, and held it to Dr Proctor's head while he fussed with his keyring. A manacle fell, and Dr Proctor waved his hand about to get rid of an ache.

"One move, Otto..." Gilhooly stood behind the man in the chair, his gun cocked and pointed at Dr Proctor's pineal gland. "I'd like it, you know."

Dr Proctor leafed through the Jessamyn Bonney data.

"Hmmn. Interesting girl. What's her score?"

"Nowhere near, Ottokar," said Wicking. "You don't have to worry about the record. Yet."

"Don't be vulgar, Francis. It's not a game, you know. It's not basketball."

"What is it then? All the killing?"

"It's an Art. It's the authentic American Folk Art."

The Tasmanian Devil looked up from the file. "Well, Monsieur Duroc?"

Duroc put his hands on the table. "We would like Jessamyn Bonney dead."

"That shouldn't make you happy, but certainly won't make you lonely."

Russell said, "Roger, I don't see where this is leading us. Your people didn't say anything about..."

Duroc raised his hand. "Silence." Russell's jaw dropped. "Thank you. Dr Proctor, we are prepared to offer you more than the deal presented by the United States of America. You have been convicted by no court recognized in Deseret. You could be awarded citizenship."

Wicking was furious. "This is fuckin' insane."

"Shush, Francis," said Dr Proctor. "I'm interested."

"You could be granted political asylum in Salt Lake City."

"I'd rather stay here. No, just kidding."

Gilhooly was confused. The sergeant's brain wasn't up to this. Good, that gave Duroc a better than 80% chance of success. The other officer, Bean, was picking his nose and scratching his belly.

"All you have to do is kill one girl. After so many, that shouldn't be difficult."

Wicking got up. "I'm ending this meeting now. I had no idea when the President's office authorized your presence that you would be taking such an extreme stance. Mr Duroc, I shall be reporting in full..."

Duroc pulled the ivory throwing star – invisible to the asylum's metal detector – and flicked it across the room.

Gilhooly's throat opened in a cloud of blood. Dr Proctor's hand was behind him in an instant, catching the falling pistol.

Wicking nearly got his gun out, but not quite.

The shot rang loudly in the room. Wicking took his chair with him as he tumbled backwards.

Duroc was on the other side of the room now, his hand over Bean's mouth, pinching the guard's nostrils. He struggled, and died.

"Don't worry, Monsieur Duroc. Everything in this place is soundproofed. Too many screams in the night."

Russell was speechless, trembling. Duroc had scooped up Gilhooly's keys, and was methodically stripping Dr Proctor of his chains.

Gilhooly twitched on the floor, still bleeding. Dr Proctor was free now. He stretched his arms and stamped around. He passed the gun to Duroc, who turned it on Russell. The Treasury man put his hands up.

Dr Proctor knelt by the sergeant, and took hold of the throwing star lodged in his windpipe.

"I told you," he said, twisting, "not to call me Otto."

The star scraped bone. Gilhooly gurgled, and stopped kicking. Dr Proctor stood up, and smiled at the Treasury Man.

"Ottokar," said Russell, "we have a relationship..."

"That's right, Julian. A very close relationship. None closer."

The Tasmanian Devil looked around for something. He saw the coffee things, and picked a teaspoon out of the sugarbowl.

"How careless," he said. "It should have been plastic. I suppose aluminium is cheaper than any petroleum by-product in these troubled times."

"Ottokar..."

Dr Proctor stood over Russell, the spoon in one hand, his other on the Treasury man's shoulder

"Dr Proctor," said Duroc. "Hurry up. We have a very brief window of opportunity here."

"It's a moment's work, Monsieur."

Even Duroc didn't want to watch the Devil at work. By the time the screaming was over, he had Bean stripped of his uniform.

"Is this your size?" he said.

"A little generous over the belly, but we can tighten his belt."

Dr Proctor stripped out of his whites, and pulled the uniform on. They would have used Gilhooly's clothes, but there was a little blood on the collar.

"Ready?"

"Yes, Monsieur." Dr Proctor held up the teaspoon. It was red.

"What are we waiting for?"

"Cook's privilege," the Devil said, "I get to lick the spoon."

VII

"JESSE, WHAT'S WRONG?"

"I don't know, Hawk. It all seems so crazy, sometimes. The Dreams, the prophecies. I'm a girl from the Denver NoGo, not some picstrip superheroine."

"You've come a long way from the NoGo."

"Have I? Have I really?"

"You know the answer. What were you? A petty criminal, a sociopath. You've killed, you've robbed..."

"That was just a phase, you know. You grow out of it."

"The people you killed won't grow out of it."

"I've never killed anyone who wouldn't have killed me."

"That's not true."

"You're right."

"How do you feel about that?"

"I don't know. It doesn't seem like the same girl. With the gangcult, it was different. You just kept riding along with the pack, you did what was expected..."

"You were the leader of the pack."

"Yes, but that just meant the others expected more of me."

"Would you go back, if you could?"

"I'd bring back Andrew Jean and Cheeks and the others, yes."

"That's not what I asked. Would you ride with the gangcults again? Waiting for the Op or the Maniak who'd take you down?"

"No. I'm too old, anyway. But no."

"And what else have you got to do?"

"Save the world?"

"Don't make that sound so bad, Jesse."

"Isn't it? This world isn't all that worth saving, if you ask me."

"You can't spend your whole life killing your father."

"What's that got to do with it?"

"Your father brought you into this world, and your father was scum, therefore you reject the world."

"That sounds too easy to me. My father wasn't the only slimeball in the world. For a start, you should meet my mother, wherever she is. Rancid Robyn."

"But the world isn't all slime."

"Isn't it? Apart from you, everybody I know is dead. Or ought to be."

"We will do our parts, and things will be better."

"I've heard that all my life."

"This time, maybe... Things are different, aren't they?"

"Different? Yes. I've never been a monster before."

"You're not a monster. You're a Spirit Warrior."

"Jesse Frankenstein's-Daughter, the Spirit Warrior."

"You must take the feelings you have for yourself and channel them. You will need all your emotional capacities."

"It's starting soon?"

"It's starting now."

VIII

DR PROCTOR SLIPPED the chip into the auto's MP7 system, and skipped to "Nessun dorma!" As the Unknown Prince, Sir Oswald Osbourne, the greatest operatic voice of the

Nineties, poured it out. Osbourne apart, the Met's *Turandot* was rather minor, he supposed, but you could never tire of the "Nessun dorma!" The aria ended, and he skipped to the finale. "C'era negli occhi tuoi" and "Diecimila anni." Then, the applause.

The incar computers told him he was in Southern Arizona. He let the machines do all the driving. He had been through this area in '15, when he was just starting out on his Devil-work. He had liked it because it reminded him of the endless mesas and sandy canyons of the Road Runner cartoons. *Zoom and Bored* (1957), *Wild About Hurry* (1959), *Fastest With the Mostest* (1960), *Tired and Feathered* (1965).

There had been a gangcult then. The Backburners. They had flagged him down to kill him and rob him. He must have added fifteen or twenty to his score that night. He never kept count. That was for the pettifoggers, the lawyers and the journos.

There were seventeen books in print about him, not counting his autobiography, and he'd been in five movies. He preferred Christian Bale's performance in *Tas*, the Newman version, to any of the others. Adrien Brody had been especially poor in *A Devil With Women*, and Ryan Reynolds out of his depth in *Have Axe, Will Travel*. Still, none of them were quite what he saw when he looked in the mirror.

Poor Mee-lee-oh. He would never get out of the mess he'd been left in. And heads would roll at Sunnydales. More heads, he corrected himself.

Once he had discharged his debt of honour with Seth, he might take the Elder up on the offer of a home in Deseret. But he might prefer to wander the byways of the United States, playing his tricks. He had about a hundred million dollars stashed in accounts, safe deposit boxes and secret caches throughout the country. His face could be changed.

And the Devil would dance again.

Duroc had been able to give him quite precise information regarding the whereabouts of Jessamyn Bonney. His sources must be superb. T-H-R had been after her for years, and according to them she had just dropped out of sight.

But Duroc's people must be practically inside her skull.

The Monastery of Santa de Nogueira. He had never heard of it, and it wasn't on most maps, but the Josephites had left directions in the car.

They had also left him with a stimulating array of toys, which he had put to good use already. He was pleased to discover there was a Mid-West Armaments firm called Acme Incorporated, and had tried out their electroknives on a hitch-hiker from Tucson. They were barely serviceable tools, but he kept them for the value of the name.

From a post office in Dos Cabezos, he sent a card to Rex Tendeter and the others on Monsters' Row. Tracing in the blood of the sheriff, he wrote "HAVING A LOVELY TIME, WISH YOU WERE HERE, LOVE OTTOKAR." He hoped the Sunnydales people would let the message get through. The monsters deserved a touch of hope. After all, if Dr Ottokar Proctor could get out, then so could they...

Since he reached the world, the media had been crazy. If he'd actually committed all the murders they were trying to pin on him, he ought to get a Nobel prize for inventing teleportation. They had him striking in New York and San Francisco within the same twenty minutes. He was as often reported and as seldom identified as Neil Gaiman. Perhaps, after he had carried out his current commission, he should go after the graphic novelist and collect the Pan-Islamic Congress' bounty on his head. No, that would demean his Art, importing a touch of too-crass commercialism to the hallowed process of murder.

He had given some thought to the problem of Jessamyn Bonney. He had listened through the Dead Rat tapes several times, and made notes on her capabilities and achievements. He had especially admired her methods in the cases of Susie Terhune and Bronson Manolo. Nothing showy, just a simple display of fatal force. She was no Artist, but she was certainly a competent enough craftswoman.

He read up on Dr Threadneedle, and looked at his autopsy reports. The conclusions were obvious. Jessamyn had something a little extra.

But he had killed people with bio-implants before. Plenty of them. He had sought out the strongest of the strong and left them howling, begging for merciful death.

Jessamyn would be no different.

There was only room for one God of Pain, and Dr Proctor was the ranking applicant for the position.

The moon rose over the desert.

IX

He was alone in the courtyard. It was late. Jesse was sleeping. There was a wind coming across the sands, coming nearer. And in that wind, Hawk knew, was the Devil.

"What the hell..." he said.

Faintly, he heard a voice in the wind, singing...

Singing "Se quel guerrier io fossi!... Celeste Aida", Dr Proctor drove across the sands. Santa de Nogueira was off the road, but the Josephites had given him an auto that converted into a sandcat.

The monastery stood up ahead, silhouetted against the night sky like an Arabian Nights palace. Aida was most apt.

If Duroc's information was correct, Jessamyn Bonney was in that ancient castle, a princess waiting for her dragon.

Dr Proctor's smile turned into a grin, and his eyebrows lowered. Those few witnesses left alive who had seen this expression come over his face had testified that he truly did resemble the cartoon character from whom he had taken his nom de homicide.

He chuckled in the back of his throat, his eyeteeth digging into his lips, and relaxed. He was the economist again, the calm pundit of the teevee shows and the press conferences, the smooth liar who had gently pushed the richest, most powerful nation in the world into a monetary cesspool from which it would take centuries to recover.

He looked at himself in the mirror, and twisted his mouth like Daffy Duck. "You know what," he said to himself, "you're dethpicable!"

He felt the killing excitement building in his water.

IN THE SALT *Lake City tabernacle, Nguyen Seth picked up his spectacles, and slipped them on. The darkness cleared, and he peered into the pool of blood in the font.*

The smoke cleared, and he saw the monastery. Duroc had chosen his catspaw well.

This was a fit night to raise the Devil.

JESSE SHIFTED, DISTURBED. Faces were coming at her at great speed. The crocodile whispered in her ear, calling ladybug, ladybug. He urged her to fly away home...

Your house is on fire, your children are gone.

Her eye opened in the darkness, and she saw that Hawk-That-Settles had gone from their cell.

Moonlight was flooding in through the windowslit.

IN THE OUTER *Darkness, the Ancient Adversary strained towards the wormhole. It was time to be spat out into the physical universe, to join with its Vessel, then seek out its prey...*

* * *

Dr Proctor turned off the sound system, and concentrated. He found the Devil inside himself, and summoned the creature up. His friends on Monsters' Row would be proud of him.

Hawk-That-Settles sang at the moon, a song his father had taught him. He called for the crocodile. He fancied that the yellow circle in the sky was distending, becoming an oval, disgorging a snout, sprouting a lashing tail. His song continued, and the spirits of his ancestors joined him.

Duroc awoke, and reached for the knife under his pillow. He had been dreaming of his uncle, of Dien Bien Phu, again. The woman beside him sat up, grumbling, and stroked his back.

"Roger, you're soaking."

His heart calmed. He put the blade back. "It is nothing, Sister Harrison," he said, "get back to sleep."

"You're feverish."

"No, it's just… a family matter."

In the Sea of Tranquillity, the dome of Camp Pournelle reflected the sun's rays, visible to the naked eye on earth as a twinkle in the face of the man in the moon.

Abandoned for ten years, since the discontinuance of the United States space program, the camp was home only to anonymous ranks of calculating machines.

A change in the temperature of the lunar subsoil triggered a mechanism, and a printer began to process a strip for the eyes of a staff long gone earthside for desk jobs.

Sensors swivelled. Events took place. They were noted down, filed away, and forgotten…

On the Reservation, Two-Dogs-Fucking was wracked with another coughing fit. He was four-fifths of the way through a pint of Old Thunderblast, an especially subtle vintage manufactured as a side-effect during the processing of cattle-feed and sold off for fifty cents a bottle to the less discerning citizens of the South-West.

Two-Dogs was lying on a garbage dump, surrounded by refuse for which even the scavenger dogs of the Navaho had no use. Next to his head was the screen of an obsolete personal computer, cracked diagonally.

In the glass, he saw the moon broken in half like a plate. It shifted, and he knew his vision was going again. He drained the bottle, and tossed it away. It broke. Soon, he would be vomiting. That was the way it always was these days. Drink, then puke. He had been badly named at birth, and now he was fulfilling his father's poor choice.

The moon twisted.

Suddenly, he was sober. He turned onto his back, and looked up at the grinning face in the sky.

He opened his mouth, and felt an explosion coming up from his stomach. He took a deep breath, and joined voice with his son, three hundred miles to the south, singing the song of the moon, the song of their family...

The moon crocodile grinned.

NGUYEN SETH CLUNG *to the shaking font as the Tabernacle shook. It was a small earthquake. The blood splashed his face.*

He remembered Bruno Bonney, saw him through his daughter's eyes as her nails went into his throat.

The Dark Ones swarmed in the beyond, great wings flapping, tentacles uncoiling...

FORT APACHE, LAKE Havasu. Trooper Stack realized Leona was awake. He rolled over to kiss her, and saw tears on her face.

"Nathan," she said, "it's over. Us, I mean."

Dr Proctor braked, and got out of the car. There was a

voice in the night, howling. He opened the trunk, and distributed weapons about his person.

It wasn't Jessamyn screaming. It must be the Indian, Hawk-That-Settles. He had glanced over his stats, and discounted him. He was negligible.

He walked up the gentle incline towards the gate of Santa de Nogueira.

"HOLINESS, HOLINESS..."

On the other side of the world, Father Declan O'Shaughnessy approached Pope Georgi I in one of the inner chambers of the Vatican. The Holy Father was studying reports from Jesuit agents in Central America.

"What is it, Declan?"

"A disturbance. A big one. Our espers are speaking in tongues, and frothing at the mouth."

"Is it an attack?"

"Who can say?"

"Call the inner council. Is Chantal available?"

"I think not."

"A pity. Open a line to San Francisco. I would like to confer with Kazuko Hara."

"Immediately, Holiness."

As he left the Pope, O'Shaugnessy heard the Holy Father muttering to himself in Latin.

Powerful prayers, he hoped.

"HOUSTON, HOUSTON, DO you read?"

"Sure, Cloudbase. What's the buzz? You may be on Japan time up there, but it's four in the ayem Earthside you know."

"Weird shit coming down, Houston. All our instruments went crazy just now."

"Sounds like Japtech error to me. We have no anomalies."

"Have you looked at the moon recently?"

"Sure, it's just out the window, what do you mean?"

"Take a look."

"Fuckin' hell."

"Yeah."

"Let's just class this as a monitor error, hey? Get some sleep, and it'll be better in the morning."

"We told you. That's all we had to do. It's up to you now. Good night, Houston."

"Good night, Digby."

THE ANCIENT ADVERSARY *stretched out its invisible, insubstantial form and detached itself from the chunk of rock. It was just a satellite, after all, more important as the focus of men's dreams and beliefs than as a collection of geological data.*

It brushed through Camp Pournelle, comforted by the tininess of its mechanisms, the limits of their measures.

Tick-tock, tick-tock, tick-tock.

"MISS... IS THERE something?"

It was like coming awake. She hadn't been in a fugue or anything, but she did seem to have wandered off on some impulse.

"Miss?"

"It's all right, thank you, comrade."

The zookeeper straightened his cap and walked away. Chantal Juillerat, S J, leaned against the railings, and wondered what she was doing in the Moscow Zoo.

This wasn't a holiday. She was with Cardinal Brandreth's delegation. There was a demonic presence of some sort infesting the semi-secure database in the Roman Catholic church on Pushkin Prospekt. She was supposed to attend the preliminary exorcism, and give assistance.

She wasn't supposed to go to the zoo.

A party of chattering children pressed around her, faces to the railings, pointing.

The reptile opened its snout, and showed its teeth. The children backed away.

Chantal looked into the crocodile's mouth, and felt as if someone had walked over her grave.

She remembered a song from a film.

"Never Smile at a Crocodile."

THE MOON WAS round again. Hawk's song was nearly done. His part in the pattern was almost over.

IN MEMPHIS, TENNESSEE, an aged Op was up late in his tiny apartment, listening to his old records, drinking too much.

From the stereo, his own, younger voice breathed "Are You Lonesome Tonight?"

The thing is, he was.

DR PROCTOR HAD expected a drawbridge, but there were just a pair of eaten-through wooden gates.

"Little pigs, little pigs," he said to himself, "let me come in."

IN THE OUTER *Darkness, the wisp that was the spirit projection of Nguyen Seth was blown this way and that by the angry breaths of the Dark Ones. The Ancient Adversary had escaped. The Great Work was in jeopardy. One among the titans came forward, and latched onto Seth, hooks sinking into the Summoner's soul.*

This was the one they called the Jibbenainosay.

Seth was pulled back through the wormhole to the tabernacle, and found himself in his body again.

He took off his spectacles.

Just beyond the Gateway, the Jibbenainosay waited. In more years than a man should remember, Nguyen Seth had encountered many things, but he had never truly known fear before.

Now, he had met the Jibbenainosay.

★ ★ ★

"HEY, CHOP-CHOP, LOOK at the drunken old Indian!"

They were Maniax, bored and hung-over from smacksynth and white lightning. They'd stumbled out of the Happy Chief Diner, where they'd stoked up on burro burritos and chilli dogs. They'd heard the Navahos had good drugs, but they'd heard wrong.

"Don't he howl, though?"

"Ain't that a Mothers of Violence track?"

"Nahh, sounds Sove to me."

"D'ya reckon he's a Red Indian?"

"Could be."

"Fuckin' commie."

"Bet I kin plug his guts from here."

"Way off, Chop-Chop. Let me try."

"Hey, no fair. You gotta ScumStopper."

"You gots the tools, Chop-Chop, you use them."

The handgun spat flame and lead. The shot resounded through the valley, amplified in its echo as it bounced off the sugarloaf mountains.

"Shit, but that's a mess you've made."

"Hell, I bet we can still lift his scalp."

"Way to go."

DUROC LAY NAKED on the stone floor, willing his every muscle to relax. It was a trick his uncle had taught him. Sometimes, it made the fear go away. Sometimes…

4.30AM, WESTERN CENTRAL Time. 95 mph. 'Nola Gay nudged the first Fratmobile, almost gently, and the spikes went in low. Redd veered sharply to the left and the Delta Gamma Epsilon ve-hickle lifted up off the freeway. She used her lightweight Combat Lase surgically, slicing off one of the Fratmobile's wheels. The ve-hickle spun end over end, and fell by the wayside. 'Nola Gay was three hundred yards down the road by the time the gastank blew. There were three other Delta Gamma Epsilon ve-hickles in this race, and then it would be the end of them.

The crewcut gangcult of fresh-faced fascists in letter sweaters and football helmets had been staging too many "panty raids" on T-H-R clients' holdings between Pueblo and Trinidad. They hadn't got the message after the first few T-H-R team strikes, and now they were getting the top lady, Redd Harvest. She'd picked the assignment herself, cruising down from Denver to handle it personally.

'Nola Gay, her customized G-mek V12, held the road like a clean dream. She took out the slowest of the remaining Fratmobiles with a popped package from her grenade launcher, and upped her speed. Often, she just raced the bandits until they cracked up, not even bothering with the roof-mounted chaingun or the 15mm autocannon.

One of the lettermen fouled up, bad. A tyre blew out at 120 m.p.h, and ragged tatters of metal and panzerboy were spread over a mile or so of the blacktop. One left.

There were explosions around her, but she swerved through them, sustaining only a little singed paintwork.

She held the wheel with her left hand, and tapped keys on the dashtop board with the fingers of her right. It was like a vidgame. Get the target centre, and then blast.

"Hey, carrot-top," a pleasant voice came over the intercom, "how's about we call this chicken run a tie and cruise over to a make-out motel for some party action. We've got brews, broads and bennies to spare.'

Without thinking about it, she stabbed the chain gun control, and made a pass. The entire rear section of the Fratmobile came apart.

Redd passed the wreckage, knowing there would be no survivors, and kept on speeding. She fired off her remaining ammo into the desert dark.

The chase was over, and she was coming down from it. But for now, she kept her pedal to the floor, and sped into the dark.

Some night, there would be a brick wall across the road, and that would be an end of it.

Some night, but not tonight.

Hawk-That-Settles felt emptied of his song, as if he had poured his spirit out into the sand with the ancient words. The Devil was at the door, and he didn't have the strength to wake up Jesse.

The one-eyed white girl was on her own.

"Houston, if you think I'm going to let you wake up the President with some glitches from a base we should have decommissioned in the last century, you have got another thing coming. E-mail him in the morning."

"What's that I hear, little pigs? Not on the hair of your chinny-chin-chins? Well, I'll huff, and I'll puff, and I'll blow your house in..."

"This is Lola Stechkin, bringing you the Middle of the Night Bulletin, and informing you that absolutely nothing is happening around the world, thank God. Soon, it's back to the *Late Nite Lingerie Lounge* with Lynne Cramer, but first, here's a message from GenTech, the BioDiv that really cares..."

There was someone down in the courtyard. One of the men from her dreams. Jesse carefully pulled on her clothes. It would be dawn soon.

The moon was going down.

★ ★ ★

X

FROM THE SHADOWS, Hawk-That-Settles saw the Devil come into the courtyard of Santa de Nogueira. He looked like a man, but Hawk saw the spirit writhing inside him.

The Devil sauntered across the open space, apparently unconcerned.

This was Jesse's test. Hawk had no part in it. Although he knew that if she failed, the Devil would surely kill him too.

Again, he was an expendable innocent bystander for the one-eyed white girl's elevation to a higher plane of being. This little Indian was getting fed up with that.

"Tonto," said the Devil. "I see you."

Hawk came out of the shadows. "My name's not Tonto."

"No, of course not. You are Hawk-That-Settles, son of Two-Dogs-Fucking, of the line of Armijah. You could be a Chief of the Navaho."

"But I'm not."

"No. You are not. You are just something in my way."

"And who are you?"

The Devil smiled. "Dr Ottokar Proctor, at your service."

"The killer?"

"The Artist."

They had been circling each other. The sky was getting light. The shadows were receding. Hawk could see the Devil's face more clearly now. It was quite a famous face, a television face, a newspaper face. Bland and unreadable, it concealed his horns, his forked tongue...

"Have you heard the one about Roy Rogers?"

"No." Hawk tried to remember the Song of his Dying, but it would not come to him. He could only sing it once, and he had to do it right.

"Well, Roy is coming home from Santa Fe on the stage-coach one night – he's been away on business – and he stops off in town before heading out to his ranch..."

The Devil stood in the open, hands visible, as relaxed as a professional golfer.

"'Mr Rogers, Mr Rogers,' says the town drunk, 'where are you going?'"

"'Well, Gabby, I'm going out to my ranch…'"

Hawk heard Jesse coming from a long way away. She was making her way cautiously down to the courtyard.

"'But Mr Rogers, the Apaches rode through yesterday, and they burned your ranch down!'

"'In that case, I guess I'd better go look out for my wife…'

"'But Mr Rogers, when the Apaches were gone, the Wild Bunch rode through, and they whipped your wife to death.'"

Hawk saw Jesse standing behind Dr Proctor.

"'In that case, I'll mosey out and see to my three children…'

"'But Mr Rogers, after the Wild Bunch were through, Mexican bandidos came up from below the border, and they took your three children and hanged them from the old oak tree…'"

Jesse was calm, ready for the move. Hawk knew that Dr Proctor knew she was behind him.

"'In that case, I'd better look after my cattle..'

"'Oh, Mr Rogers, I hate to be the one to tell you this, but once the bandidos headed out of here, the rustlers came through and stampeded your herd the hell out of the valley…'"

It was the hour of the wolf, the quiet moment between nightset and sunrise. The desert was still.

"'In that case, I'll go give Trigger his oats…'

"'But Mr Rogers, when the rustlers were finished Black Bart turned up spoiling for a fight, and he shot Trigger right between the eyes, killed him deader than a skunk…'"

Jesse walked into the open. Dr Proctor nodded to her, but kept on with the story.

"And Roy looks at the ground and says 'well, I guess I'll go out to the ruins of my ranch, count my missing cattle and then bury my wife, my horse and my kids.'"

Jesse wasn't armed, but that shouldn't mean anything. Hawk knew she was as deadly as Dr Proctor.

"So Gabby says, 'Roy, there's just one more thing…'"

In the killing game, Dr Proctor was the Artist, but Jesse was the Grand Master.

"'What is it, Gabby?'"

Dr Proctor's eyes shone. Jesse's hands rested lightly on her hips. It was her fighting stance.

"'Roy, how about giving us a song?'"

XI

NOBODY LAUGHED.

On the outside, Seth's man was a disappointment. He looked like a prosperous accountant. He had to be more than that, of course. The Elder had sent him to do a job that an entire Agency had failed to accomplish.

He turned to look at her. She looked from his ordinary face to Hawk-That-Settles. He was to stay out of it.

"Miss Bonney, how nice to meet you."

He extended his hand. She didn't take it.

"I'm Dr Proctor."

"Your name doesn't matter to me."

"You should know it before you die. I always let them know who I am."

She had a bad feeling about this one. She closed her right eye, and studied his heat pattern. He was literally cool, with none of the orange hotspots she would have expected from a man about to fight for his life.

"I've never heard of you."

That fazed him, offended him. He pursed his lips in a tiny moue. "A shame. It would mean much more."

The sun was rising over the walls. The monks should have been at their devotions hours earlier.

"I am going to give you a species of immortality, Miss Bonney. Who would remember Mary Kelly, Elizabeth Stride or Polly Nicholls had they not been blessed..."

"I don't know who those women are either."

"They were nothings, Miss Bonney. Drab tarts. But they were killed by Jack the Ripper."

"Him, I've heard of."

Dr Proctor pulled a knife out of his jacket, and threw it. She snatched it out of the air, and tossed it aside. He smiled.

"Just testing."

"You know I'm stronger than I look."

"I know a lot about you, Miss Bonney. I probably couldn't break your bones with a sledgehammer, and your flesh is reinforced with durium thread. And you have some other surprises implanted in your body. You're a proud cyborg. Your fathers made you well. Bruno Bonney made your mind, and Simon Threadneedle your body."

"I'm unbreakable, then?"

Dr Proctor cocked his head, as if considering. "Probably. I'll concede that."

"And yet you've come here to break me?"

A sly grin appeared. "No, to kill you."

"You're an honest man."

"That's the first time anyone's ever said that to me, but it's a perceptive comment. I am perhaps the only honest man. I do what I want, and I'm not ashamed of it. You were much the same, Jazzbeaux. I've read your records. But you've changed."

"You've said it." She clenched her fist in the air, feeling the metal through her palm.

"Not just like that. Inside." He tapped his head and heart. "You don't do what you want any more. You do what is wanted of you. That's why you have to die. If you'd been content to be just another high-speed sociopath, you might have lived to a ripe old age, but you had to get that old-time religion, you had to save the world..."

"I'm not interested in saving the world."

"That's what you say, Jessamyn, but your actions tell a different story."

"It's me or Seth. That's it."

Dr Proctor laughed. "You can't really be that naive. Universes are grinding together to point you two at each other. You have nothing more to say about it than the sea has about the tidal pull of the moon."

Jesse's head hurt. This was worse than she had expected.

"You know, I was expecting some super Op, Redd Harvest or Woody Rutledge. You're not like that. You're like the soce workers back in Denver. You just want to talk."

"Talk is important, Jesse."

She had an urge to tear his throat out, just as she had torn her father's windpipe away. She fought it. You don't reach the Fifth Spiritual Plane without getting some control.

"In another world, we could have worked together," Dr Proctor said. "I have the brains, and you have the body..."

He made his first move.

"We could have slaughtered *millions* of the sheep."

XII

SHE WOULDN'T BREAK, but she could bend.

Dr Proctor got her in a sumo hold, hands clasped in the small of her back, and pushed forwards with his forehead. He didn't need to be especially strong to exert the maximum pressure this way. He felt her spinesheath shifting. It was a good product, a GenTech speciality, but it was just a jacket. There were bones inside, and a slender, vulnerable cord inside them. He found the pressure spots in her lower back, and jammed the heels of his hands into them.

An inch before his face, her teeth clenched.

"Pain?" he whispered. "Remember it?"

He had her arms straitjacketed to her sides. He lifted her feet off the floor. She was off-balanced.

"See, no leverage. You can't kick me."

She pulled her head back, and struck his forehead, twice. Blood ran into his eyebrows, but he wasn't hurt.

"That won't get you anywhere."

He walked her around the courtyard in a parody dance. She was as light as any other girl. Threadneedle preferred minimum-weight technology.

She squirmed, and eased her knees up inside his bearhug, pushing them into his stomach. He felt the strain in his laced fingers, his elbows and his shoulders.

He knew she would break the hold, and decided to use it to inflict a little preliminary damage. He unlocked his fingers, made fists, and struck thumbs-first into the small of her back, then dropped her.

That should get her unaltered insides jarring, and put a bit of a crimp into her pelvic girdle.

She was up, keeping her hurt to herself, and lashing out. He backed away. For all her strength and devastating power, she wasn't an especially skilled martial artist. Streetfighting was about all she knew, with perhaps a touch of jeet kune do. Brawlers' business.

He stepped through her blows, and tapped her collarbones, hooking his forefingers into the nerve points.

Jesse yelped, and floundered. He gave her an elbow in the side of the head, and repeated the procedure three times within the space of a single breath.

"Tired? I can keep this up all day."

She still hadn't really touched him.

"You'll have had Threadneedle undermesh your stomach muscles, so we won't bother hitting you there," he said.

He saw his opportunity, and jabbed a knuckle-pointed punch at her solar plexus. It would be armoured, of course, but he didn't want to break it, just to send a shock through her whole skeleton.

"You see, all that metal inside you can rattle around. It can hurt you as badly as I can."

He pressed her ribs, his hands moving faster than perception.

"A few more of those, and all your boneshields will be loose. That'll be like having breadknives floating around the inside of your chest. You won't care for it. I can promise you that."

She stepped back, away from him. She had worked up a sweat. The sun was up there now. It looked like the thirty-nine thousand six hundred and fifteenth sunny day in a row in Arizona.

"Are you enjoying this little game of Sally Go Round the Roses? I am."

"Fuck you."

"Tut tut. Such language. You should gain a command of more elaborate invective."

She made a reach for his throat, which he dodged. Her fingers closed just under his jaw, nails scraping his adam's apple.

"Nice try. Your favourite move, isn't it? Your father's autopsy reports show an especially fine specimen of the throat-grab. And you did something similar to that Daughter of the American Revolution in Moroni."

He pulled out a derringer, and shot at her heart. Her jacket exploded, and he saw blackened flesh below.

"You might be wondering why I did that?"

She was snarling now, not looking like a girl at all.

"I knew it wouldn't kill you..."

She tightened her padded pyjamas, modestly shifting the hole from blueing ribs to smooth skin.

"It didn't even hurt you, really. You've had your nerves deadened to reduce your pain perception..."

He threw the useless gun away.

"But it did some damage, Jesse. Believe me, inside, you're leaking a little. Nothing serious. It'll clear up on its own thanks to Dr Threadneedle's micro-organisms. But you'd be well advised not to exert yourself further."

He brushed her cheek with his toecap.

"Trust me, I'm a doctor."

His heel slammed into her jaw, knocking her head to one side.

"Of course, my PhD is in economics, but I have an amateur's informed interest in bioengineering."

She got a good hold on his ankle, but not good enough. He pulled free.

"Did that dislocate your thumbs? No, well I'm sure it hurt them a lot."

She tucked her thumbs inside her fists, and tried to land a couple of punches on him. If they had connected, they would have broken bones and punctured organs, but he was out of the way and had made sure there would be a stone pillar where her fists landed.

"Did you know that Dr Threadneedle's experimental subjects had a 76% mental breakdown rate when he was with GenTech? Still, I'm sure he made some startling advances before opening you up."

Jesse fell back, her knuckles bloodied, steel glinting in the ruined flesh. There were distinct imprints in the stone where she had punched.

"And that must have been very unpleasant. You know, this is an interesting approach. I'm not really killing you, I'm just seducing you into a slow, painful suicide..."

Dr Proctor knew that everyone else who had faced up to her had been too scared of her ferocity, of her bio-amendments.

Too bad Threadneedle hadn't tried some of the new IQ-boost chromosomes on her greymass. If Jessamyn Bonney were intelligent, she could have been a real threat.

She went for one of his knees, and got lucky. No, he had to give her credit. She had seen an oppportunity, and taken it well.

Pain flared up, and he slowed momentarily. She got a kick into his side, and he had to dart back, out of range.

She wasn't really unintelligent, just uninformed. She hadn't even heard of him. Probably didn't follow the newsies, stuck out here in the sand. Like most of the sheep, she was going to die because she was ignorant, not because she was undeserving...

He'd been fought before. He didn't always favour helpless prey. He'd stalked and struggled with the best of them. Others had resisted more than this.

His side throbbed, and he realized she'd done better than he'd thought at first. With a cold anger, he stepped up to her, and used his elbows on her neck, face, shoulders and chest.

Again, he was out of her range before she really knew what he had done to her.

Her face was beginning to blacken.

"Some of those are ordinary bruises, but some of those are nice little pockets filling up with blood from the ruptured vessels."

She wiped her face off with the back of her hand.

"I can mash your face against your durium skull, Jesse. That's what I'm doing. Then I'll get to your greymass through your eyesockets."

She pulled her eyepatch off. He had wondered when she'd try that.

The red lens of the burner winked as it warmed up. He slipped his hand into his side-pocket and palmed the circular mirror.

The beam came, and he had his hand up to deflect it. The angle was off, so it didn't bounce back straight and burn the implant out, but it did pass through her hair, raising some smoke.

"Do you want to try that again? I thought not."

He made a fist, and crushed the mirror to shards, which he rubbed into her jaw.

"Let's get some air into the wounds, Jesse. You've a pretty face. I think we can make it interesting, give it some character, a few lines here, a few holes there…"

She tried for his throat again.

"Persistent little minx, eh? I was impressed with the Dead Rat roster, by the way. Especially Rodriguez. Fingers through the eyes. I always like that one myself. Of course, I don't have bolts in my knuckles to make it easy."

He bent under her fingerthrust.

"Takes the sport out of it, somehow."

A stone sang against the stones beside his head. He hadn't forgotten the Indian. He wasn't relevant to this situation, but he could be a minor danger.

"Why don't you just give up, Jesse? You can't live through this day. I'll tell you what, I'll make it painless. You can't say fairer than that."

She didn't answer him, just made a few passes in the air.

Dr Proctor felt stings on his face. And trickling blood.

"Neat. You got the glass out, and used it. You have resources."

It was time to finish it.

XIII

HAWK-THAT-SETTLES WATCHED JESSE fight with Dr Proctor. His contribution had been meagre, and unappreciated by either of the participants.

Overhead, the sun had stopped moving. That was the signal. Now, it was his part in the ritual.

He drew a circle in the sand…

Dr Proctor got a hold on Jesse, forcing her down.

He sang the song of the moon and the crocodile once more.

A cloud appeared in the sky, a black dot above the horizon, burping upwards.

Jesse's face was in the sand, which blew away from the flagstones beneath. She was coughing. Dr Proctor had one hand at the back of her neck, the other free. She was pinned beneath his body. He was scientifically killing her.

The cloud came through the sky like a bird of prey. It seemed to grow bigger as it got nearer. It didn't look like a cloud any more. It was a dart of ink shafting through a clear liquid, bubbling behind, pointed in front.

Hawk sang of the triumph of the crocodile.

Jesse's hands pushed at the sandy stones.

Dr Proctor exerted more pressure. He was only touching the nape of her neck, but blood was leaking from around her optic implant.

The cloud was overhead, blotting out the sun.

A shadow fell on Santa de Nogueira.

JESSE HAD SAND up her nose. She didn't believe she had lost so easily. Dr Proctor was fast, and he knew things about pain she would never even begin to comprehend.

Her visions had been wrong. She would die today, and never know who the other faces were, the man with the guitar, the dark-faced foreigner and the nun with the clear-handled pistol. Perhaps they were just the figments of a dream.

Her brain was turning in on itself. Dr Proctor was using her body as an instrument, and playing upon it a concerto of agony. His fingers found nerves, and sent signals through them.

He was indeed getting past her bones, pushing tendrils of death into her brain.

She struggled, but he had her as surely as if she were in a strait-jacket. The weight of his body held her down.

As he killed her, he crooned in her ear. They were tunes she didn't recognize. Opera, she thought.

A blackness fell over her vision, and she assumed this was the moment of parting from her flesh…

"QUAL TERRIBLE MOMENTO," Dr Proctor sang, "piu formar non so parole; densa nube di spavento per che copra i rai del sole! Come rosa inaridita ella sta tra morte e vita; chi per lei non e commosso ha di tigre in petto il cor!"

This terrible moment, he translated mentally, my words cannot describe; a dense cloud of terror seems to obscure the sun's rays…

There was a shadow.

… like a fading rose, she lies twixt life and death!

A cold dark fell upon him.

… he who does not pity her has a tiger's heart in his breast!

He pressed Jessamyn Bonney to the stones, squeezing her life out drop by drop.

When he was done, he would go to work on her, mutilating the corpse. The Indian would appreciate that. Of course, the Navaho spirit world would hardly welcome one who had, in life, replaced so much of her original body.

The shadow fell on his shoulders like a heavy weight, freezing him where it touched. He felt as if something were passing through him. The darkness sank through his body, leaving ice behind.

His grip on Jesse's neck relaxed.

THE ANCIENT ADVERSARY *slipped through the meat-thing, and into the Vessel. Enfleshed, it was overwhelmed by the sensations of the world…*

* * *

Hawk's song ended, and he stood, watching in awe as the transformation took place.

Jesse felt fire burst inside her heart, spreading through her body. The weight was gone from her back, and she could move again. She wiped the remaining glass out of her face. She felt her wounds closing over.

In her mind, she was a long-jawed reptile, fastening rows of teeth into a struggling hog, refusing to let him go.

Jessamyn Bonney faded to nothing inside her own brain, and the new tenant took over.

Lashing as if she had a tail, she turned over, and held fast to the hog.

Dr Proctor gulped as Jesse grabbed his throat. His aria was stopped. He saw something new in her eye as she stood up, taking him with her.

He struck her, but his well-aimed blows were feeble. She ignored whatever pain she felt.

She was changing.

For the first time, Dr Ottokar Proctor considered the possibility of his own death. It was not a pleasant thought.

What if the sheep lived on somehow? What if they were waiting for him on the other side? Once he was dead, what could they not do to him?

Jesse opened her mouth, and roared. Dr Proctor thought he saw endless rows of needle-sharp teeth.

The shadow was gone, and they were struggling in the sun.

Hawk-That-Settles crossed his legs, and watched the end. The sounds coming from Jesse's mouth were barely human. Dr Proctor was quiet now, nearly unconscious.

It was a good day to end it.

* * *

The Ancient Adversary and the Vessel were inside one another like a snake swallowing its tail. Both changed as they flowed together. It adjusted fast to the comforts and discomforts of physical form. Her spirit swelled as the being from the Outer Darkness combined with every particle of her body.

Jazzbeaux, Bonney, Jessamyn, Jesse, Frankenstein's Daughter. She flipped through her names, her faces, her identities. They were all faint now, indistinct.

And yet the Ancient Adversary was fading too, diluted by the strength of the Vessel.

It had never been a crocodile. That came from somewhere else, giving it the rudiments of a form.

She had never really been any of the people others had thought her, never felt comfortable with her own picture of herself.

Now she was something harder, as sharp and bright as a diamond. Jessamyn Bonney was dead.

She was something else...

Dr Proctor gave up the struggle, and hung limp in her embrace. She had spared his spine, but snapped his mind.

Psychiatrists had debated his sanity at length. He had joined in their arguments as a way of amusing himself back in Sunnydales. He had had no opinion either way.

Now, he drooled a thin line of spittle. Inside his head, the last bars of Lucia di Lammermoor faded away. The iris closed over Porky Pig.

They would have no question to solve now. If he hadn't been mad when he left the asylum, he certainly would be if they took him back.

She dropped him, not even bothering to administer a killing blow. Whatever she had become, she couldn't be bothered with crushing insects under her feet.

* * *

In Salt Lake *City, Elder Nguyen Seth screamed, as if icicles had been jabbed into his brain. Within him, talons curved, digging deeper into his heart. The Ancient Adversary was upon the Earth, and the Dark Ones were angry. He staggered from the font of blood, pain coursing through his entire body, and made his agonized way to the isolation chamber. The tank was always ready.*

He felt the pull of the Outer Darkness, the call of his masters. Their wrath was terrible.

The tank opened, and Seth, his robes dropped to the floor, hauled himself in. The lid descended like the slab of a tomb, and the fluid seeped in, lapping around his tormented body. He fumbled with the life-support monitor electrodes, pinning them to his flesh with little fishhooks. The warm waters rose.

Seth sank into himself, and his pain was eased.

Hawk-That-Settles got up and walked over. He was not sure what Jesse was now, but she had defeated the Devil. She stood over him, bearing the fallen creature no malice.

For a moment, he thought her face green and long, with eyes on the sides and dripping teeth. Then she was herself again, bleeding a little, her one eye clear.

"Jesse..."

She turned to look at him. She didn't recognize him for a moment. Then, she smiled.

"No, you're... you're not Jesse."

She shrugged and turned away.

It was becoming clearer.

"What have you done to her?"

She turned. She spoke in her own voice. "Nothing, Hawk. I'm different, but I'm still me."

"And who's me?"

Dr Proctor rolled away, and lay face up, staring at the sun.

"Me? I'm your Jesse, Hawk."

"No, you have enacted the prophecy of the Moon and the Crocodile. You can be named Jesse no more."

"So, I'll take a new name, like one of those ghetto kids trying to be a Russian musickie."

Hawk was afraid of this new Jesse, but he fought his fear. "I shall call myself…"

There was no cloud in the sky now.

"Krokodil."

part five
krokodil

I

Joaquin Salazar took off his straw hat and rubbed his sweaty forehead with an oily rag, squinting in the noonday sun. Hawk-That-Settles checked the cartons Joaquin had brought out to Santa de Nogueira in his battered pick-up. Canned goods, mostly, and twenty five-litre plastic containers of guaranteed pure-ish water.

"Will she sit up there all day?" Joaquin asked, peering up at the figure squatting on the roof of the chapel.

"Maybe," Hawk shrugged. "Help me get the water inside before it boils in this heat."

"Sure thing, Señor."

Hawk picked up two containers, and humped them into the main hall of the monastery.

The hollow man was inside, just sitting at the table, carving intricate statuettes of cartoon characters with a pocketshiv.

"Ottokar," Hawk said. "Give us a hand."

Dr Proctor looked up, smiled and went out to help Joaquin without saying a word.

Sometimes, Hawk felt he was sharing Santa de Nogueira with a pair of voiceless robots. Krokodil sat on the roof all day and all night, looking to the horizon. Dr Proctor made his carvings. And Hawk-That-Settles looked after the pair of them.

When the water was safely stowed in the perpetually shaded depths of the building, and Joaquin was loaded up with last month's empties, the Mexican deliveryman drove off. He was obviously uncomfortable around the monsters, and wouldn't even consider Hawk's offer of tequila.

Hawk was drinking more now. It was the boredom. That was what had nudged Two-Dogs-Fucking towards the bottle on the Reservation. Hawk couldn't get enough tequila brought out to Santa de Nogueira to keep him as drunk as his father had usually been, but he rationed his supply carefully and usually managed to keep the fug in his brain and the fire on his tongue.

Hawk watched Joaquin go. He couldn't remember whether Krokodil or Dr Proctor had spoken at all this month. Joaquin was probably the only person he ever had a conversation with these days. And Indians were supposed to be iron-willed men of few words and many deeds.

The pick-up zig-zagged across the desert, keeping to the rocky patches and away from the treacherous sands. On his first trip out, Joaquin had brought his sons and taken away Dr Proctor's sandcat and all its contents. That had been enough to cover six months provisions. The Salazar family were probably the highest-charging grocery service in the world, Hawk suspected. Last month, Joaquin had announced that the funds generated by the sandcat were at an end, and Hawk had had to hand over the DeLorean Agency tank Krokodil had been driving when they first met. He had negotiated nine months worth of food and water in return for a machine that, with all its inbuilt weapons systems, should pick up twenty or thirty million dollars when smuggled down into Mexico and sold to some would-be generalissimo. When the nine months were up, Hawk didn't know what he would do. By then, he hoped Krokodil would have decided the time had come to return to the world and they could rob a few yakuza filling stations for a grubstake. If not, he would have to fashion a bow and arrows and go out for desert game. He had eaten a catrat or two in his time, but had no wish to revert to the diet. Also, he was a terrible shot.

Joaquin bounced over the horizon, and his sputtering engine noise faded out. Santa de Nogueira was as still and silent as the depths of the sea. This had all been under the sea once. You could still find seashells out under the sand, and the fossil remnants of marine creatures. That had been before the Americas rose out of the water. Hawk had heard that the continent was going down again. Most of the South-East was under a foot of rancid saltwater, and there was a tidal barrage wall around New York City. Eventually, the waters would rush back in a deluge, and swamp everything. After a million years, the tide would come back in. In one of the newspapers Joaquin packed his beets in, Hawk read that scientists were rediscovering species long thought extinct. Back in the 1920s, they had found the coelacanth, but now there were shoals of trilobites in the Florida Keys. It was as if evolution were throwing itself into reverse gear, as the planet readapted itself for a new prehistory.

He turned away from the gates, and walked back to the hall. Dr Proctor was slumped against one of the interior walls, taking one of his siestas, a makeshift coolie hat of threaded newsprint over his head. He had lost some of his bulk, and tanned like a Mexican. In his torn white pyjamas, he could easily slip over the Rio Grande wall and get lost down amid the latino millions, evading forever the vast, country-wide manhunt that was still searching for him. He hadn't killed anybody since last year, so many of the authorities were listing him as "presumed dead". Krokodil could have killed him at any time, but had never bothered with it. Sometimes, Hawk wondered just how harmless Dr Ottokar Proctor had become since his defeat. He was like a bright four year-old, mainly keeping to himself but genuinely eager to please. Hawk supposed he was cured, but it was a cure he himself wouldn't have been happy to take. Remembering their guest's earlier career, Hawk occasionally considered slitting his throat just in case. But he didn't. He was an Indian, and he couldn't get rid of all the old ways. The insane were touched by the Great Spirits, and thus sacred.

Krokodil had changed too. Since her elevation to the Sixth Level of Spirituality, the former Jessamyn Bonney had had very little to do with the world. She drank her water and ate her beans, and she stared at the sun and the moon like a ship's look-out waiting for a sail to appear in the blue distance. Otherwise, she just sat while her clothes rotted on her back and her hair grew down to her ankles. She didn't come to his cot in the night any more, having outgrown love when she progressed beyond all other human concerns. Five times in the first four months after Jesse's transformation, Hawk-That-Settles had left the monsters to their own devices for a few days and walked to Firecreek, the nearest collection of three huts and a gas station that called itself a town, where he traded catrat pelts for tequila, smacksynth and a night with a half-Mex, half-white girl who called herself the Hot Enchilada. But each time he had been more concerned with what Krokodil and Dr Proctor might get up to in his absence. When Krokodil's sail appeared, he knew he had to be there.

His father had come to him in a dream, half his head hanging loose, and told him that he was the last of his line, and that he must stay with the moon woman until the end of her evolutionary cycle. When she surpassed the Seventh Level, he would be allowed to go free and return to the Reservation to bury Two-Dogs with honour. Oh, incidentally, his father added, I'm dead now.

Still, sometimes he wondered whether the Hot Enchilada couldn't be persuaded to move out to Santa de Nogueira for the while.

Dr Proctor had stopped calling him "Tonto," but that was who he was beginning to feel like as he cooked, washed up and housekept for Krokodil. He had been her teacher when they first met, and now he was her domestic slave, never told anything but expected to be at the ready when Kemo Sabe decided it was time to ride off on Silver and rout the rustlers.

It was not yet one in the afternoon. Hawk looked, as he did hundreds of times every day, through the window at Krokodil's perch. She was so unmoving, she might as well have been a statue of the Blessed Virgin. Her hair was growing around her like a luxurious tent.

He opened up a carton with his fingernail, and pulled out a bottle. His last one had been empty a week ago.

He broke the seal and twisted off the cap, then tipped the liquid into his mouth.

Ugh, he thought, firewater heap mighty medicine!

II

SINCE ELDER SETH went into his coma, on the night Dr Proctor had failed to kill Jessamyn Bonney, there had been a certain amount of panic in Deseret. Roger Duroc had had to cancel a long-planned-for trip to the Antarctic to stay in Salt Lake City. This was a crucial stage of the Great Work, and the Elder's spiritual absence was much felt. There had been a minor revolt among the resettlers in the outlying homesteads, triggered by the backfiring of an enzyme-augmented wheat strain that had failed to yield a worthy harvest but had spread a species of croprot among the farmhands. The farmers had marched on the Tabernacle in their dungarees, waving their American Gothic pitchforks while their faces fell off, demanding that the Elder come out and address them. Duroc had had to have some of the ringleaders publicly stoned by his security force, the grim-faced, black-clad Elders whom he had personally trained and drilled in the Old Testament system of law enforcement. Since then, there had been a few stormy council meetings, and a few families had tried to pull up stakes and make it back through the desert to the United States. None of them had managed to cross the state line yet, thanks to Blevins Barricune and the other hunter-killers Duroc had stationed along the border. There had been an information containment problem too, but he had dealt with that by ensuring the accidental crash-landing of a chopperload of newsies and freelance hacker/journalists.

But things were overextended. The Church of Joseph could not continue much longer without its figurehead, its fountainhead and its mastermind. Duroc spent a portion of each day in the tankroom, looking at the relaxed, unlined face of the ageless Elder, wondering what dreams he had lost himself in.

He thought it had something to do with the Bonney girl. They were still linked at some psychic level, and her continued existence was draining him of vitally-needed energies. He had considered several programs for eliminating the problem, but given the failure of the Manolo and Proctor options, he did not want to put anything into action without the Elder's say-so. Two failures were quite enough. Another might put his position in jeopardy. Elder Beach had been speaking against him in the councils rather too often lately, and a faction had been gathering around him. Beach would dearly love to take Seth's spectacles for his own, and shoulder the burden of the Great Work. He had his supporters.

Sometimes, Duroc questioned the wisdom of using a church to further the Great Work. The Josephites attracted too many impractical fanatics, too many focused but tiny minds, too many desperate need-to-believe lost souls. But Seth had been an accomplice in the creation of the sect, and had nurtured it for more than a hundred and fifty years. It was the instrument he had chosen, shaped and prepared. The Elder knew best.

Duroc paced the isolation chamber. It was as cold as a tomb, and slightly damp, but otherwise resembled a striplit hospital waiting room. The tank was like a cross between a fridge-freezer and an Egyptian sarcophagus, with a clear-glass faceplate inset. The Elder's clothes hung on a curly-hooked old-fashioned coatstand in one corner.

Yesterday, Duroc had had to allow the stoning of Sister Harrison, who had been caught in adultery. In Nguyen Seth's absence, he had been called upon to cast the first stone. Coralie had looked him in the eyes as he tossed the rock, showing the hurt before he struck her. He had tried to make it quick, but the Council of Elders had decreed that she must lie bleeding in front of the Tabernacle for a day and a night. This morning, she was gone, spirited away by the frog-chinned Brother Harrison. Later, Duroc would check up. He wasn't sure whether it would be best for the Sister to live or die. Whatever, he could have no more to do with her. He had engineered the evidence against her, keeping his own name out of it but making sure Brother Shipman and Elder Pompheret were disgraced. She had to suffer, not for her immorality – that was not a question that entered into his thinking – but because she had been with him the night it started to go wrong. She had seen him shivering with terror, and that must be driven from her head.

There were droplets of condensation on the outside of the isolation tank, and the temperature dials were misted over.

While in his deepsleep, the Elder drew the little nourishment he found necessary from a biosolution pumped into the waters that lapped around his body. Duroc checked the biosupport system, wiping the glass of the tubefeed monitor. The condensation came off, but the dial was still clouded. It had been abraded until opaque.

A terrible calm descended upon his mind.

He pressed the glass until it shattered. A red-tipped shard speared into the meat of his thumb. He sucked it loose and spat it out. The red froth was startling against the white floor.

It was as he had suspected, the tubefeed had been blocked and the nutrients witheld.

The double doors opened, and men clad in the dark suits of the Josephite Council of Elders pressed in, surrounding him. They had some security staff with them, discreetly armed.

"Elder Beach?" Duroc greeted their obvious leader.

"Blessed be, Brother Duroc. It has been decided. I am to head the Council until Elder Seth has recovered. We have taken a vote. It was unanimous."

Duroc looked from face to face. They were mostly unrepentant, but Elder Wiggs glanced away from his gaze at the crucial moment. His body tensed. The confined space would tell in his favour, and he thought he could kill Beach and most of the others before the security people shot him down. But he couldn't risk a ricochet puncturing the tank. The Elder might be comatose almost to the point of catalepsy, but he still clung to life.

"We have come for your approval," Beach said. "As the Elder's Executive Assistant, your palmprint is necessary to access the datanets. You must realize that this is the only path we can take."

The biosupport unit hummed, and something gurgled inside. Wiggs was pointing with a shaking finger.

"Look..."

Duroc turned. There were clear refuse tubes leading from the tank to the floor, feeding into the drains. Purple-threaded liquid was passing through the tubes. The tank was emptying.

Beach's tanned face paled in an instant. Someone began to mutter a prayer. Duroc wondered whether he was pleading with God for the Elder's return to life or consignment to death.

"I cannot give my approval to your suggestion, Elder Beach," said Duroc. "Matters such as this are not in my jurisdiction. If you want to take over the council, you will have to settle the affair with Elder Seth himself."

There was a hydraulic hiss, and the tankseal was broken. Dry-ice smoke puffed out and descended like white candyfloss to the floor.

Duroc turned. A thin, naked arm stretched out of the tank, pushing up the lid.

Nguyen Seth sat up, the electrodes falling from his white, hairless chest.

The Elder smiled. "A welcoming committee?"

Beach bowed low, trembling. "Yes, Elder."

"How gratifying. Roger, bring me my robe."

Duroc handed him a black kimono from the coatstand. He knotted it about his middle, and stepped out of the tank as spryly as if he had just lain down for a mid-day catnap and awoken refreshed rather than been in a near-death state for the better part of a year.

"Elder Beach," Seth said. "I am calling a Council meeting in the Central Conclave of the Tabernacle. See to it that the Inner Circle are all assembled within an hour. The timing is vital."

Beach backed out through his crowd of supporters, most of whom trailed after him, crushing through the doors in an undignified retreat. Elder Wiggs remained, speechless, his eyes fixed on Seth.

"Elder Wiggs?" said Nguyen Seth. "Have you no business to be about?"

Wiggs apologized, and ran off.

Seth laughed, and Duroc felt the chill of the room.

"Roger, we must be strong. This day's work will not be easeful, nor overly pleasant."

Duroc bowed his head.

"We must call to one of the Dark Ones to deal with the Moon Woman..."

A shiver began in Duroc's spine, but he held it in, refusing to let his shoulders shake.

"We must summon up the Jibbenainosay."

III

Dr Ottokar Proctor was content with his life. He had food, shelter and an interest. He needed nothing more. His knife flicked away at the hardwood, etching in the eyes of Michigan J Frog, one-time-only star of Chuck Jones classic *One Froggy Evening* (1955). First, he found the character inside the wood, then he cut away to create a rough approximation, and finally he did the fine work with the knifepoint. In the last few months, he had whittled away at the remnants of furniture which still cluttered up the monastery, creating a horde of Bugs Bunnies, Daffy Ducks, Road Runners, Coyotes, Sylvesters, Tweety-Pies, Elmer Fudds, Foghorn Leghorns, Pepe le Pews, Speedy Gonzalezes, Yosemite Sams and Porky Pigs. He kept returning to these archetypes, rendering them in each and every one of their multifarious moods. He had a Daffy with pointed teeth bared in his bill, building up to an explosive rage, and a Coyote with eyeballs twice the size of the rest of him, appalled at the approaching doom unleashed by an inexpressive, beep-beeping bird. Now, he had run through the roster of Warner Brothers' major characters, he was applying himself to the lesser-known greats: forgotten stars from the Thirties like Bosko the Talkink Kid and his girlfriend Honey, Foxy, Piggy and Fluffy, Goopy Geer, Buddy and Cookie, and that proto-Elmer Fudd, Egghead; and memorable but unprolific creations like Marvin the Martian, Witch Hazel, Hippety Hopper, Private Snafu, Spike and Chester, Claude Cat, Henery Hawk, Ralph Wolf and Sam Sheepdog from *Ready, Woolen and Able* (1960), the pathetic Merlin the Magic Mouse, Second Banana and Cool Cat. If there was anyone missing from the line-up, he couldn't think of him...

Inside his mind, there was a non-stop chase, as his carvings pursued each other through doors in the ceiling, dodged falling battleships, pulled off and replaced their heads, dressed up as busty cheerleaders with lipsticky, heart-shaped mouths and spit curls, swallowed exploding firecrackers, were reduced to charcoal briquettes and reassembled, switched on and off the lightbulbs over their heads, shot each other with ever larger guns, and reduced rivals to their essential atoms. Elmer Fudd shushed the audience with "be vewwy quiet, I'm hunting wabbits!" Marvin the Martian disappeared in the beam of a disintegrator ray as Space Cadet Porky Pig sneered "Take that, you thing from another world you!" Daffy Duck dropped 126 storeys inside an icebox while Bugs snickered "Ain't I the stinker?" The Road Runner beep-beeped, and the Coyote ordered earthquake pills, boulder suits ('impress your friends – be a rock!') and economy-size holes from the Acme Mail Order company. It was Rabbit Season, it was Duck Season. There was non-stop music, and bright colour, and no one was ever hurt. His creations were destroyed and remade in the time it takes to cut from one shot to another.

Dr Ottokar Proctor smiled to himself. He had finally found the world of his dreams.

But on the wharf, waiting for Bugs and Daffy, was a parcel, freighted all the way from Tasmania, with breathing holes cut into it. Inside the parcel, bright eyes shone with hunger, with greed, with irrational and unstoppable violence...

Soon, Bugs and Daffy would open the crate, and the Devil would be free again.

IV

NGUYEN SETH WAS *much relaxed by his spell in the isolation tank. His spirit had been drawn to the edge of the Outer Darkness and been in communion with the Dark Ones. Ba'alberith, the Mythwrhn, Nyarlathotep and the Jibbenainosay were gathered on the lip of the funnel that led down to the Earth, vast and formless, their energies gathering as they merged into one mass of power, then recreated themselves as distinct entities. Too much time spent in the world of men had robbed Seth of his appreciation for those whom he served. It was too easy to be distracted by the petty concerns of the Elders of Joseph, by the ridiculous politicking of the countries and corps of the world, by the confused tangle of personal relationships. His mindlink with Jessamyn Bonney had dragged him too deep into the mire of humanity, tainted his purpose with hatred, love, desire. When the girl became one with the Ancient Adversary, his entire being had screamed in an inexpressible agony. He had nearly been dislodged from his earthly form, and only been able to survive by slipping into his trance, allowing his spirit to wander, unfettered by the concerns of his flesh...*

The Dark Ones had been angered by the ascendancy of their enemy, and Seth had a mind-stretching vision of the eternal wars, feuds, rivalries and alliances of the Outer Darkness. The business to which his everlasting life was devoted was but one of a series of skirmishes fought on planes beyond even his understanding, between forces he could only vaguely comprehend. As Ba'alberith and the Mythwrhn combined their essences like gases creating a liquid, Seth realized just how alien these beings were, not only to his human perceptions – it took a spell in the Outer Darkness to remind him how close to humankind he really was, just one step beyond their tininess – but to the entire matter of the physical universe through which the Earth spun like a forgotten ball of mud and water. The Dark Ones had their histories, their cultures, their tragedies, their humours, but they were beyond anything he could even imagine. Time had no meaning in the Darkness, but the entire span of terrestrial history was but a brief armistice in the war between the Three Shades of Dark and the forces of Nullification. A myriad parallel universes were bunched together in a knot tied by Azathoth, the Crawling Chaos, and the Dark Ones were penetrating his own reality just as the Nullifiers were infiltrating other timelines. He had a vision of other Nguyen Seths, living through other eternities, under other names, and he was able to pick out the billion specks that were the multiple souls his lives had touched.

As a lesson to him, Ba'alberith had allowed him to dip into an alternate in which he was a fearsome sorcerer, rotting behind a mask in a seven-turreted castle at the edge of a great empire, doing battle with swordsmen, magicians and a leech lady. Seth was whipped through this life in an instant, from a violent clash on a primordial plane to another, fifteen thousand blood-soaked years later, in the heart of his castle. It was over within the blinking of an eye. From this experience, Seth learned the futility of a pure devotion to self. In that life, he had been simply obsessed with his continuing existence, with the gratification of his every whim and impulse. Upon his death, he had left nothing behind him in that universe except dust and bad memories. When he returned to his Earth, to the course of his history, he would be humbled. He would live purely to do the bidding of the Dark Ones, happy in the knowledge that in his servitude his life would mean something. He was the man born to end the world, and he would leave behind him the void through which the Dark Ones could have access to his physical universe, the predestined site of their Great Tourneys, the killing games from which would emerge the Three Champions of the Night who would join battle with the Nullifiers for the fate of the eternally expanding Empire of the Actual and its infinite number of Shadow Selves.

All this was far in the future, far beyond any physical life he could expect, but he knew he would be present in some altered form at the end of the conflict. From the lip of the funnel, he saw the timelines spiralling away into the Darkness. The culmination of his struggles was within his grasp, and beyond that was the restful blackness of the Nothing that would be the lot of the peoples of the Earth. He would bring them a merciful oblivion, freeing them from the need to endure through another cycle of pain and suffering as the whole story was played out again.

This was the future, he knew; but it was also the past. The Outer Darkness was set sideways against the progress of time...

He stepped back into his body at various points through his long career, reinforcing his original decisions, initiating sequences of action whose consequences would only become apparent as the 20th Century drew to its fiery close. He relived his finest moments, his memories becoming the realer as he sped through them, cannonballing through his own life towards the Nguyen Seth who waited in his tank in Salt Lake City.

Back in the world, he was possessed by the needs of his flesh, and took the time to satiate himself before gathering the Twelve Elders of Joseph in the Central Chamber of the Tabernacle.

Back on the lip of the funnel, the Jibbenainosay gathered itself, the alien matter of a hundred universes concentrating in the centre of its cloud, vast discharges of world-shattering electricity signifying its thought processes.

Seth had taken a tendril of the Jibbenainosay with him to the world, and now he would have to pull the whole being through the funnel, and turn it loose...

As he strode through the corridors of the Tabernacle, Roger Duroc at his side, Seth felt the ache in his gut where the tendril ended in a diamond-hard fragment of concentrated matter.

The hurt was growing as the Jibbenainosay squeezed itself towards reality, lusting titanically for the destruction of its adversary. Its Ancient Adversary.

V

A CLAWED HAND reached into his dream, and shook him awake.

Hawk-That-Settles started up in his cot, the blanket falling away from his nakedness, and the claw was around his heart, squeezing.

He forgot his dream, but the world he awoke to was nightmare enough.

The room was full of moonlight, and Krokodil was standing there, cloaked by her hair.

He saw a woman, but he felt the presence of a ghost.

She spoke, in her old voice. "Something is coming through," she said. "We must fight again."

He didn't know what to say. He had emptied a bottle before stumbling to his cot. His thinking was muddied by sleep and tequila, and he felt worse than he would have if he'd been kicked in the head by a mule.

She walked over to the bed, seeming to glide, her hair rippling.

She knelt, hair parting over her body as she stretched her arms out to him. Pale in the light of the full moon, she was lovely.

This was part of the story of the Moon Woman. His father had told him many times of the lucky brave whom the Goddess selected as her lover, and of the many heroic deeds he would later perform.

He wanted her – not just physically, his entire spirit wanted to join with this unearthly creature – and yet he was afraid. When her cool fingers touched him, he stiffened, and shrank away, feeling the stone wall behind his back.

She was not offended by his reluctance, and slipped easily into the narrow cot, pressing the length of her body against his.

Underneath her hair, she wore nothing.

She kissed him on the lips, passing a little of her cool to him. She wasn't even wearing her eyepatch. His eyes open as they kissed, he found himself looking past her fluttering eyelids, first at her clear, green right eye, alive and intelligent, then at the blue crystal facet of her optic burner, dead and deadly. He shut his eyes, and she sucked his tongue into her mouth. Her hands moved up and down his body, tracing the lines of old sandfighting scars, probing the untidiness under his right lung where his ribs had been broken and set out of true.

He touched her, smoothing her flesh. Krokodil felt different from Jesse. He could no longer feel the machinery inside her, as if it had been digested, truly becoming one with her living tissue and bone. Her skin felt silky and cool like a beautiful snake's, and her muscle tone was superb, no longer that of a soldier but of an athlete, a dancer.

With Jesse, lovemaking had been often hurried, rough. She hadn't known her newfound strength, and often left him bruised or even bleeding. They had found pleasure in sex, but no true union. Had their son been born, his spirit would have been divided against itself, the product of two people too wrapped up in themselves to care fully for each other. Now, with Krokodil, it was different. She was confident enough to take him slowly, to caress and cajole him, to prolong their climaxes. Hawk couldn't think of himself as he moved together with her. The memories that came to him were of her; no, they were hers. She was leaking her past into him, just as she was sipping his spirit...

Jessamyn, Jazzbeaux, Jesse, Frankenstein's Daughter. He loved all the fragments of the person she was still becoming...

If only, he wondered, he could love Krokodil.

When it was over, they lay awake in each other's arms, their bodies too charged and relaxed for sleep, and Hawk's fugitive spirit returned, plunging him back into himself.

They didn't move. The moonlight fell on their bodies, dappling them as if with a skin disease.

Hating himself for it, Hawk wondered if he was being rewarded, consoled or persuaded.

The moon set, and daylight inched into the room.

"Tonight," she said to him. "It will come. Hawk-That-Settles, you must help me get ready for it."

VI

The Inner Circle sat around the table, nervously waiting. Elder Beach was doodling on a notepad, crosses, goats, and skulls with Josephite hats. Roger Duroc stood by the door as Nguyen Seth walked around the room, taking a full, slow circuit of the table. He seemed to pause momentarily behind each Elder, and to a man they tensed as if expecting a killing blow.

"Brothers," said Seth, assuming his seat. "I have gathered you here to demonstrate that the Path of Joseph is never smooth."

The Elders mumbled in collective agreement. Seth smiled, and adjusted his mirrorshades. He still seemed bleached from his spell in the tank, and the mirrorholes made his face look like a grinning skull.

"We must make sacrifices if our Great Work is to be achieved."

Someone said "amen", and other people nodded.

"Blood sacrifices."

This was nothing new.

Seth signalled to Duroc, and he stepped forward.

"Please remove any belongings you have left on the table," he said.

Beach picked up his pad. Elder Hawkins, the financial comptroller of the church, shifted his briefcase. The table was covered with a stiff circle of linoleum. Duroc rolled it up, and took it away.

The table beneath was inset with a series of shallow channels, all feeding into a central funnel.

Everyone looked at the hole in the middle of the table. Suspended in the air by no apparent means was an irregular lump of crystal. It spun slowly, silvery chips in its core catching the light.

Duroc dimmed the lights. The Inner Circle were enraptured by the crystal.

"This is a simple tool for the focusing of our spiritual energies," Seth said. "It is not especially elaborate. I did not foresee that such a great effort on our part would be necessary until some time nearer the fulfilment of our purpose, but Monsieur Duroc has done his best with the materials at hand."

Nobody turned to look at Duroc. He knew this was where the spooky stuff began again.

The crystal rose a little, floating a few inches above the level of the table. It pulsed now, seeming to change its solid form as it spun, faster and faster.

"I would ask you to concentrate your prayers on the Cynosure."

Beach was sweating, but could not take his eyes away from the crystal. The others mainly seemed hypnotized, completely lost in the Cynosure's spell.

There was a blot of darkness in the centre of the Cynosure now, an absence of matter.

"Roger," Seth said. "Bring it to me."

Duroc took the dagger out of his pocket. It was old, and he had no idea what its culture of origin could have been. The handle had once been covered in carved designs, but many hands had worn these away to suggestive shapes. The blade was long, thin and honed to perfection. Carefully, Duroc gave the instrument to Seth. The Elder held it up, catching the light along its silvered edge.

With his left hand, Seth unfastened the tags on his kimono and bared his chest. The Inner Circle observed with interest, and just a touch of dread.

Duroc's hand settled on the butt of the revolver slung in the small of his back, under his coat. He had orders not to allow anyone to break the circle.

"Brothers, I beseech your blessings upon the endeavour of this day."

The chorused "amen" was ragged, unenthusiastic.

Seth stood up, allowing his robe to fall open. He touched the point of the dagger to a spot an inch above his knotted navel, and eased the tip inside him. His jaw was set, and he contained a groan as he slipped the metal into his flesh.

Elder Curran put a hand over his mouth to contain his disgust.

Inch by inch, Nguyen Seth fed the dagger into his body. No blood flowed from the wound. Seth's shoulders heaved as he probed the inside of his stomach, and he choked back yelps of pain.

Elder Javna tried to stand up, but Duroc placed a hand on his shoulder, gently forcing him back into his seat.

Seth gave out a cry and put out his hands to steady himself against the table. The dagger shook, and slowly slid out of the wound, as if pushed by something inside the man's vitals.

He grabbed the handle, and shifted the blade in the hole, enlarging it. A light came from inside him, a violet-white light. He withdrew the dagger and dropped it. His stomach was heaving now, the slit pulsating as something inside tried to be born.

With his fingers, he peeled the lips of the aperture away, and the light shot out. It moved fast, and struck the Cynosure.

There was a flash and everyone covered their eyes. Blinking, Duroc looked at the crystal. The darkness at its heart was replaced with the light from inside Seth, and the light was rhythmically pounding like a beating heart.

Seth was chanting now, in a language Duroc had heard before but could not identify. He spoke the words of a ritual that was old when continents were young.

As he chanted, some of the Elders joined in, infiltrating newer prayers into his rite. The words didn't matter, just the feelings. Seth massaged his wound, smoothing it shut, and it seemed to shrink, to pucker into a second navel.

Yellow fluid was leaking from the corner of his mouth as he continued to speak the words of power.

Elder Wiggs had his hands locked together in traditional prayer, and his eyes jammed shut. Nothing he could do could make this go away.

Apart from the ceremony, Duroc was awed by its beauty. He tried to look away from the Cynosure, but was incapable of heeding any distraction. The crystal was expanding now, almost like an egg swelled to the point of bursting by a hatchling.

Hawkins screamed, his cry lost in the rising chant. Many voices were issuing from Seth's mouth now, a choir lodged in his throat. Hawkins grabbed his chest and struggled in his seat. The man had a history of angina, Duroc knew. He was having a seizure. Perhaps a fatal seizure. Nobody made a move to help him. He spasmed, kicking the tablelegs, his hands twitching on the table, fingertips scrabbling at the channels.

Seth held out the dagger, and passed it to the Elder on his right hand, Curran. The handsome man, a former televangelist, examined it as if it were a fine cigar, but had no idea what to do with it. Duroc stepped in and showed him, pulling Curran's sleeve away from his wrist, and tracing a line along the artery from hand's heel to the inside of the elbow.

He had once explained it in a lecture to the Violent Tendency on avoiding torture. "Find something sharp, and bare your arm. Remember, across – for the hospital. Along – for the morgue."

Poking his tongue out with concentration, Curran stuck the dagger into his wrist, and pulled it down. He was inexpert, but he severed the artery. Blood gushed, and fell onto the table. His hand fell, and the wrist continued to pump out blood. The red trickle flowed into the channel, and towards the Cynosure.

Wiggs picked up the knife, crossed himself, and struck down with such force that he nearly severed his left hand. He smiled as if relieved, and his blood joined Curran's.

"No," said the next Elder, half-rising. Duroc thumb-jabbed him in the back of the neck, forced his head down onto the table, and slit his throat. The channels were thick with blood now.

Seth's chanting was a deafening thunder now.

"Joseph is merciful," said Elder Javna, surgically opening his wrist, "Joseph is..."

Next was Hawkins. Duroc put the dagger in his leaping hand, but he couldn't get a proper grip on it. Duroc made as if to take the knife himself, but suddenly the Elder found his last strength. He took the blade, and thrust it at his burning heart. Duroc heard metal scrape bone. After a brief and bloody frenzy, Hawkins fell forwards. He must have been the first of the Inner Circle to die.

Most of them didn't have to be prompted. Those who hesitated, shut their eyes and did the deed after a touch from Duroc.

Beach was the last. He opened his throat with resignation, knowing he had no choice. Duroc took the dagger from him, and wiped it off with a handkerchief.

Seth's chant slowed to a whisper.

The twelve Elders of Joseph slowly emptied, their flowing blood picking out intricate patterns in the shallow bowl of the table. The Cynosure was splattered red, and still pulsed.

Then, it imploded, shrinking to a red dot with an audible pop as air rushed into the vacuum where the crystal had been. Electrical discharges crackled, and the dead and dying men writhed, cries wrung from their throats. Beach stood up, a bib of blood standing out on his black vest. He half-turned and collapsed, as if the life were suddenly whipped out of him.

There was a smell of ozone in the air. Duroc saw Elder Curran's plump face shrink onto his skull in an instant, all the moisture sucked somehow out of his corpse.

The red dot shot up into the air like a firefly, and exploded. Nguyen Seth finished his rite, and sat down, exhausted, among his dead followers.

Duroc saw the dot whizzing up into the vaulted arches of the Tabernacle. The central chamber was a hundred and twenty feet high, and the light was careening off the ceiling.

There was a great wind. Hawkins' briefcase came open, and a storm of papers circled like a tornado.

Duroc suddenly felt tired, as if all his strength were being sapped in a single draught. He sank to his knees, his head swimming, and held fast to one of the chairs. A great weight seemed to fall upon him, pushing him downwards. The floor was covered in sticky blood.

He tried to raise his head, to look up, but couldn't.

Above him, floating under the domes of the Tabernacle was something vast, unearthly and hungry. It had forced itself through into the world with Nguyen Seth, and nourished itself on the lives of the Elders of Joseph.

Duroc was surrounded by hanging tentacles, as if an unimaginably huge jellyfish were hovering above him. The tendrils brushed him, but did no harm. He felt almost lulled by the contact. The sensations they brought were entirely new, beyond pleasure or pain. It would be easy to sit here forever under this shower, exploring the new feelings.

Then the tentacles were gone.

"Roger," said Seth. "Permit me to present to you one of the Dark Ones whom we serve."

Duroc forced himself to look up at the enormous, amorphous entity that hung above them. It was beautiful, it was terrible. He had been expecting an angel, a demon or a monster, but this was none of those. This was a prodigy, an anomaly. He wasn't sure it actually existed. Its surface rippled as if it were a liquid, or a turbulent gas contained in a molecule-thin balloon of living matter. It had eyes, faces, mouths, hands, but they were like nothing Duroc had seen on any earthly creature. Inside it somewhere, organs pumped and pulsed and squirted. It had a smell, a taste, a sound.

For the first time since leaving the seminary, Roger Duroc felt like worshipping something.

The Jibbenainosay descended. No, it expanded downwards, extruding thick feelers with tips like clawed mouths. One slunk towards Duroc, but his raised hand warded it away, and it fastened instead on the dead head of Elder Hawkins.

Other tentacles came for the other corpses. Some burrowed through the black cloth covering the backs of men who had fallen face-forward onto the table, some attached to hands, some to shoulders, some to stomachs. One clasped Beach by the face, and dug through his head, swelling his neck as it latched onto the inside of his chest.

"It needs flesh, Roger," said Seth.

"Why have you brought it here?"

The Elder took off his dark glasses. His eyes gleamed.

"The Krokodil must die."

* * *

VII

KROKODIL NEEDED HIM now. She used up three days' water cleaning herself off, and asked him to cut her hair. Using a stiletto she gave him, he did his best to shear away her black tent, and then she tied what was left up in a knot. She looked a little like some of the women on the Reservation. She found her eyepatch, and slipped it on. Then she dressed in clean clothes, and sat cross-legged in the courtyard. Hawk-That-Settles sensed her nervousness, her uncertainty. If this was the Sixth Level of Spirituality, he was glad to remain comparatively unenlightened. For a moment, she was the old Jesse, then she was the cold-blooded reptile woman again. The song was drawing to its close. In some old movie he had seen, there was an Indian who got up every morning, looked around, and said "this is a good day to die." He had thought that absurd. He had a bottle of tequila left, but he just poured it out and watched it seep into the sand.

"Gentlemen, I'm afraid this is all completely beyond me. My background is purely in the military uses of satellite technology."

"Mr President, this is completely beyond all of us. It's an anomaly we can't explain, like the business with the Sea of Tranquillity last year."

"Run the stats by me again, General Pendarves."

"Well, one of our geostationary spy satellites was knocked off course last year by an electrical failure. Its orbit has been deteriorating ever since, and we expect it to burn up sometime in late 2025. We have not been able to control it, but we have still been able to get data from its sensors."

"So we've been peeking in backyards?"

"More or less. Until recently, we've just been able to track a few wolves and trappers in the Canadian wastes.

But three weeks ago, we had another kink in the course, and the damn thing ended up over Utah."

"Deseret, General. Deseret. We renamed it, remember? It was a plank of the election platform."

"Yes, sir, Deseret. Since it's only notionally United States territory, we saw no harm in taking a look. Some of the reports that have been creeping back have been disturbing."

"I have every confidence in Nguyen Seth, gentlemen. He is a true example of the pioneer spirit that has made this country great."

"Yes, yes, yes… but there are things going on in Salt Lake that we have no explanations for. Mr Fenin has been monitoring them."

"There have been disturbances."

"What, earthquakes? Typhoons?"

"Maybe, Mr President. But along with that they have an assortment of phenomena we have no handle on. Mr Fenin is from our ESP division."

"Mr Fenin?"

"Mr President."

"We turned the data over to him."

"And?"

"And I have a few precedents for this, but nothing that makes sense. There's an immense power source of some sort in Salt Lake City, apparently in the depths of the Josephite Tabernacle itself."

"But the Josephites are back-to-the-land types, surely. They're not tekkies. They wouldn't set up a nuclear power plant, would they?"

"Not that kind of power, sir. Non-physical power. We haven't really got a name for it. Psychic force, spiritual energy, call it what you will."

"The United States of America does not recognize ghosties and ghoulies, Mr Fenin. And I can't recall authorizing any expenditure for a department of magical crackpots!"

"Sir, if you'll recall, the Soviets are very advanced in this field. The previous administration felt there was a psychic gap. President Heston appointed James Earl Carter to head the Commission."

"Balloon juice, gentlemen. I won't hear any of this."

"But, Mr President, there is every possibility of some cataclysmic force being unleashed..."

"That is abject nonsense, and you are aware of it. I believe it might be time to relieve you of your command, General."

"Mr President..."

"I'll hear no more of this. Mr Fenin, good day. General Pendarves, you will report to this office tomorrow for reassignment. The issue is closed. Ghosts... pah!"

Dr Ottokar Proctor saw the Indian cutting the woman's hair, and kept out of their way. Afterwards, he went into the cell, and gathered up the hair. It was soft, and smelled sweet. He wanted it.

Inside his mind, a crate from Tasmania shook. Nails came loose.

His eyes focused properly. His knife slipped as he was working on Bugs's teeth, and he cut himself.

Licking his finger, he tasted blood.

"Your holiness, we believe the ground zero will be in Southern Arizona, near the Mexican border. In the Gila Desert."

Pope Georgi I looked at the mapscreen. Father O'Shaughnessy amplified the projection and narrowed down the area.

"Somewhere about here." He tapped the screen with his pointer.

"What's this name?"

"Santa de Nogueira. It's an old monastery."

"Ours?"

"It was, but it's been empty for over a century and a half. We still own the ground, but only through a Spanish land grant that probably has no legal status."

"Is anybody there?"

"Somebody must be, or the demon wouldn't be on its way."

"Who?"

O'Shaugnessy lit his pipe. "There, Holy Father, you have me. Cardinal Mapache is scouting the area…"

"The prophet?"

"He's an esper, Holiness."

"Indeed."

"He is trying to divine any presences in the monastery."

"Results?"

O'Shaugnessy exhaled smoke. "Mixed. There are at least three people in the building, probably refugees from justice. The deserts are full of criminal factions, juvenile delinquents. But it's not the people who interest Mapache."

The Pope frowned. "Continue."

"There seems to be a supernatural presence."

"A demon?"

"That's hard to say. It is attached somehow to one of the people, but not in a standard possession. Mapache says they have formed some sort of gestalt."

"Is that orthodox?"

"The Holy Spirit has spoken through human beings before. The son of God took mortal flesh."

"You are flirting with blasphemy."

"Blasphemy and I are just good friends, Holy Father."

The Pope smiled.

"Can we get anyone there in time?"

"Mapache says no. Sister Chantal is busy in Kamchatka, and Mother Kazuko Hara is still convalescing. I don't think we have anyone else qualified to handle something like this."

"Your suggestions?"

O'Shaughnessy spread his hands. "Prayer, Holy Father."

DUROC WATCHED THE Jibbenainosay disappear into the sky like a Montgolfier balloon, and was relieved to see the thing getting further away from him. It still trailed its corpses like puppets, and had sprouted some non-organic looking appendages that seemed capable of doing plenty of severe damage. He got the impression that even Nguyen Seth wasn't exactly unhappy to see the Dark One off on its way to get Jessamyn Bonney.

Duroc couldn't believe that it had come to this. The Jibbenainosay was something you called up if you wanted to sink Antarctica, not take out an eighteen-year-old girl. Of course, the Manolo and Proctor options hadn't proved effective. Jessamyn – Krokodil, she was calling herself now – was demonstrating an unsuspected resilience. Still, she would have no chance against the Dark One.

Then, Duroc supposed, Seth would have the problem of finding something else to keep the Jibbenainosay occupied.

IT DIDN'T RAIN any more, but sometimes this part of the desert was visited by violent sandstorms. Hawk-That-Settles thought one was coming along. At the height of the afternoon, the wind began to blow gently, and sand drifted against the walls of Santa de Nogueira. He hadn't seen Dr Proctor around all day, but that didn't worry him. It would probably be time to gather the womenfolks indoors, board up the windows and sit tight until it blew over. But he knew Krokodil wasn't going to be be the proper squaw and let him protect her from the elements. She stood on her chapel roof, looking unblinking to the North as the sand blew in her face.

ERICH VON RICHTER, born Ethan Ryker, pulled back the joystick and lifted his Fokker up over the turbulence. He had been with the Red Baron for three years now, giving air cover for the Flying Circus's raids. They only had two planes, but the rest made do with Kustom Kars kitted out with razor-edged biplane wings and machete-blade propellors.

The convoy was down on the road, drawing level with a couple of eighteen-wheelers. He was alone in the skies today, because the Baron had some business with the yaks in Welcome. He was turning over a percentage of the scav for a tankerload of fuel, and an extension of the warranty on the Fokkers.

Von Richter loved flying, but he didn't care for the aerobatics that were the Baron's special thrill. He much preferred laying down a blanket of napalm in front of an interstate wrapper, or opening up with his twin burpguns, kicking up ruts in the road and puncturing the running groundrats.

His old man had sprayed crops for a living, back when there were crops. This was a much better way to use the skies.

"Yo, Rikki," said Heidi in his earchip. She was groundleader for the day. "We have the camels in sight. Are you available?"

"There's some weird whirlwind effect up here."

"If you can't handle it, we'll be okay without you, flyboy."

Heidi was always taunting him, jockeying for his plane. "Nothing I can't breeze through, roadcrawler. Remember, you're talking to an ace."

He dipped the bird's nose into the turbulence and swooped down. It was rougher than he had thought. The stick jarred in his hands, bruising his palms.

The motors cut out and the Fokker fell thirty feet like a deadweight before they cut in again. That shouldn't happen.

"Flyboy, what are you fucking around for? This is combat, here. Squirt some lighter fluid on those trucks and leave it to the Arizona Korps."

He didn't answer Heidi. He was too busy with the stick, trying to regain control of the biplane.

Suddenly, he was surrounded by a cloud. No, there were no clouds in the Big Empty. It must be smoke. It was black and thick, as if night had fallen in an instant. It wasn't like regular air. The instruments weren't responding properly.

Von Richter shivered as the temperature fell. Ice formed inside his goggles, and his sweat crystallized.

The engine stopped, and he tried to scream. A gust froze his throat.

The Fokker didn't fall. It was suspended in the black cloud.

"Rikki, what is that fucking thing up there? Tell me I'm having a GloJo flashback."

Von Richter thumbed his gun controls and the guns chattered, spinning bullets and cartridge casings into the black. They emptied quickly, but he still kept pressing.

This was serious weird shit.

A face ten feet across appeared in the blackness. It was more or less human. Von Richter screamed, and beat his hands against the ribbed canvas.

The face's thick lips opened, and a white beak pushed out, opening three ways. A violet thing shot out of the beak, and latched onto Von Richter's face.

Tiny filaments threaded instantaneously through his entire body, and there was a mighty tug as the black thing turned him inside-out.

The Fokker fell out of the sky, and crashed into the sand, surrounded by chunks of ice. Pieces of Erich von Richter rained down around the wreckage.

The Jibbenainosay sped onwards, towards the South, thinking less of its latest prey than a desert wanderer does a single grain of sand.

The Arizona Korps didn't stop to bury their ace.

Dr Proctor had been polishing his knife. When the Indian came into the wine cellar, he looked up, teeth bared again.

"Hello, Tonto," he said.

The Ancient Adversary was puzzled. The Vessel was not what he had expected, not the titanic being that could bestride a world and wrestle mind-to-mind with the Dark Ones.

This Jessamyn Bonney was so fragile, so slim, like a butterfly. It knew a moment of doubt. Then, it firmed its resolve.

It was shrunken inside Jessamyn now, inside Krokodil.

Alone, Nguyen Seth *sat in his library. The Jibbenainosay was on the loose, and Krokodil could not withstand it.*

Inside his mind, he could still hear her: tick-tock, tick-tock, tick-tock...

He opened a book, but could not concentrate on the text, could not even recognize the language in which it was written.

This distraction must end soon. There were things to be done. He had another demon to summon, a subtler fiend, and a more complicated enemy to be struck down.

The Jesuits were becoming a nuisance. He would have to do something about the Vatican.

The sand was blowing hard, stinging her face. This was the first sign of the Jibbenainosay.

She remembered her dead foes: Daddy Bruno, Miss Liberty, eyeless Holm Rodriguez, Susie Spam-in-the-Can Terhune, Bronson Manolo. And Dr Proctor, not dead but neutralized.

Behind all the faces, she saw Elder Seth.

The Krokodil part of her knew what was coming, what the Jibbenainosay was, and it was afraid. That was a first for it.

The Jessamyn Bonney part didn't care any more.

On the road, Trooper Nathan Stack was concentrating on the screen, wondering again whether he should try to be reassigned. He didn't know whether riding with Leona was a good idea after their break-up, but he wasn't sure if he could stand the thought of some other grunt drawing the duty. Sergeant Leona Tyree handled the United States Cavalry cruiser with expert ease. They had had a call-in from an interstate convoy, out of Phoenix for the East. Someone hadn't paid off the yaks, and a polite oriental gentleman in a suit had made a scrambled telephone call, and the Arizona Korps were cutting loose again.

Stack saw a shower of blips on the screen. "Dead ahead, Leona. Five ve-hickles. They're stalled."

Then, the whole screen lit up, a solid mass of light.

The cruiser swerved as Tyree looked over at the radar, but she got it back on the hardtop.

The glitch was gone.

"What was that?"

Stack tapped the screen. "According to this heap of junk, that was a flying object the size of the U S S Nimitz."

Tyree laughed. "You startled me there. I'll have the system stripped and overhauled when we get back to Fort Apache."

"Yeah."

A thought occurred to him. "Say, Leona, do you want me to log it as a UFO?"

Tyree sneered. "Nahhh. That gag's stale already."

THE JIBBENAINOSAY CLEAVED through the air, gradually delighting in the unfamiliar sensations of physical existence. The human brains it had absorbed taught it much about this universe. Its new form was awkward in some ways, but there were things about it that offered possibilities.

It had never had things to hurt before. It found that it enjoyed inflicting pain. Even more, it relished taking away the spark of life from these scumspeck beings.

Soon, this universe would belong to the Dark Ones.

"DR PROCTOR, YOU'RE?"

"Better?" The Devil laughed in his face. "Yes, I suppose I am."

Hawk-That-Settles was backed up against a winerack. The bottles were long gone, but in their nests were a series of figurines. This was where Dr Proctor stored his cartoon creations.

The Devil had his whittling knife, and was making leisurely passes with it, just under Hawk's nose.

"There's a storm coming, isn't there Tonto? I can feel it in the air."

"Yes. A bad one."

"Do you perhaps know anything about the history of your people?"

Hawk gulped, the shining knifepoint a hair's breadth away from his adam's apple.

"Of course you do. You are a Son of Geronimo, are you not?"

Hawk nodded his head.

"Do you know what General Phil Sheridan, the war hero, said?"

Hawk knew what was coming next.

"'The only good Indians I ever saw,' old Phil said, 'were dead.'"

Hawk's eyes went to the doorway. It was too far off. He would never make it.

"Tonto, how would you like to be a good Indian?"

She remembered Doc Threadneedle trying to tell her to stay human. She supposed he wouldn't have been proud of her.

The horizon was invisible now, the air thick with sand. She could hear the Jibbenainosay coming through the whirling winds.

Krokodil hoped there was a way she could make it up to the Doc.

Where was Hawk-That-Settles? He should be here to see her take the final steps, to see her progress to the Seventh Level of Spirituality and beyond.

It loomed out of the sands like a whale, and towered over her. There was a face in the middle of it.

She recognized the likeness of Nguyen Seth.

It smiled, feelers leaking from its black eyelids.

She remembered her father's favourite saying from Nietzsche. What does not kill me makes me stronger.

"Come on, Jib," she said. "Make me stronger."

VIII

Dr Proctor's knife shook, the point just under Hawk's chin.

Then, the world turned upside-down.

The Devil was pulled across the room, as the wineracks wrapped around him. Hawk was struck to his knees by a flying brick. He saw the stones of the ceiling shake loose. Ancient mortar fell as white dust.

Hawk choked, and held an arm up to ward off falling masonry. The whole monastery was going to come down on his head, thousands of tons of European stone.

Sand was blowing through in a throat-filling hurricane. Hawk covered his mouth. You could drown in this thick swirl.

He couldn't see Dr Proctor any more, but he could hear the man thrashing around, breaking the wineracks like matchwood. A carved Yosemite Sam hit him in the face. There was a lot of debris flying around, as if the cellar were the focus of a giant whirlwind.

The floor fell, like an aircraft hitting a pocket of turbulence, and Hawk plunged down with it, landing hard. He thought his ankle might be broken.

He knew this wasn't an earthquake.

A chunk of ceiling struck the flagstones, and burst like a stone frag grenade. Hawk heard Dr Proctor scream as the shrapnel hit him.

Hawk looked up, and saw light through the hole. Stones disappeared, pulled upwards, and sunlight, filtered through sand, streamed in. The whole of Santa de Nogueira was being pulled apart and tossed into the air. This was in the cellars. Hawk couldn't imagine what it would take to pick the structure apart piece by piece and still keep the chunks in the air.

Then he was seized by hands of wind, and tugged upright like a marionette. Pain lanced through his chest. He must have broken his ribs again.

The sand got into his eyes, his nose, his mouth. He shook his head, trying to fight the smothering blasts. There was nothing solid under his feet any more, and yet he was being drawn upwards.

Stones bounced off his head and shoulders as he rose through the storm. It was only a question of how soon he would be smashed against a lump large enough to do serious damage.

Through the sand, he could see Dr Proctor, also floating steadily upwards. The madman's limbs flailed, and he was screeching. To think that Hawk had feared Dr Proctor, had imagined that this pathetic puppet was the Devil.

They were well out of the cellars now. Hawk couldn't see any ground below, but thought it must be hundreds of feet beneath him. They were above the layer of the whirling stones. The skeleton of the monastery still stood, stripped of its bulk.

Hawk had flown in his spirit dreams, but this was the first time his physical form had been so elevated. In his dreams, he had walked the winds with the wendigo and the eagle ghosts. Now, he was helpless, a kite without strings, buffeted this way and that. Rising slowly, he had the sensation of falling from a great height, picking up speed as he shot towards the iron-hard ground.

Then, suddenly, he was above the sandcloud, floating in the still air. Dr Proctor broke the surface of the sandstorm at the same time, and the two men shouted to each other.

There was calm here, and a light breeze. The storm below was like a sea of agitated grit. Stones, wooden beams and gravemarkers were tossed on the surface of the clouds, being thrown up and sucked down. Krokodil was down there somewhere, swimming through the sand. The sky stretched away to a blue infinity, and the sun bore down on them.

In the gentle warmth, Hawk suddenly felt all the injuries he had sustained in his flight upwards. His face had been effectively sandblasted, and one of his legs hung useless.

He couldn't hear what Dr Proctor was shouting, but it didn't matter. Words were no good. All the songs Two-Dogs-Fucking had taught his son were no good. There was no adequate response.

The thing that hung above the storm, its tendrils dangling into the sandclouds, was unquestionably a gitche manitou. Hawk couldn't bear to look at it, and yet he was unable to turn his head away. The Jibbenainosay was dark beyond darkness. Hawk supposed that a black hole must look like this, concentrated and yet immense. It was not a being Hawk could ever have shared a universe with.

It made the sky seem small.

IX

It left the chapel alone, but tore up everything else in sight. Millions of tons of sand tossed around her, but she was in a bubble of empty air. The Jibbenainosay was cloaked in its storm now, but she could sense its bulk beyond the chaos. The entity was big enough to be infested with Godzillas the way a dog has ticks. For all its size, it appeared light, almost insubstantial. Krokodil knew it was from another place entirely, and she didn't mean Oz, Heaven or Akron, Ohio.

She saw its summoning in her mind. There was Elder Seth cutting himself open, surrounded by the bleeding dead. And there was the Jibbenainosay billowing inside a cathedral, squirming into the universe, the foul-smelling shit of some other reality.

Also, she knew that inside her was something that recognized the Dark One, that knew its secret names and the nature of its multiple existence. Something which, in another life, could even claim kinship with the Jibbenainosay. This was the thing that had helped her best Dr Proctor, had hauled her up to the Sixth Level, had made her Krokodil.

Whatever it was that possessed her, she hoped it would have the resources to fight this world-gobbling thing.

A tentacle shot out of the sand, and she brushed it aside. Its sweat stung.

She swung down from the perch, and dived into the sand. She expected to be engulfed, but her bubble travelled with her. Standing in front of the door to the chapel, she braced herself. The chapel must be the last of Santa de Nogueira. There were excavations in the earth where the storm had uprooted and scattered the monastery's subterranean cellars and passageways.

The bubble expanded, and she saw the ruin that was left where the courtyard had been. The flagstones were gone, and even the sand stripped away. The surface was uneven, strewn with detritus. A dome of sand-thick air curved over the area. Krokodil looked up, and saw the bodies sinking through the storm to the fragile bubble.

Several sets of legs dangled into the bubble, and were followed by man-shaped things. They were puppet-strung on tentacles, and twitched like galvanized frogs' legs.

Twelve corpses, dressed in bloodied black, touched down, and bobbed on their tentacles. They were all broken in various ways, but they were sprouting new organs from their rotten flesh. They were poison fungi, Krokodil knew, the stings of the Jibbenainosay.

The Dead Dozen stood in ranks, unsteady but mainly upright. Most of them didn't have faces any more, but those she could see were ordinary. They were dressed in the remains of outfits like the one she always saw Nguyen Seth wearing. One zombie, hunched over because of the tentacle stuck through his spine, even still retained his wide-brimmed pilgrim hat. These people had been Josephites, like Seth's fools from Spanish Fork. She knew more had been sacrificed for the benefit of the Elder's Great Mission.

She looked up at the boiling sand roof of the bubble. The face was there again, between the dangling tentacles.

"Fuck you," she said, opening her optic. Her patch burned away, and the lase struck upwards, striking Seth's laughing face dead centre. It was broken apart, and a shower of sand fell into the bubble, dusting the zombies with muddy dandruff. Krokodil wiped her face off.

The nearest of the Dead Dozen made a grab for her, a bloated scorpion tail uncurling from its mouth. She twisted its neck with both hands, and the body fell lifeless. The disembodied head and its poison appendage still whipped around on its tentacle. The eyes popped on stalks. With an optic blast, she singed it to a skullcinder, and the tentacle was withdrawn in a whipping movement.

She unslung the machine pistol from its shoulder harness, and drew it out from beneath her padded jacket. It was old-fashioned and she doubted whether it would be much use against a Dark One, but there was still a Jazzbeaux part of her that took comfort in Twenty-first century deathware.

She gave the zombies a burst at chest height, and flesh-flowers burst open where her slugs struck home. One or two were damaged beyond repair, and just hung useless, but the rest were still mobile enough to come for her. Her next spray was at head-height, and she gave a few lase jabs with her optic as well.

About half of the Dozen were out of commission. The rest were not recognizable even as former human beings. One scuttled towards her on its hands and the myriad crablegs that sprouted from its hips. Its Josephite hat bobbed as its head receded into the chest cavity. She emptied her clip into it, and it leaped like a Mexican jumping bean, green fluid splashing in spirals. It kept moving until she brought her booted foot down on its spine and pinned it to the ground. She swept with her lase, and severed the tentacle. The Josephite convulsed, and went limp, cockroaches bursting from its split mouths.

The remaining five corpses fell back into a close formation. She slipped a new clip into the pistol, and spattered them with fire. They still stood, linking arms, their tentacle strings twining together like the strands of a rope. They were growing together, forming a composite creature. Arms and legs reached out to steady the roughly spherical, multiply-headed beast. Its umbilical tentacle was thick and rough-skinned, like an elephant's trunk. Skins burst, and organic weapons poked through: stings, claws, mouths. A stiff tube spat pips at her. The tiny things exploded in the air, puffing sick-smelling smoke.

She held her breath and got out of the way. She put another burst of fire into the thing, and it swallowed the bullets with pleasure. Her laser blasts made smoking pinholes, but did no damage.

There were still human heads in the morass, and they were whispering to her.

The thing stumped towards her, agitated, and she danced back towards the chapel. She was always at the centre of the bubble, she noticed. She could not run into the storm and take her chances there.

The thing knew which way she would go, and kept pace with her. The Jibbenainosay was playing around, she realized. It could snip her head off with a single stroke, but it was prolonging the game.

A tightness was growing in her chest. Without knowing why, she opened her mouth and began to suck in air. Her lungs filled, but still she sucked. She inflated a little, but was able to take it. With the wind, she tasted power.

The thing stopped, and stood ten yards away from her, its appendages waving in the draught.

She sucked in more.

Stones came away from the chapel wall, a hundred feet away, and flew through the air.

Her inbreath continued.

She was Krokodil. The Ancient Adversary. She lived only to bring down the Dark Ones.

The thing was shaking now, pulled out of shape by the wind. Its tentacle was tangled, and the strands were parting.

Through her mouth and her nostrils, through the apertures of her eyesockets, through the pores of her skin, Krokodil drew in air…

The thing was struggling with itself. One of its components tore free and, manlike, made a dash for the edge of the Bubble. A pincer struck out, and sheared it in half.

Krokodil paused, and held the breath. There was a terrible quiet.

Then, she exhaled.

X

IN THE TABERNACLE, Nguyen Seth was preaching. He eulogized the sacrifice of the Inner Circle, and vowed to his congregation that their deaths would not be in vain, that their bodies would be foundation stones for the greatness of Deseret. Choirs sang as he spoke, filling the vast space with heavenly music. He was eloquent. His words flew like birds.

Roger Duroc sat near the back, exhausted, not hearing the Elder's speech. His world had been transformed completely by the manifestation of the Jibbenainosay. He was sobered. Now, for the first time, he fully appreciated the vastness of the work upon which he was engaged. Nothing else mattered. Literally, nothing else in the entire history of the universe had ever mattered. His own life was less than nothing, and he was one of the handful of human beings who had anything at all to contribute to the Purpose.

Seth was enthusing the congregation. Tomorrow, when Krokodil was dead, he would select a new Inner Circle, and the process of initiation would begin. Duroc was impressed by the Elder's attention to petty details. A lesser immortal would have sunk to his knees in the presence of the Dark One and let everything else disappear from his mind, but Seth knew how important it was to retain his grip on the minutiae of the Great Work.

Duroc could not think of anything but the Jibbenainosay. When he closed his eyes, he saw the blackness of the thing. Behind the beautiful harmonies of the Josephite Tabernacle Choir, he heard the Dark One's symphonic roar.

Elder Seth recounted the good deeds – manufactured especially for this service – of the martyrs, and listed their names among the saints. Above him, on the cross, a stone Jesus was forgotten, His tear-filled eyes averted from the preacher. This had nothing to do with Him, either.

Then, in the midst of his flight, Seth paused. He put out his hands to the lectern to steady himself, and shook his head.

He did not resume his speech.

Duroc was alerted, and looked up. He left his seat, and joined the throng pressing towards the Elder.

Nguyen Seth was shaking, in the throes of a grand mal seizure. Duroc had seen him like this before, when Krokodil bested Dr Proctor. But this was more serious.

Duroc realized that the finish of the battle being waged to the South would tell heavily on the Elder, whichever way it came out.

Seth staggered away from the altar. His jacket was open, and Duroc saw he was bleeding from the wound in his belly. Yellow tears crept from behind his dark glasses, and trickled down his white cheeks.

Duroc pushed his way through the Josephites. They fell back, reverentially. He knelt by the Elder, and hugged him. Seth was trembling. Duroc held him fast.

He waved his hand. "Clear the Tabernacle," he whispered. His order was taken up, turned into a cry, "Clear the Tabernacle! Clear the Tabernacle! Clear the Tabernacle!"

The people flooded out, until they were alone.

Seth didn't speak. Duroc took his spectacles off, and saw the naked pain in his master's eyes.

Seth's hand found Duroc's arm, and grasped. His fingers fixed painfully into Duroc's flesh.

He was speaking now, an outrush of words in a dead language.

The battle continued...

THE COMPOSITE CREATURE burst like a squashed puffball when Krokodil's blast hit it. Bodies peeled away from its mass, and were smashed into the sandstorm, where they were lost. The tentacle pulled it up off the ground, and its limbs kicked. There were shreds of bone and fleshmatter swirling around, and it was destroyed completely.

Krokodil yelled in her triumph, and seemed to expand inside herself. She was not just her tiny physical form, she was a vast jacket of energy. Her body was simply the core.

Her consciousness spread inside her extended sphere of power. She outgrew the bubble the Jibbenainosay had left her, and spread out through the storm.

The Dark One could not hide from the Ancient Adversary that way.

HAWK-THAT-SETTLES SAW DR Proctor drop into the storm, and felt unsteady. With nothing beneath his feet, it was hard to balance. Then, the sand came up for him, engulfing him completely. He did not know whether he was falling, shooting upwards or flying through the skies. But he was moving.

The Jibbenainosay raised another million tons of sand and held it in the air, thickening the atmosphere. The business with the human tools had been a feint, designed to dislodge the Pawn of the Nullifiers from the womanspeck, Krokodil. It had drawn out its Adversary now, and swelled in readiness for the serious fight.

As its passion built, continua were created and destroyed in the discharges of its energy. Dark thunderbolts struck all over the desert, blasting stretches of sand into polished glass dark-mirrors the size of small cities.

Time stopped, then jerked backwards, then forwards again. The Jibbenainosay chewed at the fabric of reality, sucking in the Chaos from the Beyond, and spitting it out in phlegmy dollops.

Throughout Creation, the cacophonies were heard.

DR PROCTOR HAD stopped struggling as soon as the impossibilities started. He accepted his fate as a cartoon character, and allowed the world to stretch like elastic around him. His head had exploded like a firecracker, but instantly reassembled. Anvils, safes and pianos plunged towards hapless citizens, but he was ascending like a hot air balloon.

He knew that, so long as he did not look down, he would never fall like the Coyote to the canyon floor miles below.

The Indian bobbed about, maybe twenty feet away. In Dr Proctor's mindsight, Hawk-That-Settles was three figures: a wiry, gaunt, nearly middle-aged Navaho in bloodied denims, covered in sand; a large bird of prey, wings outspread, talons pointed for a strike; and a tubby cartoon redskin with a big nose, a feather in his oiled black hair, warpaint on his cheeks, and fluffy moccasins on his feet.

In the storm, he heard the Warner Brothers' Orchestra race through a Spike Jones arrangement of "What Do They Do on a Rainy Night in Rio?" before doing a segue into "Tell the Doc to Stick to His Practice, Tell the Lawyer to Settle His Case, and Send the Indian Chief and His Tommy-Hawk Back to Little-Rain-In-My-Face".

The Tasmanian Devil howled for his dinner. He wanted Devilled Hare!

He leaped at the Indian, his legs kicking the air, his claws out. Stretched horizontal, he saw the boiling clouds of sand below, and felt the pull of gravity tugging at his face.

He was frozen for a second, and then the whoosh pulled him down. The sand hit him hard as he sank into it, and then he was plunging through the unknown darkness towards a rocky ground.

It would be all right. He might flatten like a pancake on impact, but he would pull himself together double-quick and bubble back to his original shape within a few beats.

Dr Ottokar Proctor fell...

THROUGHOUT THE WORLD, seismic instruments exploded at the same instant. Clocks stopped, or raced towards an unimaginable future. Millions subject to epileptic fits fell frothing, and hundreds of thousands of others, hitherto unaffected, joined them. It was as if a maxiscreamer the size of Saturn had been let off next to the planet.

Globally, a number of people equal to the population of the largest megapolis on the planet, died. Heart attacks, spontaneous human combustion, asphyxiation, a new species of instantaneous cancer, cerebral haemorrhage, suicides, massive discharges of bodily electricity, and simple shut-down were the major causes of death, but there was an increase of hostile activity in all the world's war zones, and an epidemic of murder that swept around from country to country like a contagious disease for weeks afterwards.

The computer records of a major corporation, located in a site under Nevada secure against nuclear holocaust, were wiped, precipitating an international money-market collapse that even rocked the solid foundations of the GenTech corporate empire.

Firestorms raged throughout the arctic tundra, and chunks of ice the size and shape of Silbury Hill poked through the sands of the Sahara Desert.

A ring of spy satellites recently put in place by a Gottschalk Geselleschaft in conjunction with the Soviet

Union as an attempt to counterbalance GenTech's orbital superiority burned out at the cost of nine hundred billion Euros. Every nation in the no-longer-terribly-exclusive Doomsday Club opened their silo doors and chained button-pushers to their consoles in readiness for an attack from the unknown.

A stretch of the Caribbean rose to the surface, bearing with it the wrecks of numberless ships and the ruins of a pre-human civilization, while a wave of water rippled across Louisiana, carrying away what little was left there. Solar flares jetted a million miles into space.

Beyond the galaxy, stars went spectacularly nova, snuffing out tens of thousands of life-bearing planets in a fireworks display whose light would not reach the earth for a billion years.

There was no one in the entire world, in the entire universe, who did not hear, feel or experience somehow the side-effects of the moment.

"Wilma, what was that?"

"Oh, honey, don't you bother. It was just another air crash out at Edwards. Why those wingboys bother, I don't know."

"Aw, Cheeze, I thought it was the Trump of fuckin' Doom or somethin'. I near shit in my pants."

"Oh, honey, don't talk crude. You know Mama don't like it."

"Shaddup, and get me a brewsky, Wilma."

"Another beer?"

"Wilma..."

"'Kay, honey."

Hawk-That-Settles thought he was travelling horizontally until the ground loomed up like a wall, and he found himself stuck to it by gravity.

His head spun, and he knew which way was down again, thank the Lord. His ankle was still crushed, and he had other broken bones. But he was not spread out on the desert like a paste.

Sand was falling around him like rain, and he had to struggle not to be buried.

It was like trying to keep on the surface of a sea. He pushed himself upwards, letting the sand flood in below him, thrashing with his good leg and his arms.

Then, the rain was over. The winds were passing. Somewhere, Krokodil and the Jibbenainosay were wrestling, but Hawk was being left behind.

He rolled over, broken, and saw someone coming across the desert. At first, he thought it was Dr Proctor ready to finish him off. He almost wasn't sorry about that. Relieved, he pulled his shirt away from his throat. Being a good Indian was better than trying to stay alive and sane after today.

But it wasn't Dr Proctor. It was someone riding a horse.

Laughing painfully, he propped himself up on his elbows, and waved.

The horseman wore a battered stetson, and had his kerchief up over his face. Like his steed, he was thickly coated with desert dust. But he was reassuringly solid. The horse had a firm footing, and trod carefully across the sands. Hawk had a funny feeling about the horseman, as if he were seeing the earthly aspect of a manitou, or the spirit of a great warrior from the days of his ancestors.

"Stranger," he shouted. "Over here."

Rider and horse heard him at the same time, and both heads turned to look.

The horseman twisted his reins, and dug in his heels, spurring his animal to a gallop.

The stranger rode across the desert to Hawk, and the Indian felt safe again.

God was in his Heaven, it snowed in Indianapolis in the wintertime, the President of the United States was a good and honest man, you could get a free lunch, a buck could buy four quarters, the white man always honoured his treaties with the red, nobody got cancer, his father was hailed as a great chief, Jennifer White Dove fucked on a first date, a good Navaho could always hold his liquor, and…

"Friend," the horseman said, his voice rich and deep, "you look as if you could use a hand."

And there was a Lone Ranger.

"MR PRESIDENT, YOU are cleared for the red phone. The connection is being made… now."

"Roman, talk to me."

"Our people tell us they're on DefCon 3, too. The missiles are not in the air."

"Roman, what the fuck are you guys playing at? What do you mean, 'what are you doing?' This has nothing to do with us, either…"

"He'll be in the bunker under the Kremlin, Mr President. Soviet chain of command has been established. If we struck at the Minsk switchboard intersection, we could gain perhaps five or ten minutes on our first strike."

"Roman, I've got scientists out my ass telling me the world is ending. We're the only guys big enough to do anything about it, except maybe one or two Japcorps, and the UEC, of course, and maybe a couple of Muslims, and… Hell, you know what I mean. I have to think you know what's going down, you know. What…? 'Going down?' It's an American expression, it means, like… uh, happening, I guess…"

"Is that a no, Mr President?"

"Yes, goddammit, Alex. I mean, yes that's a no… Roman, I'm sorry. I have someone shouting at me."

"The think tank suggest you act."

"Look, Roman, I'll put it this way. You stand down, and we'll stand down and maybe we'll get to go to the Quarter-Millennial in a couple of years."

"Our sleepers in GenTech Tokyo just woke up, sir. They report that the corp are taking advantage of this window to sink a couple of Russkie ships in the Sea of Japan. We could go in with them..."

"Alex, shut up. Roman, look, we have some information that may be of use to you."

"Sir, we have a secret treaty with GenTech confirming our neutrality in any corporate war with the Soviet Union. You are bound by the terms of that agreement not to share the intelligence I have just given you with Premier Abramovich."

"I'm the President, Alex, I can do any fucking thing I want to... Roman, look behind you. Off your Asian seacoast. This has nothing to do with us. We're sharing intelligence, here. We're helping you, now could you please just stand down and we'll stand down... Roman, you know I can't speak Russian."

"Mr President, I would like to tender my resignation."

"Shut the fuck up, Alex! Roman, have you got that? We're sending you charts on the satellite hook-up. The Sea of Japan. Get it to your navy."

"Sir, they've stepped back to DefCon 2."

"Roman, thank you, I love you! Roman? Roman? He's hung up! He can't hang up on me, the commie bastard!"

"Sir, we're still at DefCon 3. We could still hit Minsk. This way, we'd have twelve full minutes."

"I'm the President! He can't hang up on the President, can he?"

"Sir..."

"Oh, fuck it, Alex, stand down. Get me a press aide. I need someone to write me a speech..."

* * *

Dr Proctor was the mouse. Above him, a giant-sized housecat was tangling with an equally huge bulldog.

He stumbled across the littered desert, trying to keep out from underfoot as the growling, snarling, miaowing monsters locked in their mutually destructive embrace.

Chase, catch and eat! That was the cycle of all life. Chase, catch and eat!

Dr Proctor would not be eaten today. He was too small a morsel.

"Holiness, we have the latest data from Mapache. I'm not sure, but there may be some help. Meanwhile, we have some reports from our man in Salt Lake City."

Pope Georgi studied the strip-prints. Cardinal Brandreth, the camerlengo, took them from him and studied them himself.

Outside, the square of St Peter's was full. People had just stopped what they were doing and flooded towards the Vatican. They knew something was happening, but weren't sure what.

The Pope considered. "We must send Sister Chantal to Arizona. Have her summoned."

Father O'Shaughnessy bowed, and kissed the Pope's ring.

Elder Seth was *back in Jessamyn's childhood, her backstripes stinging. The nightmares poured in, as he clung to his disciple.*

The focal point within his body, where the Jibbenainosay had lodged, was open again, and the Darkness was pressing at it. He was himself a gateway to the Outer Darkness.

In the beyond, the Dark Ones swarmed.

The Jibbenainosay reeled under the counterattack. The Ancient Adversary was turning its form against it. It realized how little it knew of the physical being of this universe. It had to concentrate, to pull its cloaking Darkness around its Cynosure. The Pawn of the Nullifiers had melded with the woman, and was its superior in terms of this universe. In the Outer Darkness, the Jibbenainosay would have dwarfed the Adversary, but here the match was disturbingly even. It funnelled its power into a vast tentacle, and thrust it through the Adversary's energy field, pumping the Darkness through...

ON MONSTERS' ROW, they were going wild. Jason had wrenched his door off, and was being held down by a dozen officers. Rex Tendenter hung naked from his bars like a monkey, chattering like a mad creature. Staig, Mizzi, McClean and Brosnan were howling like beasts. Etchison was laughing uncontrollably, plucking his eyelashes out one by one. Myers just stared at the walls of his cell, unperturbed by it all.

Jason got a cattleprod away from one of the officers, and shoved it through a uniformed chest. Hector Childress clapped as the blood sprayed, and called for more. Tendenter leaped to the floor. His bars had been bloodied. He licked the fast-drying red greedily, smearing his face. Colonel Reynard Pershing Fraylman lay on his military-perfect bunk, his tongue lolling, his face blackening. He had been struck dead early in the riot, brought down by a burst blood vessel. Herman Katz shouted in a womanish, high-pitched voice.

Jason had killed five of the guards, by now. Tear gas canisters exploded and Staig swallowed his tongue, choking quickly to death. Three hefty officers in transpex riot gear jogged through the door, and levelled their guns. Rubber bullets bounced off the killer's broad chest, and spanged against the bars.

"Don't fuck around," shouted a sergeant who was trying to hold his arm onto his shoulder, "kill the motherfucker..."

Herman Katz cringed at the bad language.

The riot bulls levelled semi-automatics, and filled Jason's chest. The hulking moron kept stumbling onwards.

"Come on guys," shouted the sergeant, "plug the fat..." He was cut off by the next burst. Ricochet bullets slammed into him, and he relaxed, his arm slipping into his lap. Three other officers died in that volley, but Jason kept walking.

The riot bulls put ScumStoppers through Jason's eyes, and the back of his bald head exploded.

"What a mess," said Herman. "This will never wash out, you know, never. This dress is ruined!"

They were still screaming. Tendenter dipped his fingers in Jason's spilled blood and brains, and raised the chunks to his eager lips.

"Fuck," said Officer Kerr, "it's time we settled these bastards' hash once and for all."

He shot Tendenter between the eyes, and the Bachelor Boy slumped, still smiling, in his cell.

Childress realized what was happening, and ran to the back of his cell, hiding behind his bunk. Officers shoved their rifles through the bars and shot the chainsaw murderer through his bedding.

"Who's got the keys?" asked Kerr.

"No one."

"We do it through the bars then," said Kerr. "Sandall, you take Myers with the burpgun. He's the worst of them."

Sandall shoved his weapon through the bars, and looked into the empty eyes of the Haddonfield Horror. Even without a mask, his face was a blank. He flipped the safety catch, but the murderer moved too fast for him, and he found himself hugged to the iron. His head wouldn't fit through the gap, but Myers pulled it into the cell anyway, leaving ears, hair and chunks of flesh on the metal.

"Myers has got a gun. Take him."

The sirens stopped, and more officers arrived. Myers tossed the gun into the corridor, and sat down again.

"What's going on here?" asked Deputy Warden Crighton.

"The monst... the inmates attempted escape, sir."

"There'll be a full enquiry, Kerr."

"Yes, sir."

Crighton looked down Monsters' Row, at the corpses jumbled against the walls.

"Shit, what a mess! This is worse than the Tasmanian Devil's leftovers."

Rex Tendenter was buried in the asylum grounds while an overwhelmingly female crowd of over 300 piled lavish floral tributes against the walls of the institution. The widow of Officer Lyndon Sandall, who had been one of five mourners at his modest funeral a week earlier, threw a petrol bomb into the crowd. Sixteen died, forty-one sustained serious burns, and Clara Sandall moved into Sunnydales' Low Security Wing.

The home had kept Dr Proctor's "confinement area" empty for him, just in case he was ever recaptured. Nobody really wanted him back.

Meanwhile, Jason's body disappeared from the morgue.

Krokodil felt the Jibbenainosay's arm pumping lethal filth into her spirit body. Concentrating, she reversed the flow, and sent the darkness rushing back through the tentacle into the body of the demon.

Physically, she was just standing there, the Jibbenainosay towering over her. But spiritually, she was containing the Dark One, spreading her power around the invader.

This must be the Seventh Level.

Dr Proctor thought he wanted to go home now. He wanted his books, and his cartoons, and his lawyers, psychiatrists and interviewers.

He turned away from the dog-and-cat fight, and walked into the desert. His home was out there, somewhere.

IN THE SURFSIDE Pyramid, Gari the Guru raised his arms, and the Congregation joined in one long "ommm". The House of Worship was on the strip, within sight of the best surfing beach on the coast.

Gari told his tanned and even-teethed flock that it was okay to make money and still be spiritually healthy. He put them in touch with their selves, and purged them of any residual feelings of guilt they might have over their worldly success. He taught them to actualize their potential, and not to look out for the other guy. After all, in life there were winners and losers, and there weren't any Gods for losers.

In his audience were the heads of three Hollywood media conglomerates, four ostentatiously anonymous movie stars, a world-renowned porno stud who had recently turned devout, a Beverly Hills plastic surgeon who claimed to be second only to Dr Zarathustra in the field, Sonny Pigg of the Mothers of Violence, Hayley Duff's personal astrologer, a gaggle of surfie chicks and dudes Gari could have sworn were runaway sex-clones, the CEO of the LA GenTech subsidiary, the West Coast editor of Guns and Killing, ZeeBeeCee TV personality Lynne Cramer, author of best-selling roadway action fiction Derek Duck, bonsai tycoon Mike Miyagi, sonic sculptor Ritchie Bassett, the Deputy Governor of California, and the religious affairs correspondent of the *Los Angeles Times*, Harlan Ellison, who would be writing the Pyramid up in his Church of the Week column.

"Today, I want to rap with you about one of our former co-worshippers," Gari said, waving his crystal-tipped wand.

He pulled down the poster-size picture of Bronson Manolo. The Op was standing beside a surfboard, with a bikini babe, caught by the camera in mid-jiggle, on either side. His teeth shone, and his implanted chest hairs could have been painted on his sculptured pectorals. His ballsack swimming pouch made him look as modest as Michelangelo's David.

"When you look at Bronson Manolo, guys," the guru said, "I want you to see a loser!"

The Pyramid People hissed like Dracula confronted with a crucifix.

"Loser, loser, loser," they chanted. Some people threw things of little value: gold fountain pens, diamond earrings, last year's wristwatches. Gari would have them picked up later.

"Here was a cat who seemed to have it, but inside he was just a zeroid waster or else he would be here today."

They were shouting now, screaming their hatred at the outcast.

"Remember, guys, the beautiful never die!"

"Never die, never die, never die!"

Gari was happy. He had his people at the pitch he wanted them. The collection later would be his best yet.

"Winners never die," he shouted, "never die, never die, never die!"

He stopped shouting, and let the Pyramid People's adulation get to him. It hit him like a cocaine rush, but it was better than that. It gave him a thrill in his penis, and he knew he could convert this feeling into anything. Afterwards, he could have any of them, have all of them if he wanted. Promise people eternity, and there was nothing you couldn't get out of them. Nothing.

"Never die! Never die! Never die!"

Gari showed his teeth and extended his arms. His multicoloured robes caught the light.

From the back of the Pyramid, looking out through the clear-glass windows down to the beach, Gari the guru was the only one who saw the tidal wave coming.

"Never die, never die, never die," chanted the Pyramid People.

It was a pity Bronson Manolo was dead. This was one wave he would have given anything to be on top of.

Raging against the Adversary, the Jibbenainosay dwindled, its matter being compressed in on itself. The process introduced it to the concept of agony. It felt the whole physical universe pressing against it, and yet knew there was no way back with honour into the Outer Darkness.

The Ancient Adversary squeezed.

"This is Lola Stechkin, interrupting your scheduled broadcast to ask the question that's on everybody's lips this afternoon, October 8th, 2023. Just what the fuck is happening? Later, we'll be going over to our weather bureau, our correspondents in Washington, Moscow, Tokyo and Rome, to our espers and to experts from the Universities of the world. And we'll be asking you to interface with your datanets to give us your suggestions. But first, here's a message from GenTech…"

... and squeezed...

"Musterr Banks, Musterr Banks, 'tis turruble, turruble, turruble. Wullie the Whale's alive, alive, alive. And the Bolivian ambassadurr's burruthdae partie's still on insaide hus stummuch! We're doomed, doomed!"

"Fuck off, Jock, I'm counting money."

... and squeezed...

"Chantal, it's Father O'Shaughnessy…"

"Father, I'm pleased to hear from you. I've been working through those Glenzugge theorems, and I've had some thoughts."

"Papa Georgi wants to see you. It's important."

"I'll be there directly."

... and squeezed...

Dr Proctor stumbled through the sand. He had lost one of his shoes, and was leaving bloody footprints.

He pushed on, the desert swallowing him.

... and squeezed...

Nguyen Seth convulsed, and his eyes shot open.

"Roger, we've lost."

That couldn't be.

... and squeezed...

Hawk-That-Settles had been drifting in and out of consciousness. Now, he snapped awake. The horseman was gone, but his wounds were bound. He felt better. The storm had passed.

... and squeezed...

The Ancient Adversary held the collapsed mass of the Jibbenainosay in its aura, and felt the Dark One lose its grip on the universe. The wormhole opened up, and the Jibbenainosay was sucked back through it, its being unravelling as it jetted back up the funnel into the Outer Darkness. There, Ba'alberith, the Mythwrhyn and Nyarlathotep would be awaiting it, waiting to chastise it for its failure. Strengthened by its victory, the Ancient Adversary allowed itself to shrink, to recede, to spiral down.

* * *

Krokodil stood alone in the vast space of the desert. The remains of the monastery of Santa de Nogueira were a mile or so in the distance.

She was tired, but unhurt. The thing she had found in herself, and let loose, was coiled safe in her chest again.

At her feet was a lump of crystal, clear but shot through with threads of red. She picked it up, and was transported...

She floated in the midst of an eternal Darkness, sensing titanic presences, witnessing their eternal struggles. Aeons passed, and the course of the battle swept across the expanse of the Multiple Creation and back, but nothing really changed. The Dark Ones and the Nullifiers still struggled, but there was no victory, nor did either side truly desire the destruction of the other...

She dropped the crystal, and it sank into the sands.

That was not an experience she wanted to repeat in a hurry.

"No," Seth said, "we haven't lost. Yet. The Dark Ones are angry, but their wrath is for one of their number. We are excused. The Great Work still goes on. Roger, we must prepare to summon a demon. Quickly. You must nurture this one with your blood. We must strike."

Seth stood up, and straightened his mirrorshades. Inside, he could still hear the tick-tock of the crocodile.

He raised the knuckle of his right forefinger to his mouth, and bit. The finger came off and fell away. A feeble spurt of blood splashed on the table, and he drew a sign of protection with it.

He sucked the stump. The finger would grow back soon.

Hawk-That-Settles sat up, and sang his song of life. He felt no triumph, for he had not truly overcome anything. But he was alive, when he had had no chance of survival. From now on, his life was blessed, the gift of the manitou. He must be careful with it.

Krokodil heard him and walked across the sand to find him.

ABOUT THE AUTHOR

Besides his contributions to BL Publishing's Warhammer and Dark Future series, the seldom-seen Jack Yeovil is the author of a single novel, *Orgy of the Blood Parasites*, and used to fill in occasionally as a film reviewer for *Empire* and the *NME*. Kim Newman seems to have Jack under control at the moment, but the stubborn beast flesh occasionally comes creeping back.